JENNI F

Falling Fast

PENGUIN BOOKS

For Michael. Finally a sport we both like!

PENGUIN BOOKS

UK | USA | Canada | Ireland | Australia
India | New Zealand | South Africa

Penguin Books is part of the Penguin Random House group of companies whose addresses can be found at global.penguinrandomhouse.com

www.penguin.co.uk
www.puffin.co.uk
www.ladybird.co.uk

First published 2025

001

Text copyright © Jenni Fletcher, 2025

The moral right of the author has been asserted

Penguin Random House values and supports copyright. Copyright fuels creativity, encourages diverse voices, promotes freedom of expression and supports a vibrant culture. Thank you for purchasing an authorized edition of this book and for respecting intellectual property laws by not reproducing, scanning or distributing any part of it by any means without permission. You are supporting authors and enabling Penguin Random House to continue to publish books for everyone. No part of this book may be used or reproduced in any manner for the purpose of training artificial intelligence technologies or systems. In accordance with Article 4(3) of the DSM Directive 2019/790, Penguin Random House expressly reserves this work from the text and data mining exception.

Set in 11/14.5 pt Baskerville MT Pro
Typeset by Jouve (UK), Milton Keynes
Printed and bound in Great Britain by Clays Ltd, Elcograf S.p.A.

The authorized representative in the EEA is Penguin Random House Ireland, Morrison Chambers, 32 Nassau Street, Dublin D02 YH68

A CIP catalogue record for this book is available from the British Library

ISBN: 978–0–241–71466–9

All correspondence to:
Penguin Books
Penguin Random House Children's
One Embassy Gardens, 8 Viaduct Gardens, London SW11 7BW

Penguin Random House is committed to a sustainable future for our business, our readers and our planet. This book is made from Forest Stewardship Council® certified paper.

Books by Jenni Fletcher

How to Lose an Earl in 10 Weeks

Two Dukes and a Debutante

A Duke for Christmas

Lights Out

Falling Fast

Now that New Year celebrations are out of the way, we motorsport fans can get down to business. F1 is back at the end of February, and I can't wait!

Single Seat News, 6 January

PROLOGUE

THERE'S A SCENE NEAR the start of *The Wizard of Oz* when Dorothy opens her front door and the grey world of 1930s Kansas has been replaced by one of glorious technicolour. That's how I feel at this moment as the lift doors open to reveal a large, open-plan office decorated in shades of sunflower yellow and bright sparkling white. Only this isn't Oz, Wonderland or any other fantastical realm hidden behind an ordinary-looking door. This is the Quezada Formula 1 team UK headquarters, and I've never seen anything so beautiful in my life.

I'm so impressed I can't move. I just stand and stare, pulse racing, until the lift doors start closing again and I have to quickly wriggle through the gap to avoid missing my floor. It's not the most dignified start to my interview, but thankfully nobody is looking in my direction. They're all busy, doing important Quezada-related things, so I smooth my hands down my black blazer, check that my long auburn hair is still neatly restrained in a sleek ponytail and allow myself a moment to breathe in the atmosphere.

It's not quite the mothership, since this office is near

Milton Keynes and the team's main base is on the outskirts of Barcelona, but it is home to the managerial and public-relations departments, and that's good enough. The fact that I've made it this far, to a job interview with arguably the greatest team in F1 history, renders me breathless with excitement. All I have to do now is convince Jasper Ramirez, director of Global Communications, to take me on.

I think I have a reasonable shot. I'm efficient, organized and meticulous. I make planning into an art form. I'm also dedicated, motivated and prepared to work every hour in the day, with only catnaps and black coffee to sustain me, because I've wanted a job in Formula 1 – specifically with Quezada – since I was fifteen years old. And, seeing as my driving skills are disappointingly average, being part of their communications team – talking about F1, persuading others to talk about F1 and spending my days generally enthusing about F1 – is the next best thing.

I want this job so badly I can taste it.

Since it's going to look weird if I don't move soon, however, I straighten my shoulders and head for the nearest desk. All the furnishings are yellow, making the office look like the interior of some gigantic beehive, buzzing with activity. But then Quezada isn't just a racing team; they're a global brand. Even people who don't like cars have heard of them.

I knew they were the team for me the moment I first saw them race. It was a defining moment of my life, like being adrift in the middle of a vast ocean and glimpsing a lifeboat ahead. If it wasn't for Quezada, I might still be lying on a sofa, too depressed to get up, let alone make a plan for my future. Yellow has been my favourite colour ever since, even though it does nothing for my pink-toned complexion. If required, I'm prepared to give an impromptu lecture on the history of the company (founded by two brothers, Adan and Pedro Quezada in 1962) along with the dates and details of their thirty-seven world championships and thirty-five Constructors' titles. Basically, I'm the most passionate candidate they could ever hope to meet, but I'm also not above begging on my hands and knees if that's what it takes.

'Hi.' I greet the receptionist. 'I have a ten o'clock appointment with Jasper Ramirez.'

'That's me.' A man of around forty, with green eyes and shoulder-length dark hair, answers from a few feet away, standing up from where he's perched on the edge of a desk. 'You're right on time.'

'Ava Yearwood.' I give him a firm handshake.

'Also known as Single Seat News.' He smiles as he says the name of my podcast. 'Welcome to Quezada, Ava.'

I smile back because the words sound like music to my ears. 'Thank you. I'm happy to be here.'

'The feeling is mutual. Let's get the formalities over with, shall we?' He waves a hand, gesturing for me to follow him. 'Come this way.'

Jasper's corner office is glass on all four sides – two of which have views of landscaped gardens – with an impractical white carpet and minimal decor. There are only three pieces of furniture in the room: a shiny curved desk that looks space age, and two yellow leather chairs on either side. Everything looks expensive and spotless, just like I always imagined it would.

'I'm afraid I haven't had a chance to look over your CV properly yet.' Jasper sits down at the desk and opens one of four laptops, his eyes flitting over the screen for a few seconds before turning back to me. 'But your name was passed to me by Giovanni Bauer. You two are friends, is that right?'

'Yes.' Technically, I know Gio through his former fake, now real, girlfriend, Maisie, but even if their situation wasn't a secret, it would be way too complicated to explain.

'And you want to work in Formula 1?'

'I do.' I answer emphatically because it's impossible to overstate this. 'As well as my podcast, I've done some volunteering at local motorsport events and I'm in a lot of online forums. I'm basically obsessed.'

'I know the feeling.' Jasper chuckles. 'Although I have to ask, if you're friends with the current world champion, why doesn't Gio get you a job at Fraser?'

'Because he knows I support Quezada. It's been my favourite team ever since I watched Torres beat Sullivan in Melbourne.'

'Torres?' Jasper leans back in his chair. 'When was that, six seasons ago?'

'Yes. It was his last year before he retired. That was the race that hooked me. I've been loyal to Quezada ever since.'

'But your podcast is on F1 in general?'

I nod. 'I try to be objective and fair.'

'Good. Fair is important.' He looks down at his laptop again. 'So, like I told Gio, we have an entry-level position in our Communications department, but there are lots of opportunities for progression. I see you have an A-level in Spanish?'

'I do. I thought it might be useful some day.'

'And your degree is in Media Studies?'

'It will be. I sit my final exams in May.'

'Ah . . .' His brow knits. 'May?'

'Yes.' I'm afraid to ask what his tone means. 'Is that a problem?'

He hesitates, drumming his fingers on the desk. 'I'll be honest with you, Ava. I think you'd fit in perfectly here.'

'I would.' I shuffle forward to the edge of my chair. 'I know I would.'

'Unfortunately, I need people right now, and I definitely can't keep a position open until May. The season begins next month and there's still a lot of preparation to do. We're launching the new car on Valentine's Day.'

I swallow hard as my vision of a bright yellow future starts to fade before my eyes. I can't let this opportunity slip through my fingers. 'Would it be possible to work remotely or part-time until my exams are over? I'm confident that I could do both. I have excellent time-management skills.'

'I'm afraid not.' He shakes his head. 'F1 is a way of life; you need to be all in. If you want the job, you'll need to start immediately.'

I tense because one thing I'm *not* half-hearted about is this. I'm already all in. I just need five more months to finish my degree. Unless . . . My breath hitches as it occurs to me that I *could* leave university, abandon my finals. Who needs qualifications anyway? I could simply walk away and come here . . .

My entire being rebels at the idea. I have a life plan, and the prospect of changing any part of it – even in pursuit of my end goal – causes an immediate flare of panic. If I give up my degree now, all I'll have to show for hundreds of hours of study is thirty-five thousand pounds' worth of debt and two extremely disappointed parents. If I even suggest leaving university, they'll instantly assume I'm having another breakdown and come rushing home from the eleven-month round-the-world holiday they've been planning for literally decades, to take care of me – and they've only been gone a week.

But this is Quezada!

I'm so conflicted I can't even articulate an answer. I just sit, tapping my three-inch stiletto heels against the carpet as I stare wordlessly at Jasper.

'Look, I'm not asking you to abandon your studies. In fact, I insist that you don't.' He seems to understand my hesitation. 'There's obviously been a misunderstanding between Gio and I. I thought he meant you were available now.' He snaps his laptop shut. 'So call me at the end of the season and we'll talk again.'

'Thank you. That's very generous.' I clear my throat. It's obvious there's nothing further I can do to change his mind right now, but I'm determined to make one last request. 'And if anything comes up over the summer . . .'

'I'll keep you in mind.'

I force a smile as I reach for my Monos Metro tote – a recent birthday present from my brother. I seem to be moving in slow motion, like I subconsciously think if I give Jasper more time he'll reconsider.

This is a setback, that's all, I tell myself. I need to hold on to the fact that Jasper's invited me back. I'm still in control and I can't – *won't* – let this stop me or get me down. If I stick to the plan, then everything will work out. I've waited this long to get into F1, so I can wait a little longer. Eleven months, to be exact.

It sounds like an eternity.

'I appreciate your time, Mr Ramirez.' I push myself to my feet, though it takes all my willpower to do so. 'See you in December.'

Three months into the F1 season and anyone who expected Fraser to run away with the trophy this year must be feeling disappointed. Quezada are back on form, turning the competition into a fight between the current world champion, Fraser's Giovanni Bauer, and the two-time former champion, Quezada's Jaxon Marr.

The other big news this weekend is the possible resurgence of Rask Racing. After an amazing start to the season, Rask have been plagued by mechanical issues, pushing them way down the grid table. But, after taking P3 in qualifying yesterday, it seems Norwegian driver Leif Olsen is fighting back.

On a personal note, I can't believe I'm actually in Monaco to see it!

Single Seat News, 25 May

ONE

'ARE YOU OK?'

I lower my sunglasses to peer at my best friend and former flatmate, Maisie. She may be the only person in the world who would ask such an insane question on a day like this.

We're lying at opposite ends of a large cream-coloured daybed, beneath the canopy of a luxury super yacht, lined up alongside dozens of other impossibly huge yachts in the crystal-clear azure waters of Monaco harbour, waiting for the start of the most glamorous Grand Prix in the entire Formula 1 calendar. What kind of person – correction, what kind of F1 fan – would *not* be OK with this?

But the honest answer is no, I'm not OK. It's been over four months since I walked out of Jasper Ramirez's office and not a single day has passed when I haven't wondered if it was the biggest mistake of my life. Being here as a spectator is both an amazing, once-in-a-lifetime experience and a painful, heart-wrenching reminder of what might have been. It just seems ungrateful to say so out loud.

'I'm fine.' I twist my face away so she can't tell I'm lying. Maisie and I met in halls during our first year at university and have been able to read each other's expressions ever since. From the moment we met, I knew we were on the same wavelength, possibly because we've both been through stuff in our pasts that makes our lives . . . complicated, for want of a better word.

'You don't have to say that. I know it must be tough.' She sounds sympathetic.

'Maybe a little,' I admit. 'But I'm still thrilled to be here. Thank you for inviting me.'

'You're welcome! I just wish the timing wasn't so terrible.' She flings her iPad aside and shakes her chestnut curls with a groan of frustration. 'I feel like my head is going to burst and I still have so much to revise. I wanted to finish another chapter before the race starts.'

I glance at my phone. There are only five minutes to go before lights out. Barely time to order a champagne cocktail and make our way to the stern to watch. My own exams finished three days ago, but Maisie has two left this week and I know she's been feeling overwhelmed. It's not easy studying for your finals in sports psychology while trying to get on to a competitive MA programme *and* training for downhill mountain bike races, *as well as* dating a world champion F1 driver who spends most of his time travelling. She's being pulled in several different directions at once. That's why she recently moved out of our flat and into Gio's house, because at least that way they get to spend *some* time together when he's at home. I'm happy for her, truly, even though my own life feels a little emptier now.

'You know,' I say, swinging my legs over the side of the daybed and glancing around surreptitiously. 'You don't have to watch every second of the race. You can keep revising and I'll let you know if anything interesting happens.'

'Would you?' Her brown eyes widen. 'I feel like such a bad girlfriend, but if I keep working now then I can take tonight off.'

'You're not bad – you're busy.' I give her a wink. 'I won't tell anyone, I promise.'

'This is why I love you.'

'I love you too.' I blow her a kiss as I grab my wide-brim sunhat and head to the railing at the stern of the yacht. I look out over the red-roofed buildings of the principality and the craggy cliffs that tower behind them. As views go, it's kind of incredible. The weather is perfect as well, sunny but not too hot, with a gentle breeze stirring the hundreds of red-and-white Monégasque flags. Every grandstand and balcony is packed with spectators, and a mood of hushed expectation fills the air.

Despite my mixed feelings, I'm *very* aware how lucky I am to be here, watching from the harbourside. From this vantage point, I can see the tunnel exit and the Tabac chicane, one of the fastest sections on the narrow street circuit. If anyone tries to overtake, it'll likely be here, though the chances of that happening are small. The average race speed in Monaco is generally lower than on other circuits, and the winding roads and tight corners make overtaking difficult, as well as potentially perilous. This is the race every driver wants to win and desperation can sometimes lead to reckless decisions, but generally speaking whoever starts in pole finishes there, which in this case is good news for Gio.

I focus my attention on the giant harbour screen as the drivers climb into their cars for the formation lap – Gio for Fraser on pole, Jaxon Marr for Quezada in P2. Right behind them is the biggest surprise of the weekend. Like most pundits, I expected to see either Noa Shimizu in the other Quezada car, or Gio's new teammate, Hayden Quaid, in

P3, but instead it's Leif Olsen for Rask, whose impressive qualifying time sent shockwaves through the entire paddock.

Of all the eleven teams, Rask Racing have had the most tumultuous start to the season. Alongside their mechanical problems, it's no secret that their billionaire former owner disapproved of the appointment of the new team principal. But nobody expected him to sell his remaining stake a month ago and simply walk away, along with a large percentage of the staff, leaving his former team in free-fall.

Personally, I like Bastian Aalto, a softly spoken Finn who's worked in F1 for almost two decades – first as an engineer, then as a racing director. Given a chance, I think he'll do great things as team principal at Rask. Leif Olsen, too. Of all the new drivers on the grid, he's the one I'm most intrigued by. Though, apart from Gio, I don't support individual drivers.

My loyalty is still to Quezada, which means I support whoever's driving for them, no matter who they are or what I think of their racing style. But something about Leif Olsen appeals to me, and not just because, as a reserve driver for Chiltern, he overtook Luc Farron on the last lap of the Japanese Grand Prix last year – a move which gave Gio the championship.

It doesn't hurt that he looks like a modern-day Viking, all square jaw, high cheekbones and platinum-blonde hair. In interviews he comes across as polite but reserved – the kind of driver who keeps to himself and avoids the spotlight when he can. But, in a car, his style is utterly compelling – sleek and smooth rather than aggressive – the closest thing I've ever seen to poetry on a race track.

When his car behaves, like it did back in the very first Grand Prix of the year in Australia, he's up there with the best. Admittedly, he was helped out that day by a sudden rainstorm that sent five other drivers into the wall, but he still came third in only his second F1 race. *Then* Rask's mechanical issues began, and he's had to withdraw from three of the six races since. Fingers crossed he can go the distance today.

I hold my breath as the cars finish the formation lap and line up back on the grid. There's a moment of stillness before the screen cuts to the five lights on the gantry above the track, turning red, one by one. Waiting for them to go out never fails to send a shiver down my spine. The majority of car-to-car contact takes place on the first lap, as the drivers jockey for position, so if there's going to be a significant change to the running order, it's usually now.

The lights go out. Engines roar, the crowd cheers and away they go.

'WOW!' MAISIE DECLARES, STANDING in the doorway of my cabin five hours later.

'Do you think?' I slide one last hair grip into my low bun and then pluck anxiously at the scooped neckline of my black jumpsuit. I don't remember it clinging to my curves quite so snugly when I bought it, but I have done a lot of stress-eating recently.

'Yes!' She bats my hands away. 'You look gorgeous.'

'So do you.' I step back to admire her shiny blue mini-dress. 'I can't believe how toned you are from cycling. Your legs look incredible.'

'Thanks.' She strikes a model pose. 'If you can't dress up for Monaco, when can you?' She checks her phone for the time. 'We'd better go. We have a lot of celebrating to do.'

'I guess Gio's in a good mood after his win?' I say, reaching for my clutch before we head up the stairs to the main deck. 'I won't ask where you two went after he got back. I barely had a chance to say hi!'

'Yeah, sorry about that.' She gives me a teasing smile. 'But you can congratulate him at the club – he's meeting us there.'

We leave the yacht via a gangplank. It's bizarre to think the street beside the quayside was a race track this afternoon. The clear-up is already well underway, as the temporary barriers are taken down and life returns to normal, but there are still plenty of people around, giving the whole place a party atmosphere.

Personally, I wish we could stay out here in the open air, but this is Gio's night so I don't complain when a member of Fraser's PR team takes us to a club on a side street. It's guarded by a small army of doormen, who give us suspicious looks as we squeeze past them to the dance floor. There's a raised booth in the centre, flashing with gold and green lights, where a DJ is playing dance music, but it's hard to tell how big the room is because there are mirrors on all the walls, reflecting everything back on itself. Bizarrely, there are also trees placed randomly about the floor, actual palm trees stretching up towards a domed glass ceiling. I daren't ask how much it costs to get in here because I already know I can't afford it. Fortunately, tonight is courtesy of Mark Haddon, Gio's boss.

'There he is!' Maisie shouts over the thump of the music, pointing towards a private area beside the bar. 'Come on.'

I take a deep breath to calm myself before following her. Experience has taught me to keep a tight rein on my emotions in crowded spaces like this. The last thing I need is any old memories leaping out to sabotage my progress, but thankfully, after six years of practice, I'm an expert at staying in control.

'Heyyyy!' Gio steps forward to greet us, dressed in a rumpled button-up and white chinos, looking as handsome as ever with his curly dark hair and striking, turquoise-blue eyes. 'You two look stunning!'

'Thanks.' I smile, though I know he only has eyes for Maisie. 'And congratulations. That's two wins in a row. You should really give the other drivers a chance.'

'Ha! Maybe next year.' He wraps an arm around Maisie's waist and presses his lips to her forehead, like he can't get enough of her. 'It was a good day for Fraser, especially since Hayden came second. And who came third?' He smirks at me. 'Oh, that's right, *not* Quezada.'

'They made a couple of mistakes with their pit stops, that's all,' I reply defiantly. One of the Gold Dart drivers finished third, putting the Quezada cars in fourth and sixth place.

'*Sure.* Anyway, come and meet Leif and Corey from Rask.' Gio waves in the direction of the bar. 'I invited them along.'

I clamp a hand around his arm. 'Leif Olsen?'

'Yes.' He does a double take. 'Why? Are you interested? I'm pretty sure he's single.'

'That's not why I want to meet him. He's just *such* an incredible driver,' I enthuse, before remembering who I'm talking to and biting my tongue. 'Like you, obviously.'

'Uh-huh. Nice save.' Gio laughs, before looking suspiciously at Maisie. 'Was she this starstruck the first time she met me?'

'Oh, I'm so not getting involved in this.' Maisie chuckles. 'If it helps, you're still *my* favourite driver.'

'It does help.' He gives her yet another kiss and then grins at me. 'Come on, I'll introduce you.'

Gio strides off with Maisie, leaving me no choice but to follow. I wanted a moment to prepare, but now all I can do is clamp a hand to my chest as excitement bubbles up from my stomach because I can already see a pair of familiar faces beside the bar.

'Guys!' Gio calls out as he approaches. 'This is Maisie's friend, Ava. Ava, this is Leif and Corey.'

'Hi! It's so great to meet you both,' I say, trying to strike a blend between friendly and sympathetic because if Quezada had a bad day, Rask's was catastrophic. Leif was driving a perfect race until his gearbox broke on the twenty-first lap, while Corey finished sixteenth – not quite last, but still way out of the points.

'Hey, Ava,' Corey answers in his strong and sexy Australian accent. This is his second season in F1 and, whilst his driving style isn't particularly exciting, he's popular with the other drivers off-track and has a reputation for being the biggest flirt on the grid. And now I understand why. Not only does he manage to make a simple greeting sound *incredibly* suggestive, but he looks like a rock star, dressed in a tight dark shirt, black jeans and loads of chunky silver rings, with shoulder-length chestnut hair, golden eyes and sun-bronzed skin.

In contrast, Leif has cropped hair, twilight-blue eyes and stubble so pale it's practically invisible. He's taller than most F1 drivers, with broad shoulders and slim hips, and he's dressed casually in a baseball jersey with patina jeans. Also, unlike Corey, he doesn't say hi. He doesn't even smile. Instead his posture stiffens, his eyes widen and he just . . . *stares.*

My bubble of excitement pops. I can't interpret his expression, but it doesn't exactly say 'pleased to meet you'.

'So, Ava, do you work in F1?' Corey asks.

'Not yet, but I'm hoping to one day,' I say, smiling because at least *he's* being friendly. I don't mention Quezada.

In the end, being told to come back in eleven months isn't exactly a definite job offer. 'I'd love to work in media or communications, ideally for a team, but I only just finished my degree and I've heard it's tough finding positions midway through the season.'

'Can't Gio find you something at Fraser?'

'He's done enough,' I say quickly, because the truth is he's already offered and I've already refused. I could tell he felt conflicted about it, and I don't want to put him in an awkward position, especially since I can understand his reluctance. Quezada are Fraser's main rivals, which means that if I do end up getting a job with them in December, anything I've learned from one could potentially be passed to the other, even accidentally.

'That's a pity.' Corey winks at me. 'It might have been fun seeing you about the grid.'

'Leave her alone.' Gio breaks off from nuzzling Maisie's neck to wrap his spare arm around my shoulders. 'I'm her honorary big brother.'

I smile because that's how I feel about him too, even though I already have a big brother at home. It's good to know Gio's got my back, especially considering the way Leif just reacted to me, like he thinks I was responsible for his loss today.

My gaze drifts back towards him. He's not staring so intensely any more, but now his brows are drawn together and his eyes are wandering over me like they don't know where to settle. Blood rushes to my cheeks in a way I haven't felt for a long time. All I can think is that I've said something negative about him in one of my podcasts and he's taken it personally. Although . . . I'm wracking my brains, but I can't think of anything.

'Sorry about your gearbox,' I say, because I need to reassert control over the situation somehow.

'We're not talking about it.' Corey answers for him again. 'That's our team ethos. Forward not backwards. No blame and no regrets.' He puts a hand on Leif's shoulder. 'Even when it sucks.'

'You know, Ava has a podcast, *Single Seat News*,' Maisie says. 'You guys should be on it. That's how Gio and I officially met.'

'I'd love to.' Corey doesn't hesitate. 'Send me some details and we'll set it up.'

'That would be amazing.' I beam gratefully at him. 'Thank you.'

I glance surreptitiously in Leif's direction, but he's obviously *not* offering. He's still not said a word. The only good thing is that he's not looking at me at all any more. Instead his hard stare is fixed on the dance floor behind my head, his jaw clenched tight. If I had any doubts, I'd say that's fairly conclusive proof he doesn't want anything to do with me.

My foot taps a beat on the floor. Well, that's fine because I don't want anything to do with him now either. I don't usually take an instantaneous dislike to people, but in this case I feel it might be justified. Not only is he making me feel awkward, but I'm *so* disappointed too. Ten minutes ago he was my favourite driver, and now it turns out he's an asshole. I guess it's true what they say about never meeting your heroes.

'That's enough standing around,' Maisie declares. 'Who wants to dance?'

'I'm in.' Corey raises his bottle.

'Me too.' Gio's already heading towards the floor.

'I might get a drink first,' I say. I know how my brain works and I'm not ready to dive on to the dance floor yet. Even with Maisie here, I need time to acclimatize to my surroundings.

'OK, but don't be long.' Corey grins at me. 'Look after her, man.'

It takes me a moment to realize who he's talking to, then another to process the fact that it means Leif's not dancing either. *Shit.* I flex my hands to stop them from curling into fists. I can't believe nobody else has noticed or called him out on his rude behaviour, but then Maisie and Gio are so wrapped up in each other and maybe Corey's used to it . . .

'Just water, thanks,' I say to the hostess who approaches at that moment. I never touch alcohol in places like this because I prefer to stay in control, although for the first time in forever I'm tempted. If anyone could drive me to drink, I have a feeling it would be Leif I-stare-at-people-for-no-apparent-reason Olsen.

The silence between us seems to drag on forever. Not that it's really silent, obviously. The music is actually deafening. But standing side by side like this feels *so* uncomfortable. My skin is prickling because I'm so acutely aware of him, but I've made at least two attempts at conversation and I refuse to try again.

Thankfully, the hostess returns with my water, which I gulp down and set aside in record time. I'm still not ready to dance, but anything has to be better than this.

I'm just turning to say goodbye when somebody bumps into me from behind, knocking me straight into Leif's chest. Automatically I lift my hands, fingers splaying outwards, while his come up to grasp my triceps. I get an instant impression of rippling pectoral muscles and an earthy fragrance that bypasses my brain and rockets straight to a low-down spot in my body. We're pressed against each other so closely I can feel his heartbeat thumping hard and heavy through our clothes, making mine race in response.

I'm totally unprepared for the volcano of heat that erupts inside me at his touch. I jerk my head up in surprise, but meeting his gaze makes the situation a hundred times worse. His pupils are so dilated his eyes look thunderously black rather than blue and a muscle is twitching in his cheek, like touching me is some kind of punishment, which is kind of ironic when he's the one holding me.

'Sorry.' I yank myself backwards, wrenching my arms away.

'It's OK.' He speaks – *finally!* – and even though I've heard his voice plenty of times in interviews, hearing it in person is a shock. It's deep and accented and seems to vibrate across my skin and through my body, making me feel weirdly off-balance. Perhaps he senses it, because his gaze flickers down to my legs and then quickly up again. I have no idea how to read his expression this time either.

'Um, I'm going . . . to dance . . .' I mutter, gesturing in the direction of my friends. It's all I'm capable of at this moment. Despite the water I downed, my throat's drying up and my arms are tingling like they've been scorched by his fingertips.

Panic flashes through me. I have to go, to get as far away from Leif Olsen as possible. My composure isn't just undermined, it's utterly wrecked.

1. Shower
2. Unpack
3. Coffee
4. Find a job
5. Shopping (milk, lasagne, apples, thank-you gift for M&G)

Ava Yearwood, To-do List, 26 May

TWO

I COME TO A decision. I've pined for long enough. I need to forget Quezada (at least temporarily), be practical and get a job. Preferably one with a six-month contract.

I decide this the morning after the Monaco GP – approximately two minutes after Gio and Maisie drop me back home after our early flight – and I get straight to work. My flat, which I rent cheaply from my cousin, is as clean and tidy as I left it, so I write a brief to-do list, take a shower, unpack my small suitcase, pull on some purple leggings and my Eras Tour T-shirt and head for the kitchen.

Placing my laptop on the table, I arrange a row of cue cards and pens beside it, make an espresso and then start browsing employment websites. *I should have done this sooner*, I think – at least a couple of months ago – but I just kept hoping that some kind of opportunity would come up with Quezada. Since it hasn't, however, I need to devote today to finding employment.

An hour later, I have a list of possibilities and a satisfying sense of being back in control. It might sound weird to some people, but I find lists inherently soothing. There was a time when I maybe went a little too far with them – *get out of bed, get dressed, brush teeth* – but now I'm in a much better headspace, and I know how to stay there.

I'm halfway through my first job application when there's a distinctive knock on the door, two sharp bursts of three raps. I don't need to look to know who it is, though I'm surprised to hear it at noon on a Monday.

'Dan!' My brother's apparel is an even bigger surprise. Instead of his usual smart suit, he's dressed in blue shorts, a Nirvana T-shirt and a pair of new and expensive-looking Nike trainers. More alarmingly, he's clutching the edge of my doorframe, his copper-brown curls damp with sweat as he bends over and gasps for breath. 'Have you –' I peer closer – 'been jogging?'

'Yes.' His green eyes, the same seaweed shade as my own, glance up and then away. 'Don't look so shocked.'

'I can't help it. I thought jogging was my thing, not yours.'

'I've just started.'

'*OK.*' I make a face because he's still panting really hard. 'No offence, but I'm not sure you're doing it right.'

'Because I've *just* started. Are you going to let me in or not?'

'Well, since you asked so nicely.' I open the door wide. 'Why aren't you at work?'

'I had some holiday owing, so I took a long weekend. Then I thought I'd come and visit my little sister so she could interrogate me.'

'Sorry!' I laugh, as I lead him through to the kitchen. 'It's just that you don't usually drop by.'

I wave him into a chair as I head to the sink and pour a glass of water. Dan and I have always been close, but it can be hard to find time to hang out together when he's so busy working as a business analyst for some huge multinational, with an equally busy medical-student fiancée, Hailey.

'So, what's with the jogging?' I ask, handing him the water as I take a chair opposite.

'Thought I'd try something new.' He sprawls backwards, downing the water in a few gulps. 'You know, get into shape.'

'That's great. I can devise a programme for you, if you like?'

'No!' He answers a little too quickly. 'I mean, no offence, but I can manage.'

'Fair enough.' I lean forward. 'Now tell me the truth. Did Mum and Dad ask you to come by and make sure I'm OK, now that Maisie's moved out?'

'How –?' He puts the glass down on the table with a thud. 'All right, yes.'

'Why?' I throw my hands up in exasperation. 'I told them I was fine. I even told them I was going to Monaco. I sent Mum a photo from the yacht!'

'They still worry.' Dan looks sheepish. 'And that's not the only reason I'm here. I've been meaning to visit for a while.'

'Well, that's OK, then.' I arch an eyebrow. 'But just out of interest, how often should I expect one of these spontaneous visits? Is it an occasional thing or did you promise Mum you'd do a recce every couple of days?'

'It wasn't a formal arrangement. Not everyone is as organized as you.' He glances at my laptop and cue cards. 'What are you up to anyway?'

'Applying for jobs. Making lists and using my highlighters. You know how much I love doing that.'

'I do.' His lips twitch into a smile. 'So I know you probably have your day all planned out, but I wondered if you'd like to jog with me? I'll treat you to lunch afterwards.'

'Sorry. Wrong day. I work out on Tuesdays and Thursdays.'

'So? Break the rules a little! I won't tell anyone.'

'But *I'll* know.' I tip my head sideways. 'Although I could still lunch?'

'Even better.' He sounds relieved. 'All this exercise was beginning to hurt anyway.'

'Great.' I leap out of my chair and head to my bedroom. 'Just give me five minutes to get changed.'

HALF AN HOUR LATER, we're sitting in a cafe with two flat whites, a grilled chicken salad (mine) and a bacon and cheese toastie (his) on the table between us.

'So, how was Monaco?' Dan asks.

'Amazing.' I give him a smug look. 'It's really not so bad, hanging out with the rich and famous on a yacht for a weekend.'

'I'll bet. Gio Bauer seems like a good guy. Did you meet any other drivers?'

'A few.' Leif Olsen's unfriendly face pops into my mind. 'So, how's Hailey?' I ask to distract myself. 'She must have finished her training by now, right? It'll be useful, having a doctor in the family.'

'Yeah, about that . . .' Dan's face seems to crumple. 'Hailey and I broke up.'

'What?' I splutter on a mouthful of coffee. 'But you two were perfect together!'

'I thought so too. Only it turns out Hailey didn't totally agree. She's moving to Australia.'

I gape at him. 'Why?'

'They're offering doctors a really good deal over there. Regular shifts, decent pay, a good work–life balance.' He rubs a hand around the back of his neck. 'Honestly, I don't blame her for wanting to go.'

'But you're engaged!'

'*Were* engaged. Not any more. Apparently she's been thinking about emigrating for a while and now she's finally qualified . . .' There's a catch in his voice. 'She asked me to go too, but I said no. My career is here. So the wedding's off.'

'Oh, Dan . . .' I reach a hand across the table. 'I'm sorry.'

'So am I, but we're going to stay friends. We still love each other – we just want different things, that's all. And it's better to realize that now, instead of in a few years' time, so . . .' He shrugs his shoulders. 'She's moved back in with her parents and she's leaving in a couple of months.'

'Wait, she's already moved out?' I jerk my head backwards. 'When did you break up?'

'About three weeks ago.' He looks apologetic. 'I didn't want to tell you before your exams and then I didn't want to ruin Monaco for you.'

'You still should have told me.' I narrow my eyes at him. 'You don't have to be the one looking out for me all the time, no matter what Mum and Dad say.'

'They don't say that.'

'Really?'

'Well, only sometimes. They're just afraid you wouldn't tell us if you were feeling depressed again.'

'I'm not depressed!' I grind my teeth with annoyance. 'I haven't been for years. I know how to look after myself now, and, anyway, *I* should be the one comforting *you*. You know that jogging is a clear sign of denial, right?'

'I thought it was a sign of wanting to get into shape.'

'Unless you're trying to distract yourself, in which case . . . denial.'

'I'm trying to be healthy, that's all, and it's better than lying around being miserable all day.' He looks stricken suddenly. 'Shit. Sorry, Ava, I didn't mean –'

'It's OK.' I shake my head. 'I know you didn't. And you're right. Getting healthy *is* a better choice.'

'Thanks.' He coughs. 'So speaking of jogging . . . I bumped into Oliver in the park the other day.'

'Oh?' My throat tightens at the mention of my sort-of ex's name. *Sort of* because we only went on five dates. *Ex* because he's still the closest thing I've ever had to a boyfriend. 'How was he?'

'Good. Still confused about what happened between the two of you.'

'Nothing happened.' I roll my eyes. 'He asked me out, I gave it a try and it didn't feel right. End of story.'

'He said he thought there was something you weren't telling him.'

'What?' I stiffen in alarm.

'I didn't say anything.' Dan holds a hand up. 'But maybe *you* should have.'

'No.' I shut him down quickly. I don't want to talk about this. I talked about it a *lot* six years ago – to Dan, to my friends (before they decided to move on with their lives), to my parents, to a counsellor – and then I was done. I talked it to death and now it's over. Locked behind a door in my mind, never to be let out again.

'Ava.' Dan's voice softens. 'Don't you think what happened back then might still be affecting you when it comes to dating?'

Yes! I want to scream across the table at him. *Of course it still affects me! It changed my entire personality.* Maybe I was a relaxed, easy-going, hearts-and-flowers, love-conquers-all kind of person before I went to the park with my friends that night, but not any more. And I know some people, Oliver included, may think I'm uptight, but I also know how frightening the world can be and I won't let my guard down ever again because that way madness – or at least six months of sofa-bound depression – lies.

'Talking about it to Oliver wouldn't have made any difference,' I say.

'You don't know that.'

'Yes, I do.' I look him straight in the eye, trying to get him to understand. 'Dan, I can't handle a romantic relationship. That part of me is just . . . broken.'

'You're not broken.' His expression turns almost fierce. 'Oliver wasn't the right guy for you, that's all. It doesn't mean there isn't somebody out there who is.'

I tear my gaze away and take a forkful of salad. The way Dan's looking at me right now is pulling on my heartstrings so hard I can feel a lump building in my throat. It's a look that says he's got my back and that he'll never give up on me. He's so decent and kind and optimistic, even when he's just split up with his fiancée. I'm so grateful to him, for rescuing me six years ago and for still being here now, showing me that good guys really do exist, but I really, *really* wish he'd let this subject drop.

The thing is, objectively I know that he's right, that I shouldn't give up on love, but honestly, if I couldn't make it work with Oliver, I don't see how I can make it work with anyone.

Oliver was the perfect candidate: a gaming developer I met during my internship last summer – smart, funny, attractive. I did my best to trust him, to be like everyone else, but every time he kissed me it was like my body turned to ice. And it wasn't because I felt ashamed or afraid or any of those other self-destructive emotions that overwhelmed me for so long. It was more like detachment, like I couldn't feel *anything*. In the end, breaking up was a mutual decision. It wasn't Oliver's fault, even if it wasn't mine either. Like I said . . . broken.

My unconscious is apparently on Dan's side because a memory from last night suddenly flashes into my brain. I'm pushed up against Leif, his hands around my upper arms, his breath on my cheek. I didn't feel quite so detached and broken then. *But that was an anomaly*, I tell myself – like I told myself several times last night – *a confused reaction brought on by a combination of excitement, disappointment and dislike*. If I were to ever meet him again, I'm sure I wouldn't feel anything.

'I'm focusing on other things right now,' I answer finally. 'I don't need a relationship to be happy.'

'I never said you did. So long as you really *are* happy?' Dan gives me a meaningful look. 'Ava –'

I interrupt him. 'I have to take this call.'

'What?'

'A call.' I reach for my phone because, luckily, it really is vibrating in my jacket pocket. Normally, I would never answer an unknown number, but I'd happily chat to all the telemarketers in the world if it gets me out of this conversation.

'Hello?'

'Ava Yearwood?'

'Maybe.' I twist away from Dan's sceptical expression. 'Who's calling, please?'

'This is Vienna Szeto, director of communications at Rask Racing. Your name was passed to me by a colleague. I understand you produce the podcast *Single Seat News*?'

I sit up straighter. Rask may have plummeted in the rankings, but if they want to be featured on my podcast I'm not going to say no. 'That's right. Hi, Vienna, how can I help you?'

'Hopefully we can help each other. How soon could you come to our HQ for a chat? We're based outside Huntingdon.'

'Oh . . .' I mentally scan my diary. It's pretty empty. And Huntingdon isn't far, only half an hour's drive away. Fortunately for my podcast, there's a cluster of F1 teams around these parts. 'Well, I'm in Cambridge, so travel isn't a problem, but I'll need some time to prepare questions if you want to be on the podcast.'

'Actually, it's not for that.' Her tone is brisk. 'Long story short, we have a job opening and I think you'd be the perfect candidate.'

I have news!

Single Seat News, 26 May

THREE

MY FIRST IMPRESSION OF Rask Racing HQ is ... underwhelming. Compared to the sleek and modern facade of Quezada, it looks a lot like an industrial unit.

But it's still an F1 team and adrenaline is coursing through me so fast I'm practically vibrating. I have been ever since Vienna's phone call because I can't believe this is happening, that I got invited to an interview out of the blue! I mean, I haven't even sent in my first application yet. Gio must have given them my name and then forgotten to mention it to Maisie.

'I really appreciate you driving me,' I say to Dan, as he pulls up outside reception. In an effort to prepare, I've spent the journey brainstorming answers to hypothetical interview questions and coming up with my own. 'Are you sure you don't mind waiting around?'

'Nope. Just text when you're ready to be picked up.'

'OK.' I unclip my belt and take a deep breath. 'Wish me luck.'

'You don't need it. Whatever the job is, you're the best person for it. Who else could prep for an interview within an hour of a phone call?' He leans over, calling after me as I climb out, 'But good luck anyway!'

'Thanks!' I give him a wave, adjust the skirt of my olive-green maxi dress, toss my leather baguette bag on to my shoulder and head inside.

Fortunately, the reception area is much more impressive than the exterior, with half a dozen floor-to-ceiling display cases containing team memorabilia. There's a set of Rask overalls, as well as the specially painted helmets from this year's Australian and Miami GPs, and – *urgh* – my gaze lands on a life-size photo of Leif Olsen. Somehow, in my excitement about this job, I managed to repress the fact that working here would also mean working with him.

I give my name at reception and sit down on a red leather sofa to wait. There's a selection of autosport magazines on a coffee table, but I ignore them in favour of glaring at Leif's photo, tapping my foot and fantasizing about what I might do to it with a Sharpie. I'm still mentally graffitiing when a woman with a shoulder-length black bob and the biggest platform boots I've ever seen comes bursting through a set of double doors beside the main desk. She's dressed in various shades of grey and moves so fast it's like being confronted by a human tornado.

'Ava?' I recognize her clipped tone instantly. 'I'm Vienna.'

'Hi.' I stand up and hold a hand out. 'Thanks so much for seeing me.'

'No problem. I'm glad you could make it at short notice.' Her fingers have barely connected with mine before she's spinning around again. 'Come on in.'

I slip on the security lanyard she hands me, then follow her through the doors and up a staircase. Everything about her is efficient, from her rapid-fire way of talking to her brisk, ground-eating stride. I don't know whether to be intimidated or make her my role model, but I'm regretting my spiky heels because I practically have to jog to keep up.

'Wow!' I stop as we pass a window overlooking the factory floor. There are two bays below, divided by work stations, each containing a Formula 1 car and a group of mechanics. Everything looks so well organized I'm filled with an immediate sense of belonging. This is definitely my kind of place.

'Not a bad view, is it?' Vienna is calling over her shoulder from several metres ahead so I really do have to jog after her into a large, open-plan office. It looks welcoming enough, painted in shades of blue, red and yellow – the Rask colours – but it's weirdly empty. There's a scattering of people, but I can see at least half a dozen monitors without anyone in front of them.

'Take a seat,' Vienna says, leading me into a smaller side office. 'So, Ava, I'll get right to the point. I've listened to your podcast and you clearly know your Formula 1, which means you'll also be aware of all the jokes and comments about us. Right now, most people seem to think we'll be either bankrupt or under new management by the end of the season.'

'I've heard some rumours,' I answer tactfully, because I can't reasonably pretend otherwise. Rask's performance so far this season has provoked a lot of speculation.

'The problem is, they're not wrong. We're in the middle of a total shitstorm. But storms have to pass sometime, right?' She kicks her boots up on to the desk. 'Ordinarily I'd tell you this was all off the record, but since our situation is pretty much common knowledge I might as well be blunt. Presumably you know the team's background?'

'Yes.' I nod. 'Mika and Nova Jokkinen bought out Rask Racing at the end of last season.'

'That's right. The deal was fairly amicable at first. Unfortunately, that didn't last long. Our former owner, Philip Sawyer, wanted the money *and* to keep running the team behind the scenes. Long story short, he threw a hissy fit and left, and we ended up losing about 30 per cent of our workforce with him. We're doing our best to rebuild, but right now it feels like an uphill struggle. And Philip's still hovering in the wings, thinking that if he can cause enough trouble he'll be able to buy the team back at a cheaper price.'

'No!' I'm genuinely shocked. 'That's so sneaky.'

'Yeah, well, you know billionaires . . .' She drops her feet back on to the floor, like she can't keep still for longer than a few seconds. 'Turning a team's fortunes around isn't easy, especially mid-season, but we have some major upgrades coming. We've brought in some new engineers, and Bastian, our team principal, is confident.'

'That's great!' I say enthusiastically. 'What happened in Monaco was such a shame.'

'It was, but our number-one priority is to get some positive coverage. I want Rask to be seen as the plucky upstarts of F1 and we need to get the fans' support back. Basically, I need new staff in post as quickly as possible, which is where you come in. Like I said, I've listened to your podcast and I'm impressed. Your socials are engaging too. You have a talent for storytelling, you're obviously self-motivated and most importantly you haven't dug the boot into us the way some other pundits have.' Vienna regards me in silence for a long moment. 'So, are you interested in joining us?'

I open my mouth to give a resounding yes and then close

it again. The job might sound exactly what I need right now – a challenge to really get my teeth into, maybe even prove myself to Quezada come December – but I can't let myself get carried away. I need to keep this professional.

'I'm definitely interested. I just have a few questions.' I mentally scan through the list I made on the way here. 'First, what exactly would the job entail?'

'Everything and anything.' Vienna flings her hands out. 'Officially, your title would be communications officer, but unofficially you'd be my assistant, helping me implement a new media strategy and figuring out ways to revitalize the brand. I won't lie to you, I'll need you to hit the ground running and start coming up with ideas yesterday.' She glances at her phone as it beeps. 'It'll be full time, and an insane amount of stress, but with any luck by the end of the season it'll be worth it.'

I nod along because I hope it will be too. I'm already invested in her plucky underdog story, only I have one more important question and it's kind of a deal breaker.

'Would it be a fixed-term position, or permanent?'

'Mmm?' She pulls her gaze away from her phone. 'Oh, we'd hire you on a trial basis at first, but if things go well I can't see any reason why it couldn't become permanent.'

'I see . . .' I chew my lip. The problem is that I don't want a permanent position, not when I have another interview lined up with Jasper in December. A temporary contract with Rask, on the other hand, one without any non-compete clause, would be perfect; I'm prepared to throw myself heart and soul into this job, for six months anyway. But a trial period could easily last that long and, if not, I could stall . . .

'Is something the matter?' Vienna's fringe twitches like she's lifting an eyebrow, although I can't actually see one.

'No.' I smile, deciding quickly. If I turn down Vienna's offer, it'll be my second missed opportunity to work in F1. 'It sounds amazing.'

'Good. In that case, there's just one more thing.' She leans forward. 'It's about your podcast. I hate to ask, but if you take the job here, you'll need to put it on hiatus.'

'Oh.' I feel my body go rigid. I love *Single Seat News*. I've put so much work into it, invested so much time and research. I have twelve thousand subscribers, more than I ever expected when I launched it four years ago. I don't want to stop, but I guess it would be a conflict of interest to keep recording it while working for an actual F1 team.

'Would you object to me doing one last episode?' I ask. 'So I can tell my subscribers what's happening.'

'Not at all, provided you can do it tonight?'

I pause because today's been crazy enough, but this is a chance to show my proactive attitude. 'Yes, of course.'

'And give us a mention? It would be good PR.'

'I'd be happy to.'

'Then go ahead. I'll make sure to listen.'

'Great.' I discreetly let out a long breath. I guess this means I have a job in F1! It's so incredible it's going to take a while to sink in. 'So, when do I start?'

Vienna fixes me with a hard stare. 'How does right now sound?'

'I'LL HAVE A CONTRACT ready by the end of the day,' Vienna says, marching me out of her office and into the larger, open-plan one we passed through earlier. 'In the meantime, let me introduce you to a few of your new colleagues. Emika – chief press officer. Charlotte, who coordinates digital and print media. Yuto's in charge of marketing. Emika and Yuto also work as minders for Leif and Corey on race weekends. Like I said, at the moment we all do everything.'

'Hi,' I say, though nobody gets a chance to answer before Vienna hustles me on again.

'In here is Strategy.' She sticks her head through another door, barking out another quick introduction, before moving on the moment the last name is out of her mouth. All I can do is smile, wave and try to make mental notes as we repeat the same process with the design office, model shop, operations room, engineering office, workshop, canteen, break room and Finance department, but after ten minutes my head is spinning.

'This place is like a rabbit warren –' Vienna declares as she bolts off down another corridor – 'but you get used to it. Give it a week and you'll be fine.'

'I actually have another question.' I pant, as I scurry alongside. 'You said on the phone that a colleague recommended me?'

'That's correct.' She throws me a quick look and then somehow accelerates. 'Anyway, last stop for today . . .' She stops beside a sign that reads 'Simulation Room'.

My pulse jumps as we climb some steps into a large, dark space filled with screens of various sizes. I've always wanted to see an F1 simulator. Being in the control room is like standing on the deck of a spaceship. The volume of data being continuously recorded and analysed is mind-blowing – there are limitations on the amount of time teams can spend testing on tracks or in a wind tunnel, so simulators are vital for training. Even if I hadn't just got a job, it would have been worth coming in for this. I have a thousand questions, but everyone looks busy.

'Over here,' Vienna whispers, leading me towards a balcony. Below I can see a replica of a racing-car chassis, bumping and twisting from side to side as the driver responds to the image of a race track on a huge 180-degree screen.

'Usually the drivers get Monday off after a race, but since everything's so hectic at the moment, they had to get straight back to work this morning,' Vienna explains. 'Right now they're preparing for Barcelona. Mostly trying out different ways of approaching the track, seeing which lines to take and how the braking responds. The engineers will be throwing some tricky scenarios at them to see how they cope.'

'It looks so realistic.'

'It has to be. This is where the drivers spend most of their time when they're not on the actual track. Although, from the look of things, they're just finishing. Good timing.' She screws her eyes up. 'I can't tell if that's Leif or Corey, though.'

'It's not me,' a voice behind us says, as the car below reaches the chequered flag.

'Corey? Hi.' I turn and smile. 'We met yesterday,' I explain to Vienna, though I can hardly believe that was only last night. So much has happened since.

'In Monaco?' She presses a hand to her forehead. 'Please tell me he behaved.'

'He was a perfect gentleman,' I say, laughing at Corey's aggrieved expression. 'Not to mention a pretty good dancer.'

'Well, that's a relief.' Vienna gives him a sceptical look. 'Ava's coming to work with us.'

'Really? That's awesome! Welcome to the team.' Corey grins. 'I'd offer to show you around, but it's my turn in there.'

He waves in the direction of the simulator and my stomach plunges. Because if Corey's here, then the other driver, now removing his helmet as he heads up the steps towards us, must be . . .

'Leif?' Vienna calls out. 'Come and meet the newest member of the communications team!'

I lift my chin, trying to summon up some enthusiasm, but I'm seized with a powerful urge to run out of the room.

'Hi.' I offer a tight smile because Leif looks about as thrilled to see me now as he did last night, which is to say not at all. Judging by his stony expression, I wonder if he even recognizes me? I reintroduce myself. 'I'm Ava.'

'I know.' He stops in front of me and plants his feet wide apart.

I feel my hackles go up all over again. So I guess his objectionable behaviour last night wasn't just a one-off. He remembers me and he's *still* being an asshole, which is why he can't be bothered with basic manners. Although, I have to admit, it's kind of a relief. It makes it easier to forget any feelings of attraction I might have experienced and go back to straightforwardly disliking him in return.

'Right.' I keep pasting a fake, close-lipped smile on to my face and thrust a hand out. Suddenly I'm determined to make him acknowledge me properly. 'Nice to see you again.'

He looks down at my hand for a long moment, his shoulders visibly stiffening before he puts his helmet aside and peels off one of his leather gloves to take it. 'You too.'

I glance down at our joined hands. It shouldn't be a surprise that his is warm after an intense simulator session, but the way it sends electricity up my arm definitely is. *Shit.* That wasn't supposed to happen.

'Are you OK?' His fingers twitch against mine.

'Yes!' I let go and take a step backwards. I don't know what my body is playing at, but it needs to stop it right now. 'Why wouldn't I be?'

His gaze lingers on my blushing cheeks for a few seconds before he turns to Vienna. 'I should go and debrief.'

'And I should get in there.' Corey grins, shooting pistol fingers at me as he heads for the stairs. 'Welcome to the team, Ava!'

'So, what do you think?' Vienna asks the moment we're outside. 'You'll be working pretty closely with the drivers. Corey's easy to get along with, obviously, whereas Leif takes a little more getting used to, but he's a complete teddy bear underneath that stern exterior.'

I almost snort with incredulity. I can hardly think of anyone who fits the description less. Possibly because I've never felt either attracted to or enraged by a cuddly toy – not that I'm prepared to accept either of those reactions. If Leif and I are going to work together, then I can't let him affect me. I need to stay calm and control my feelings. Put them in a box and bury them deep in my subconscious.

'Trust me,' Vienna goes on. 'Plus he's an incredible driver. Better than the car deserves at the moment, but hopefully . . . Wait!' She stops walking so abruptly I'm several paces ahead before I realize. 'I have a brilliant idea. You should film a "First Day at Rask" segment tomorrow, a sped-up version of the tour I just gave you. It doesn't have to be long, but it means we can start posting content as soon as possible.'

'You mean, with me in it?'

'Of course! You'll be our poster girl.'

'Oh . . .' I hesitate because it sounds like jumping in at the deep end. Then again, why shouldn't I? If Rask are going to have my (temporary and dual) allegiance, why not go all-in? 'OK. That sounds great.'

'Perfect. In that case, I'll let you go for today, but I'll email the contract over later and there'll be a security pass waiting for you at reception first thing tomorrow.' She marches me to the main doors and holds them open. 'I'm relying on you to start brainstorming tonight. I can't wait to hear your ideas!'

Hi, I'm Ava Yearwood and I'm the new communications officer here at Rask Formula 1 team. This building is their headquarters, so come with me and I'll show you inside!

@ RaskRacing, 27 May

FOUR

I WAKE UP TWO hours before my alarm goes off, shocked into consciousness by a dream where I'm back in the club in Monaco with Leif. Only this time we're dancing, his strong hands gripping my waist while his blue eyes bore deep into mine, so intense it's like I'm the only person in the world. Meanwhile one of his legs is pressing between my thighs, moulding our bodies together, as we move in a slow, sensual rhythm . . .

I launch myself upright, red hot and horrified, as electric tingles race up and down my spine. I can't believe I had such an unprofessional dream! It's so . . . so . . . *so* unacceptable. I practically leap out of bed, shaking my head to repress the memory. If I had a security pass already, I'd get up and go straight to work, but since I don't – and I've planned all my outfits and meals for the rest of the week – all I can do is make coffee and start rehearsing what I'm going to say on my 'First Day at Rask' video. First days are stressful enough – especially after a spicy dream about one of my new colleagues – but I guess this is what I signed up for.

I manage to get one of the last spaces in the car park when I arrive just before nine, then film my steps leading up to the entrance. Luckily I arrive in reception at the same time as Emika, the chief press officer I met during Vienna's whistle-stop tour yesterday, and she waves at my camera as we go in together.

'Vienna told us you'd be filming a first-day bit,' she says once I've put my phone away and we're heading upstairs. She has short, tightly curled black hair and immaculate make-up, all rainbow eyeshadow and statement red lips. 'First things first. Let me show you our fuelling station.' She throws her bag and jacket on to a desk and then takes me into a kitchen with a state-of-the-art coffee machine. 'Our budget may be a little tight right now, but Vienna still insists on decent coffee.' She opens a drawer full of pods. 'Just avoid the blue ones. Yuto gets possessive of vanilla.'

'Thanks for the tip.' I choose an orange pod at random.

'Caramel? Good choice.' She smiles at me as the smell of arabica beans fills the air. 'We're so pleased to have another person on board. We've been doing our best to cope, but we're so understaffed we're behind with everything. Everyone's desperate for some time off and we're not even halfway through the season.'

'I'm excited to get started,' I say, because I really am. After recording my final (for now) podcast discussing the prospects for the Barcelona Grand Prix, I spent last night doing a deep dive into Rask: everything I could discover about their new owners, the Jokkinens (Mika and Nova are brother and sister, not a couple as most people assume), their buyout of Rask, as well as media coverage of their first eight races. Finally, I looked at their social media accounts and . . . Yeah, I hate to kick a team when they're down, but none of it was very inspiring. There are token posts after every race, thanking everyone for their efforts, with photos of the cars and a few statistics, but there's hardly any personal content, and nothing remotely eye-catching. It's not surprising, given all the recent turmoil in the team, but it's not going to win any new fans either.

Fortunately, there is *some* good news. Corey, for example, is a publicist's dream. Originally from Brisbane, he's funny and likeable, and clearly knows how to handle the media. Like most of the drivers, his main home is in Monaco and, according to his personal Instagram profile, which is in pretty good shape, his spare time is taken up with other extreme sports: surfing, skiing, sky-diving and abseiling. He's such an adrenaline junkie that there's a clause in his contract allowing him to be as crazy as he wants. I'm already envisaging some sweaty workout photoshoots.

Leif, on the other hand, is a total mystery. He's twenty-one, a year younger than Corey, but his official address is still in Norway, and I can't find *any* clues about what he enjoys outside Formula 1. As far as I can tell, he doesn't even have social media accounts and, judging by the monosyllabic answers he gives to interview questions that don't involve motor racing, he doesn't enjoy talking about himself in general. There's also a total lack of profile pieces about him. All I can discover are basic facts about his career – he got into karting at the relatively late age of twelve, won the World Karting Championship at fourteen, then entered F3, which he won at eighteen, and F2 through the Chiltern young driver training programme. Then, after serving as reserve driver for Chiltern last season, he was chosen by Bastian Aalto as a full-time driver this year.

It's . . . surprising. Most drivers come from money or have some kind of family connection to racing. That's why they call it the billionaire boys' club. It's not exactly democratic, but it's how the sport works. For a driver to succeed through talent and dedication alone is unusual. Impressive. Or it would be, if it were anyone else. I'd rather not give Leif Olsen any more credit than I have to.

'So, we usually have a team meeting mid-morning,' Emika goes on. 'Vienna's a powerhouse, but only after ten a.m. She generally doesn't arrive until then, and we absolutely don't talk to her until the caffeine kicks in.'

'Not today.' Vienna's voice makes us both jump.

'Oops.' Emika presses a hand to her mouth, though she's laughing at the same time. 'Sorry.'

'I'd fire you if it wasn't true. Or if I had any spare staff.' Vienna's glower is belied by the twinkle in her eye. 'Obviously, I'd prefer to start every day at twelve, but since we have a mammoth task ahead of us, I've decided today is an exception. You can apologize by making me coffee. You know what I like.'

'Double espresso. Will do, boss.'

'Welcome to the deep end.' Vienna gives me a wry smile before turning to address the whole office. 'Listen up, people! This is the first day of the new Rask Racing team. I want energy, optimism, focus and absolutely no mention of that bastard Philip Sawyer. Everyone to the conference room – now!'

I pick up my caramel latte and follow the others, taking a seat at a large oval table beside Charlotte. She looks like the original Barbie, with loose beach-wave blonde hair and huge baby-blue eyes that dazzle me when she turns and gives a welcoming smile. Yuto sits opposite, his dark hair flopping over his face, while Emika sits beside him. They're all dressed casually, I notice, in cargoes, jeans and T-shirts. It makes me feel overdressed in my oversized black trouser suit.

'Now, I know you're all tired from covering so many jobs,' Vienna announces once she's gulped down her double espresso. 'But from now on rebuilding our image takes priority. So . . . ideas?'

I blink as she looks straight at me. I get the impression this is a test, but it's what she hired me for, after all – to inject some new energy. And she's right – everyone else around the table looks drained. Fortunately, my head is already buzzing with ideas.

'OK.' I unlock my iPad and pull up the list I made last night. 'So until the upgrades happen, car performance may still be an issue. But we can do some things to get people's attention and change their perception of Rask. Research shows that a lot of fans support individual drivers rather than specific teams, so, first of all, we need to work on boosting Corey's and Leif's personal profiles. Then they can tell everyone what a great team this is.'

'Like one big, happy family.' Charlotte beams.

'We might have our work cut out with Leif.' Emika makes a face. 'He's not a fan of doing promo.'

'I noticed.' I try to keep my expression neutral. 'But we'll just have to find some way to persuade him.'

'Won't that be helping the drivers' brands instead of ours?' Yuto asks. 'I mean, what if they decide to change teams at the end of the season?'

'That's a good point.' I nod. 'But there'll be plenty of cross-promotional opportunities. Plus, if we can show the drivers that we're helping their careers, they'll be more likely to stay, don't you think?' I look around the table. 'I've come up with a few ideas for content – how about I throw them out and you tell me what you think?'

By lunchtime, we've come up with at least a dozen promising concepts. The best part was that once I started making suggestions, everyone else joined in too. Pop quizzes, endurance challenges, go-kart races, a mini golf competition . . . We finish with Vienna promising to set up meetings with Corey and Leif as soon as possible. The mood in the room is so positive it feels like the change of attitude is already taking effect.

Mid-afternoon, however, my blood sugar drops and worry sets in. A change of attitude here is all very well, but what if nobody else notices? The media is busy watching Fraser and Quezada battle it out at the top of the table. What if nobody spares any attention for us? But we have to try, so I banish my blues by drawing up a rough content schedule, then retrace the tour I did yesterday with Vienna on my phone. I can speed it up when I edit it later, which should be eye-catching. What would make it perfect is including one of the drivers at the end. And by one of them, I mean the driver who actually knows how to smile.

'Is Corey about?' I ask Emika. 'It would make a cute end to my video if I could accidentally bump into him.'

She shakes her head. 'He flew back to Monaco a couple of hours ago. Leif is still here, though.'

'Oh . . .' I grimace. The thought of Leif 'welcoming' me to my new job is laughable and I'm not in the mood for another of his intense looks right now. 'Never mind. I'll leave it as it is.'

'Why? You said we need to boost his online profile.'

I suddenly wish I hadn't mentioned anything. 'But like you said, he obviously doesn't enjoy doing promo and I don't want to spring it on him.'

'Leif's fine so long as nobody asks him anything personal,' Charlotte interjects, looking up from her desk. 'He's a really nice guy. I dropped my bag in the car park last week and he came running over to pick everything up for me. And when it was Yuto's birthday, he ordered the biggest ice-cream cake you've ever seen. Honestly, he's adorable. I'm sure he wouldn't mind helping you out.'

'OK, but has he had *any* media training?' I ask, annoyed because this is the second time somebody's told me how nice Leif is. 'Only he's not exactly adorable in interviews. Most of the time he just seems uncomfortable.'

'True, but it makes a good contrast with Corey,' Emika argues. 'You know, one super-friendly driver, one serious.'

'But that won't work if we're going for a one-big-happy-family vibe. Fans want the drivers to be open and accessible, not monosyllabic. I've met Leif twice now and both times it's been like getting blood from a stone. I'd have as much luck using that wall in my video. Or this cup.' I lift my empty mug, although it occurs to me that maybe I've drunk a little too much caffeine because I can feel myself getting carried away.

'Um, Ava . . .?' Emika clears her throat.

'You're right, that was unfair, but he could try lightening up a bit.'

'*Ava!*'

'What?' I follow the direction of her frantic head-nodding to where Leif is standing in the open doorway, one shoulder resting against the frame, dressed in pale jeans and a striped Rask T-shirt.

Crap.

I clamp my lips together. Of all the people to appear at this moment! Although he could have given some indication he was there – a knock or a cough or a stamp of the foot. But of course he didn't because he's Leif Olsen, king of awkward silences. And now I'm the queen of them because I have no idea what to say either. I rack my brain, but I've got nothing except a deeply unhelpful flashback to this morning's dream.

Fortunately, Leif starts the conversation for once.

'Vienna says you'd like a meeting?' His brow is puckered into a frown, only this time I can't object. Asshole or not, he has every right to frown at me. Every reason to get me fired too. I'm pretty sure that 'Do Not Insult the Drivers' is a golden rule of working in F1 communications and I just compared him to a wall. And a cup. I'm so embarrassed that I'm blushing to the very roots of my hair.

'Um . . . yes, that would be great, if you're available any time soon?' My voice is a whole octave higher than usual.

He stares down at the floor for a couple of seconds, as if his schedule is printed there, before looking up again. 'Nine a.m.?'

'Tomorrow?' I blink. 'But aren't you . . .? I mean, don't you need to . . .?' My tongue trips over the words. 'You know . . . go to Barcelona?'

'Not until midday.'

'Ah.' I lick my lips, trying to make my voice sound normal again. 'In that case, 9 a.m. is perfect. Thank you.'

'Good.' He turns to go.

'Wait!' Emika calls out, just as I'm about to sag over my desk and start banging my forehead against it. 'Would you mind being in Ava's video before you go?'

'Oh, no.' I hold my hands up as he turns round again. 'It doesn't matter. You look like you're on your way out.'

'What do you need?' He ignores my protest, lifting an eyebrow instead.

'It's a first-day-at-work short,' I say hesitantly, because apparently there's no way out of this. 'I thought it would be good if Corey could appear at the end, but he's not here so . . .'

'I can do it.' He folds his arms and nods curtly.

'You can?' I feel a need to double-check because his negative body language is so confusing.

'Yes.'

'OK! Thank you. So, the idea is that I meet you in the corridor and you say "Hi" and "Welcome to Rask" or something along those lines . . . if that works for you?'

'Sure.'

'Great.' I exchange a quick look with Emika, who gives me an encouraging thumbs-up. 'In that case . . . shall we do it now?'

He inclines his head infinitesimally, which I choose to interpret as another nod, so I get up from my desk and lead him out into the corridor, lifting my chin as I go. I'm not sure whether I'm more resentful of his behaviour or embarrassed about mine, but it's a disconcerting combination.

'So I'll carry the phone like I'm just casually walking along and then you come out of that door,' I say, trying to emulate Vienna's brisk manner as I point towards an empty store room. 'Then it'll be like we're just bumping into each other.'

'Fine.'

'And it would be great if . . .' I pause because I'm not entirely sure how to phrase this without giving offence. 'If you could maybe try to smile when you come out?'

There's a flicker of something in his eyes, something that on anybody else might be amusement. 'I can smile.'

'Yes. Right. Of course. I didn't mean to imply –' I order myself to stop talking before I make things even worse. 'So you go that way, and I'll go this way . . .'

I turn and walk off, taking a moment to gather my thoughts, before lifting my phone out in front of me. *I can do this*, I tell myself. It's just ten seconds of film, at most. No big deal. Just ten seconds and then we can go our separate ways.

Ten loooooong seconds.

I turn around to check that Leif isn't visible, then press record as I walk along the corridor, talking enthusiastically. 'So that was my first day! I've had such a great time. Everyone is really lovely and . . . Oh!' I feign shock as Leif appears around the door. 'Hi, Leif.'

He tilts his head as he comes towards me. 'Hi, Ava.'

I open my mouth to reply, but no words come out because suddenly I'm transfixed. His mouth is curving up at the corners in a smile that transforms his whole face so that he looks boyish and handsome and yet also . . . devastatingly sexy. My mind stalls and my steps falter. Now I understand why he does it so rarely. It's too powerful. His cologne fills my senses again too, a combination of earth and wood and smoke and leather all rolled into one.

Oh fuck. It hits me that I've come to a complete stop to stare at him.

'Ava?' His smile fades into a look of confusion.

'Sorry!' I let out a shaky breath and snap back to myself. 'I just . . . forgot my line – haha! Would you mind if we go again? I'll get it right this time, I promise.' I don't wait for his answer as I hurry away, cringing internally.

People say you should be careful what you wish for, but how could I have anticipated a smile like *that*? And 'forgot my line'? I need to get a grip. He's an asshole! A rude, monosyllabic asshole!

So how is it possible for him to be having this kind of effect on me?

Describe your ideal partner ...

@ LaraLovesF1, 28 May

FIVE

DESPITE BOTH EMIKA AND Charlotte's reassurances, I was expecting a phone call from Vienna all yesterday evening, telling me my trial period was cancelled and not to bother coming back. I'd even worked out what I was going to say in response, that I understood, I knew I'd acted unprofessionally and I was sorry for offending Leif, etc. I even waited until 9 p.m. to post my first-day video in case it proved too ironic. Only no call, email or text ever came, and my security pass – I hold my breath as I scan it across the pad in reception – still works.

Phew. I fling myself through the door, hyperventilating with relief. Which looks weird, I realize, when two men dressed in overalls pass by and give me curious looks, so I hurry upstairs to the communications office to get started.

'Hey.' Yuto does a double-take when he arrives at 8.45, dressed in grey shorts and a black North Face hoodie. 'You're here early.'

'I have a meeting with Leif at nine,' I explain, feeling even more overdressed than yesterday in tapered trousers, a navy blazer and my spikiest heels, with my hair in its usual high ponytail. But I *need* to look professional today. Power dressing makes me feel in control, and hopefully this way I'll avoid making a fool of myself again.

'Morning!' Charlotte comes in behind Yuto. 'There, didn't I tell you?' She smiles brightly at me. 'I said Leif wouldn't get you fired.'

'Have I missed something?' Yuto looks between us. 'Why would you think that?'

'There was an incident,' I say, clasping my elbows. 'I said some things.'

'What sort of things?'

'Just about how he can come across as a bit . . . terse.' I lower my voice and glance at the door because the last thing I want is a repeat of yesterday. 'Though obviously I wouldn't have said so if I'd known he was standing in the doorway.'

'It was pretty funny.' Charlotte giggles. 'I mean, he must have been standing there for a good thirty seconds before you noticed him, but honestly, it'll be fine. He's one of the loveliest guys I've ever met. Even Andre, my fiancé, says so, and he thinks most drivers are total divas.'

'Leif has met your fiancé?' I ask in surprise.

'He came to our engagement party.' She nods happily. 'Anyway, good luck in your meeting. I have a press release to write, but Emika and I are going to the canteen for lunch at one if you want to join us?'

'Sounds great. I'd love to.'

'Don't ask her anything about the wedding –' Yuto whispers as Charlotte heads for her desk – 'or you'll be trapped all afternoon.' He fixes me with a pained look. 'Do *you* know the top five most popular colours for bridesmaids' dresses?'

'Um . . . no.'

'I do.'

'Right,' I answer sombrely. 'Thanks for the warning.'

I pour a cup of water from the cooler and head into the conference room to get my thoughts in order before Leif arrives. On top of power dressing, I've had a long, stern talk with myself and I'm determined this meeting is going to go well. I intend to be extra polite and efficient. That means no more weirdness or tension and *absolutely* no thoughts of attraction. I refuse to let him affect me any more.

It also occurred to me, after replaying my comments from yesterday at least a dozen times during the (thankfully dreamless) night, that I never actually said sorry. Even if Leif doesn't like me, which is pretty obvious, I need to persuade him to trust me, to see me as a professional person who's trying to do the best for his career, which means an apology is the first order of business.

The one positive about yesterday is that at least now I know he *can* smile. That should make my job a little bit easier. Especially when that smile is so powerful in a slow burn, sexy kind of way . . . I tense as I realize I'm trailing a finger along the edge of my blazer in the direction of my cleavage. I really need to snap out of this.

I set out my things, placing my laptop in front of me, my notepad and papers to the left and three pens (black, green and red) to the right, beside my cup of water. Next, I take a quick peek in my compact to make sure there are no crumbs on my face from the wholewheat blueberry muffin I ate for breakfast, then place my hands, palms down, on the table and wait.

It's 8.59 when I hear Leif's voice in the office outside, accompanied by the sound of Charlotte's laughter. Obviously he's being 'adorable' again, though I'm 99 per cent certain he'll be frowning by the time he enters the room.

It takes approximately five seconds to have my theory confirmed. Leif looks like he's about to have an interview with the taxman. He's even wearing a shirt, a short-sleeved Rask polo with a collar, like he wants to keep this professional too.

'Hi.' I stand up from the table as his eyes lock on to mine. In the morning light, they look even more quicksilver pale and intense than usual. I get the sudden feeling that if he were to focus on me for too long he'd see everything, right down to all my deepest, darkest secrets. Nervous energy runs down my spine at the thought. I've never felt so acutely self-conscious with anyone in my life.

'Come in. Can I get you –' I glance at the mug in his hand and shake my head. 'Never mind. Please take a seat.'

I wait for him to sit before doing the same, folding my hands together and putting on my most professional expression. 'So before we start, I'd like to apologize for yesterday. I should never have said what I did and I'm truly sorry. It won't happen again.'

'OK,' he answers flatly.

I stare at him, waiting for something more, but there's nothing. His expression is so completely unreadable I can't tell if he really forgives me or if he's just not interested in my apology. 'OK,' I echo. 'Well, that's very kind of you. And feel free to insult me back if you like.'

He cocks his head to one side. 'What do you mean?'

'You could point out something about me that you don't like. Then we'll be even.' I try to make the words sound cajoling, but they appear to have the opposite effect because he looks genuinely shocked.

'I can't.'

'Just try. It'll clear the air.' I grit my teeth and smile. 'After yesterday, I'm sure there are lots of things you can think of.'

'No.'

'Oh.' I look down at my notes, tapping my foot under the table to vent some of my frustration. So much for 'adorable'. Either he has no sense of humour or he's simply not prepared to joke around with me. Or use sentences of more than four words. But that's fine. We don't have to be friends, just colleagues. Which means getting down to business.

'So Vienna hired me to help reinvigorate Rask's image and implement a new social media strategy,' I begin. 'Which means we need to get people's attention. Because of that, when I posted my video last night, I asked if there were any questions people would like to ask you and we got a really good response – quickly too, which is a positive sign. It shows the fans are curious.' I slide a piece of paper across the table to him. 'These are some of the best. If you're happy with them, we can shoot a short video when you have a gap in your schedule and then post it on the team's channels.'

He reaches a hand out for the paper, his bicep flexing in a way that I try not to notice but can't help because I have treacherous eyes that linger a fraction too long. Even when I drag them away, I'm still aware of his arms in the periphery of my vision. It's irritating. I'm *never* this aware of a man.

'These questions are for me?' he asks, skim-reading the paper before setting it down again. Long, tapered fingers tap the table beside it and, yep, there it is: he's frowning again.

'I know they're not very car-related,' I say, to pre-empt any criticism. 'But they're fun, quirky, perfect for fans to get to know you as a person.'

'"If you could have any animal as a pet, what animal would you have and why?"' He sounds perplexed, like I've just asked him to write a political treatise on Anglo-Norwegian relations, although judging by his expression he might have preferred that.

'We're trying to show your lighter side,' I explain, reaching for my water. 'Think of it as a kind of rebrand. Basically, we're reintroducing you to the fans.'

'You mean the ones who think I'm monosyllabic?' His eyes follow the cup to my lips.

'Right.' I swallow a little too forcefully. 'Like I said –'

'An Arctic fox.' He interrupts me.

'Pardon?'

'If I could have any animal as a pet, that's what I would choose.'

'Oh, they're lovely.' A clip from a nature documentary pops into my head of a small white fox diving headfirst into a bank of snow, along with a random fact. 'They have hair on the soles of their feet.'

'They do.' His eyes widen, like he's surprised. 'They're also mostly solitary, but monogamous once they find a mate. So . . .' He gives a firm nod. 'An Arctic fox.'

'That sounds perfect.' I make a note.

'"If you weren't a driver, what would you do?"' A shadow passes over his face as he reads from the list again.

'Yes. You know, as a job?' I prod him when the silence starts to feel uncomfortable. 'Maybe something else with cars?'

'Maybe.' He sounds brooding.

'Like being a mechanic?'

'Perhaps.'

'You know, it would be brilliant if you could do a technical video about your car sometime.'

'Sure.'

'Great.' I watch as he reads again. It's not like I'm staring, except . . . well, maybe I am a little, but I can't help noticing lots of little details about him, like that his lashes are long, but so pale you don't notice them at first. Also what looks like a chickenpox scar on the left side of his chin, just visible through his stubble. And speaking of stubble, it's longer today than it was in Monaco, like he hasn't shaved since. Give it a couple more days and it'll be a full beard. That would probably suit him, in a rugged, lumberjack kind of way . . .

I follow the line of it down his throat. F1 drivers need to have strong necks to withstand the intense G-forces of motor racing, and his looks particularly muscular. Like his arms, which are straining the sleeves of his polo shirt in a way that makes me think I ought to ask Merchandising to get him a larger size. Maybe as some kind of peace offering? A quiver of something ripples through my body.

Shit. I squirm in my chair. I promised myself this wouldn't happen again today. It shouldn't be happening at all! *What the fuck, body?*

'"Have I ever committed a crime?"' He looks up abruptly, just in time to catch me ogling him. 'Do I have to be truthful?'

'That would probably be best.' I clear my throat, as if that might somehow hide the hot flush creeping over my cheeks. 'Unless . . . do you want to leave that one out?'

'We probably should.'

'Really?' I lean forward, intrigued. 'What did you do?'

'It was a long time ago.' He looks back down at the list. '"Describe your ideal partner."'

'Right. Again, feel free to cross out any questions you don't like.'

'It's a tricky one.' He sounds thoughtful. 'But I guess it would need to be someone who likes Arctic foxes too. Then I wouldn't have to choose between her and my pet.'

'Good answer.' I smile because I feel like he's finally getting into the spirit. In which case, maybe it's time to ask the big question? 'Leif,' I say in a casual voice. 'I notice that you don't do social media, but fans really like to connect with drivers. And I'm sure your sponsors would appreciate it too . . .' I take a deep breath. 'How would you feel about setting up an Instagram account?'

'No.' He doesn't hesitate.

'You wouldn't have to do much.' I carry on like he hasn't spoken. 'We'd be happy to produce and edit the content for you. Then your assistant –'

'I don't have an assistant.'

I blink a couple of times. 'You don't?'

He shrugs. 'My manager and performance coach deal with most things.'

'So maybe one of them could do it? Or me?' I spread my hands out. 'I'd be happy to run your account for you.'

'I just want to drive.'

'I understand, but –'

'I'm *paid* to drive.'

'Well, that's not entirely true.' I try to keep my tone reasonable. 'Your contract involves certain promotional requirements, doesn't it?'

'Some.' The furrow between his eyes deepens. 'The ones I couldn't get out of.'

'Because they're good for the team. The more media you

do, the more attention it brings, which means more sponsors, fans and money.'

'Formula 1 is about driving skill and precision engineering.' His tone is clipped. 'If people don't think that's enough, then maybe they're not real fans.'

'Oh, come on.' I roll my eyes because now he's being deliberately obtuse. 'There's a lot more to it. Or do you think there ought to be some kind of test for people attending a Grand Prix? So only ones who can correctly identify all the components in a power unit can enter?'

'I'm not saying that.' His eyes flash so brightly I could almost swear they turn silver. 'All I'm saying is that I'm happy to talk about the car and the races, but as for social media and the rest of this bullshit . . .' He waves a disparaging hand at my paper. 'I don't see the relevance of some trivial interview about my favourite animal.'

'Excuse me, but I'm doing you a *favour* with this bullshit interview.' I keep my voice calm because, despite the fact he just insulted my job, I'm supposed to be building bridges, not arguing with him. 'I deliberately chose these questions so you wouldn't have to talk about your private life. And this doesn't *have* to be trivial. If you weren't so close-minded, you'd know that social media can be powerful, a platform to talk about issues you care about. You could do some good with it.' I heave a sigh. 'Look, believe it or not, we're on the same side. I'm trying to help the *team*, and right now, you're stopping me from doing my job.'

His gaze flickers briefly before he leans back in his chair. 'It matters that much to you?'

'Yes. So you should either give in now or get ready to have this conversation every time we meet.'

'Then I guess we're going to be repeating ourselves a lot.'

'If that's what it takes.' I close my laptop to demonstrate I mean business. 'Please look over the rest of those questions when you get a chance, and we'll shoot the video when you get back from Barcelona.'

'Fine.'

'Fine.' I toss my ponytail and then can't resist digging the boot in. 'And when you're being interviewed in Spain, if you could say a little more than the absolute minimum, that would be really helpful. Maybe with a hint of a smile?'

He doesn't answer, holding on to my gaze with a look that I can't interpret, but that somehow makes it harder to breathe. It feels as if the air is subtly shifting, like somebody is lighting tiny invisible matches around us. The atmosphere feels taut, tense . . . *exciting*. Heat blooms in my stomach and I'm self-consciously aware of a now familiar (and entirely unwelcome) tingling sensation racing across my skin. I have a sudden image of us both springing across the table, his arms pulling me against him, me lifting my face up to meet his . . .

Wait, what? I push the thought out of my head. It's so inappropriate I can feel myself blushing again.

Fortunately, Leif breaks the connection, pushing his chair back and standing up.

'I'll do my best.' His voice sounds different, huskier than before.

'That's all I ask.' My throat feels tight too.

Then he's gone and I have a feeling that working with Leif Olsen is going to be a bigger problem than I anticipated.

Reigning champion Gio Bauer may be on pole in Barcelona, but with every grandstand full to bursting with Quezada supporters, he'll struggle to keep Jaxon Marr behind him today.

@ MotorsportEchoNews, 1 June

SIX

'I CAN'T BELIEVE YOU'RE working for a rival team!' Maisie exclaims the moment I open my front door.

'I know.' I hang my head in mock shame. 'If you never speak to me again, I'll understand.'

'Well, I thought about it . . .' She pauses for a moment, before thrusting a plastic tub towards me. 'But then I made celebratory brownies instead. Congratulations on the new job!'

'Oooh.' I lick my lips as I open the lid. Maisie's chocolate brownies are the best. She says the secret ingredient is sour cream, which doesn't sound very appealing, but they're absolutely mouth-watering. 'In that case, you can come in.'

She pushes the door shut with her foot. 'Um, not to sound critical, but what are you wearing? Couldn't you be fired for wearing a Quezada shirt when you work for Rask?'

'Not if they don't know about it.' I suppress a pang of guilt. 'It's the *Spanish* Grand Prix! What else can I wear? Anyway, I can support *both* teams.'

'Can you?' Maisie looks sceptical. 'What if it comes to a choice?'

'It won't,' I answer confidently. Quezada are in the top

two, while Rask are stuck in the lower middle of the pack. No matter how effective their upgrades might be, something dramatic would have to happen for either Leif or Corey to challenge Jaxon Marr or Noa Shimizu.

'But theoretically?' She nudges me.

'Theoretically?' I arch an eyebrow. 'My heart belongs to Quezada.'

'I knew it! You're just flirting with Rask.' She laughs. 'Don't worry. I won't tell.'

'Thanks. Now, come on. Dan's watching the race with us.'

'Great.' She follows me through to the kitchen-lounge. 'So how's it going at Rask? I won't tell Gio, I promise.'

'I love it!' I grin at her over my shoulder. 'I still have to pinch myself every morning to check I'm not dreaming. It's pretty full-on, but it's fun and the people in my department are all super nice.'

I sigh because it's true; I really do like my new colleagues. After just a couple of days – even though Emika and Yuto left for Spain on Wednesday afternoon – I feel like I'm getting to know them well. For example, I know that Charlotte loves romance novels about vets and that she's getting married to a real-life vet in January, during the off-season. Despite Yuto's warning, I've already had several conversations with her on the subject. I also know that Emika is an identical twin, is sick of wedding talk and hates the smell of Yuto's favourite prawn cocktail crisps. As for Yuto, he's a huge Warhammer fan and, according to our new WhatsApp group, is prepared to switch to salt and vinegar on the condition he can still have prawn cocktail on Fridays.

In return for all this information, I've told them about my degree, my podcast, my friendship with Maisie and Gio and . . . Well, then I drew a blank. Not that my life is empty, but now that my main interest has also become my job, I guess maybe it's time I found a replacement hobby.

'Don't Rask need you to work today?' Maisie asks.

'Not really.' I shake my head. 'Media Day on Thursday was busy, but the team at the track handle all the communications stuff today.'

'Well, I'm really happy for you.' She looks past me to the lounge. 'Hi, Dan.'

'Hi!' My brother looks up from where he's slumped on the sofa, watching the pre-race grid walk. 'I hope you don't mind me joining you?'

'Of course not.' She flings herself down beside him. 'I didn't know you were an F1 fan?'

'I'm not, but my little sister insisted I take her to brunch, so I thought I'd hang out for a while afterwards.'

'Good idea.' She smiles sympathetically. 'By the way, I'm sorry about you and Hailey. Is there any chance of you two working things out?'

'No. She's moving to Melbourne in a couple of months.' He lifts his beer with a grimace. 'What about you? How are things with your world-champion boyfriend? Shouldn't you be in Spain cheering him on?'

Maisie bristles. 'I have my own life, thank you very much. I don't just follow Gio around the world like some kind of cheerleader –' She stops, abruptly. 'Sorry, it's a bit of a sore subject. He wanted me to go with him this weekend, but I have a big race of my own coming up soon and I need to train. It's the regional mountain-bike championships.'

'Will Gio be able to come to that?'

'No, it's the same weekend as the Austrian GP.' She pushes

her hands through her hair. 'I know he can't just drop a race, even though there are like twenty-four of them, but it feels like our schedules are completely out of sync. And I don't see why his career is so much more important than mine, even though he earns more and has millions of fans.'

'It's not.'

'Tea?' I interrupt, carrying a tray laden with mugs and brownies over to the coffee table. Listening to them both bemoan their love lives, I'm wondering if it was such a good idea to bring Maisie and my brother together. This afternoon was supposed to cheer them both up, not depress them.

'Yes, please.' Maisie looks at me, suddenly changing topic. 'I saw your "First Day at Rask" video. It was really good.'

'Thanks. It was my boss's idea, but I think it went OK.'

'You got Leif Olsen to smile on camera. I've never seen that before.'

'*Urgh.*' I roll my eyes. 'I don't know how. He still hates me.'

'I'm sure that's not true. I know you said he was weird with you in Monaco, but Gio says he's a really nice guy.'

'That's what everyone keeps telling me. I guess I just bring out the worst in him.'

'Give the guy a break,' Dan objects. 'You'd be moody too if your car kept breaking down.' He points a finger at me. 'If you want him to smile, tell your engineers to give him a better engine.'

'Hopefully they already have. Rask are introducing some new upgrades this weekend.' I give him a double look. 'How do you know about his car anyway?'

'They've just been talking about it.' He gestures at the television before tipping his head back. 'Ava, why is it so dark in here? What happened to your light?'

'What? Oh.' I look up to where some capped wires are dangling from the ceiling. 'There was something wrong with the fitting so I had to take it down. I've bought a replacement, but I need somebody qualified to install it properly for me. Maybe somebody who did an electrical apprenticeship with their dad before they decided to change career direction?' I bat my lashes at him.

'Fine.' He chuckles. 'I'll bring my tools over next time.'

'Look!' Maisie starts waving at the screen. 'There's Leif now.'

I turn my head quickly to see my least favourite driver standing next to his car, a towel round his neck and his overalls rolled down to his waist, as an interviewer shoves a microphone into his face. He had another impressive qualifying session yesterday, putting him in P9, with Corey only three spots behind in P12, but whether his gearbox will last the race is another matter. I cringe as the interviewer asks Leif about that, waiting for a terse reply, but to my amazement he only nods his head like he's processing the question, then gives a long – two sentences! – answer about how the team have been working hard and how they – *we* – are all giving 100 per cent. He even manages a small curve of his lips at the end.

'He did it again!' Maisie points at the screen. 'That's *two* smiles.'

I beam back at the television, feeling a surge of professional pride. Leif might not like me, but at least he's doing what I tell him.

'You know –' Maisie tilts her head as an orchestra starts playing the Spanish national anthem – 'he's actually pretty good-looking, if you like the brooding, strong-jawed Viking type.'

'I guess.' I tilt my head too, pretending the idea has never occurred to me before.

'Maisie, did you bake these?' Dan mumbles through a mouthful of chocolate brownie. 'They're really good.'

'I know.' She looks pleased. 'Biking and brownies are my twin talents.'

'Leave some for the rest of us!' I smack his hand away as he reaches for another. 'I thought you were getting healthy?'

'I changed my mind.' He reaches past me. 'What's the point of a break-up if I can't even drown my sorrows in sugar?'

'You can't drown them in sugar *and* beer. Pick one.'

'Fine.' He puts his bottle down, swapping it for a mug of tea. 'One at a time.'

'They're about to start!' Maisie sits forward on the sofa. 'Usual deal?'

She flicks a look at me and I nod. We made an agreement at the start of the season not to cheer in the event of a Quezada car overtaking Gio or vice versa. That way there's no risk of damaging our friendship.

The lights go out and the cars speed away. Gio keeps the lead, with Marr close behind him, but Louis Cooper in one of the Chilterns manages to overtake Shimizu on the first corner by diving up the inside. I'm surprised Shimizu allows it, but maybe the pressure of driving in front of a Quezada home crowd is getting to him. The grandstands are a sea of vivid yellow, like a field full of sunflowers. Just the sight of it causes a pang in my chest. It would be so amazing to be there, yelling and cheering along, soaking up the atmosphere. Maybe next year ... In the meantime, it's probably better that I'm watching at home. I meant what I said to Maisie about supporting both teams, but I don't want anyone at

Rask to know I have divided loyalties, and it would be hard to conceal my love for Quezada if I were there.

'Olsen got a good start,' Dan comments.

'Yes.' Maisie and I answer at the same time, both of us staring fixedly at the screen. He's right, Leif has already overtaken two cars and is causing problems for Zaragoza in the Gold Dart. He's driving really well too, closing the distance so fast it won't be long before he's in the DRS zone and can overtake.

'Oh, shit.' Dan jolts forward suddenly, and I see Maisie wince as Marr overtakes Gio on the straight. It's a brilliant move, a completely amazing piece of driving, and the Quezada crowd go crazy.

Meanwhile, Leif has gone up another place, but the cameras have been so focused on the leaders that we've missed it. I hope they show a replay later because overtaking three cars in one lap is impressive.

I settle back in my armchair, sipping my tea as the race settles into a steady rhythm. I generally watch races twice. The first time so I can fixate on the Quezada cars, the second time for all the others so I can give them equal attention in my podcast, but today I find myself uncharacteristically distracted, my gaze drawn towards the middle of the pack. It's a strange feeling, like my heart is pulling me in one direction and my head in the other.

The cars start pitting on lap 13. The track at Barcelona is notorious for tyre degradation and, by the look of it, all the teams are on a two-stop strategy. Leif is one of the first in, which puts him back half a dozen places until lap 18, when suddenly he's in fifth place. As if that isn't enough good news, Shimizu also manages to leave the pit-lane ahead of Cooper, putting him back in third, while Corey is up in tenth. I can hardly believe it's all going so well.

'What kind of upgrades did Rask give their cars?' Dan sounds impressed.

'I have no idea.' I find myself grinning. 'But I guess Bastian knows what he's doing.'

Lap 60 and I give myself permission to start getting excited. There are only six laps left, and Leif and Corey are still going strong, with no sign of any mechanical issues. That's a win in itself, but if they can finish where they are, in fifth and tenth places, it'll mean eleven points for the team.

I rest my hands on my knees and lean towards the screen. This could be the perfect result: Quezada occupying the first and third spots on the podium, with Gio between them, and both Leif and Corey scoring points. Just six more laps . . .

I'm still envisaging it when Cooper, in fourth place in front of Leif, understeers at the third corner, hurtling into the tyre barrier at high speed, flipping his car over and sending one of his wheels flying towards the track. It happens so quickly there's no time for a red flag before Leif and Zaragoza both swerve and brake. But Matti Erikkson in the other Gold Dart is close behind Zaragoza, too close, as he runs straight into the back of him. He's going so fast, almost two hundred miles an hour, the impact launches him straight up into the air. The car flips, corkscrewing over the top of Zaragoza to land . . . I shoot a hand out, gripping Maisie's arm, as my heart leaps into my throat.

'No!'

'Is that . . .?' Maisie gasps.

I hold tight, watching in horror as the Gold Dart lands on the back of Leif's car, causing it to rear up and spin off into the gravel too.

'Shit!' Dan is on his feet.

We all stare at the screen, waiting for the drivers to get out of their cars and prove they're OK. The race has been red flagged and the medical car is speeding towards the scene, but everything seems to be happening in slow motion. I can't move, can't speak, can't do anything because my heart is hammering so hard. Cooper climbs out, then Zaragoza and Erikkson, then . . . I press a hand to my chest, heaving a sigh of relief as Leif hurls his steering wheel over the side of the car and pulls himself out over the top.

'Phew.' Maisie collapses against me. 'That was scary.'

'It probably wasn't as bad as it looked,' I say, though I hear the quiver in my voice.

'It's still horrible to watch.'

'Shame – Olsen was in fifth place.' Dan sits down again. 'If he'd just been another second ahead, he probably could have dodged the whole thing. But at least Corey Hammond is still out there.'

'I guess,' I say, trying to sound positive as my phone buzzes.

Gutted! Charlotte's WhatsApp message comes with a string of crying-face emojis.

Cooper had better get some kind of penalty. Emika joins in from the media centre in Barcelona. **The stewards are looking into it now.**

I send a disappointed face back, then put my phone down and grab a cushion, wrapping my arms around it as the stewards clear the track and the race restarts. Marr, Gio and Shimizu cross the finish line a few minutes later, sending the Quezada fans wild, but I can't seem to cheer any more.

Maybe my heart is a little involved with Rask, after all.

A few days on from the accident in Barcelona, there must be mixed feelings at Rask HQ this week. Although their upgrades seem to be working – with Corey Hammond bringing home eight points for the team – it's hard to imagine Leif Olsen feeling anything other than despondent right now.

© MotorsportEchoNews, 4 June

SEVEN

'HAVE YOU HEARD OF Ashley Hart?' Yuto calls across the office.

'No.' I look up from ticking items off my to-do list. I write a new one when I arrive at work every morning and today's is almost a full page long. 'Wait, yes. She's an actress, isn't she?'

'And a huge F1 fan. Leif's manager says her people have been in touch, wanting to set up a date.'

'With Leif?' I stifle a laugh because I can't even imagine how awkward that would be.

'It's some kind of promotional thing for her new film. Like if they can be photographed together, they'll both get more exposure or something. The chances of Leif agreeing to it are probably a billion to one, but I guess we should still ask.' Yuto lifts his eyes to the ceiling. 'I just can't believe anyone would be stupid enough to fall for some fake relationship photo-op.'

'Mmm.' I make a noncommittal sound because that's exactly the way Gio and Maisie started. Not that I'm about to say so out loud. Another thing I've learned about Yuto is how much he loves to gossip.

'I can ask Leif, if you like?' I offer, pushing my chair back. 'I need to speak to him today anyway, find out if he's had second thoughts about social media yet.'

'And I thought *my* question was hopeless.' Yuto gives a bark of laughter. 'He's in the factory, but I'd save my energy if I were you.'

'I can't.' I reach for my phone and iPad. 'But don't worry, I have a strategy. I'm just going to annoy him until he gives in.'

'You evil genius, you.' Yuto is still laughing. 'In that case, yes, please, and good luck.'

'Thanks!' I stifle my trepidation and march determinedly downstairs to the factory. Given Leif's DNF result in Spain, I've waited two days before approaching him, but I can't put this conversation off any longer, no matter how much I might want to. Fortunately, I've had another stern word with myself and I'm now 100 per cent confident in my ability to stay in control of my emotions and not get distracted by eyelashes or biceps or any other physical features, *or* angry at slights to my job. I'm going to be focused and professional because Leif needs to be online and it's my job to make that happen. I've brainstormed a long list of persuasive arguments – they're all ready to be reviewed on my iPad – and I'm prepared for a long campaign. I'll pester him all summer if I have to.

For both our sakes, I really hope I don't have to.

Despite Yuto's scepticism, I'm actually cautiously optimistic because Leif already recorded the video interview I asked for, even though I said it could wait until he got back to HQ. Emika filmed it in Barcelona last Friday and we published it the night before the race. He answered nearly all of the questions too, including what hair product he uses (Hanz de Fuko Quicksand), his favourite food (kjøttkaker), and what subject he wishes people would ask him about in interviews but they never do (the collected works of George R. R. Martin). To be honest, it got a bigger response than I'd expected. After what happened on the track in Spain, a lot of people now seem to be rooting for him. They've even started using the hashtag #arcticfox when posting about him.

'Hi.' I push open the door to the factory and peer inside. 'Can I come in?'

'Hey.' A guy with cropped blonde hair and a large handlebar moustache beckons me over to where a group of about twenty mechanics are gathered round a car. 'The more, the merrier. What can we do for you?'

'I'm looking for Leif.'

'Machine shop.' He jerks his thumb to the left.

'Thanks.' I watch as the mechanics start removing and replacing tyres. They're so fast, their movements are practically a blur. 'Are you doing pit-stop practice?'

'Yep.' He holds up a timer and grins. 'You think drivers are competitive? They've got nothing on these guys.'

'I can see that.' I give him a sympathetic look. 'How are you all doing, after what happened to Leif's car last weekend?'

'Well, it sucked, obviously.' He makes a face. 'But at least Corey got points, and we know we're on the right track with the upgrades. So, on to the next race.'

'That's a great attitude.' I glance back at the mechanics. 'Hey, do you mind if I film this? It would be great for our socials.'

'Why not?' He raises his voice. 'Hey, guys, no more swearing. This one's being filmed.'

'And would you mind introducing it? Just say who you are and explain to the viewer what's going on.'

'Hell, yes!' He flexes his hands. 'I was born for this moment.'

'Ready when you are.' I hold my phone up.

'All right, folks! I'm Logan, aka the Lollipop Guy, and this is the Rask factory where we're busy practising our pit-stop times. The challenge is to replace all the tyres without getting in each other's way or dropping anything. Under two seconds and we all get a bonus. Anything over two and a half is bad news. So, on your marks, get set, go!'

'Wow.' I feel like I've barely started filming before I'm lowering my camera again. As for Logan, I think I've found a new Instagram star. 'That was seriously impressive! How often do you practise this?'

'A lot. That way we don't have to think during a race. It's like muscle memory.'

'Doesn't it get boring?'

'The alternative is worse. Imagine being the guy who messes up on the day.' His face splits in a sudden grin. 'They'd have *him* to deal with.'

'Hmm?' I turn to find Leif standing behind me, dressed in his usual pale jeans and Rask T-shirt combo. His expression is as brooding as ever, though something about him looks different today. Something I can't quite put my finger on.

'Oh yeah. He's pretty terrifying when he's in a bad mood.' Logan talks in an exaggerated whisper. 'One time he *sighed* at poor Frankie over there. It was pretty brutal.'

I force a smile. If I remember correctly, I got a little more than a sigh from Leif in our meeting last week. But then everyone else seems to get the best version of him.

'Hey, Logan!' somebody shouts. 'We're ready.'

'Gotta go.' Logan extends a hand to me. 'Nice to meet you . . .?'

'Ava.' I shake his hand with a smile. 'Thanks for the help.'

'Any time.'

I take a deep breath before I turn back to Leif, surprised to find him staring after Logan with slightly narrowed eyes. 'I wonder if I could have a word? If you're not too busy?'

His whole body tenses, like he literally hoists his shoulders back and goes completely stiff, which isn't very flattering, but whatever. I'm getting used to it. Judging by his conflicted expression, he's also trying to think up an excuse to get away from me, but too bad. If he thinks he can escape, he's got another thing coming.

'Is it about social media?' His voice is even deeper than I remember.

'Amongst other things.' I smile sweetly. 'I have a number of items to go through. It won't take long.'

'OK.' His face takes on a resigned expression. 'Come to my office.'

'You have an office?'

'Corey and I like to call it that.'

'Great.' I clutch my iPad to my chest and follow him into a large corner room with a football table, basketball hoop, a couple of black leather sofas and a kitchen area.

'This is nice.' I look around, impressed by how neat and tidy it all is. 'Very organized.'

'Yeah, well . . .' A smile tugs at the corners of his mouth. 'Corey's not here.'

'Oh.' I suddenly realize what's different about him. He has a beard, a very short, neatly trimmed and pale one, not so rugged lumberjack after all, more sexy male model. It looks so soft my fingers actually twitch with the urge to touch it, but fortunately my brain intervenes, diverting my gaze towards a pile of books on the coffee table.

'Are those yours?' I rock back on my heels in surprise. There's an autobiography of lauded architect Frank Gehry, along with a large photo book of the hundred most important buildings of the twentieth century and another about neo-futurism. 'You like architecture?'

'Yes.' He sounds suspicious, like he thinks I might turn this fact into a social-media segment.

'So do I.' I pause and then can't resist adding, 'Especially Scandinavian architecture. The Deichman Bjørvika is one of my favourite buildings in the world.'

'Mine too.' He tilts his head. 'Have you been to Norway?'

'No, but I'd like to. It sounds beautiful.'

'It is.'

There's a moment of heavy silence while we stare at each other. It feels weird to have something in common besides F1. Even weirder that we've been in the same room for over a minute and neither of us is frowning yet.

'Anyway . . .' I exhale heavily as the silence drags on. 'First of all, I wanted to say thank you for the interview video. It was really good.'

'It was an apology.' He leans back, bracing his hands against the kitchen counter. 'For what I said last week. I shouldn't have implied that your job was trivial.'

'Oh.' I'm surprised by both his candour and the length of his sentences. 'Thank you.'

'And your questions weren't bullshit. Some of them were actually quite funny. The point is, I was being a dick and I'm sorry.'

I open my mouth to agree before it occurs to me that I could get some leverage out of this. 'Well, apology accepted. Does this mean you've changed your mind about social media?'

'I value my privacy –'

'And I respect that.' I forestall him. 'I would never ask you to talk about anything you're not comfortable with, I promise. It would only be promotional stuff for the team.'

His expression wavers. 'You're really not going to give up, are you?'

'Nope.' I lift my chin.

'OK –'

'Bec– Wait. OK?' I'm so geared up to persuade him, I feel almost deflated. 'As in, you agree?'

'Yes. I haven't changed my mind about social media in general, but I have been thinking about what you said, about bringing attention to issues I care about, and you're right, I should do that.'

'Oh . . . that's, um, great!'

'Is something wrong?' His lips twitch, like he's enjoying how confounded I am.

'No-o-o.' I try to shake my head, but it kind of bobs up and down instead. 'I just thought I was going to have to persuade you a lot more.'

'I know. That's why I'm giving in now.' He quirks an eyebrow. 'You seemed very determined.'

I pull my iPad away from my chest and stare sadly at the screen. 'I made a list of arguments.'

'A list?' He looks from me to the iPad. 'How many bullet points?'

'Twenty-two.'

'Impressive.' He scratches his chin. 'Can I see?'

'Sure.' I start to hand my iPad over and then freeze. Now that I think of it, some of my points might not have been 100 per cent professional. They might even have included such persuasive arguments as 'Shut The Fuck Up And Do What I Say' and 'It Would Make You Less Of A Pigheaded Asshole If You Could Just'. To be honest, I might have had a little too much wine towards the end of my evening's brainstorm.

'Actually it's a little rough.' I yank the iPad back again. 'I should probably type it up properly before you read it.'

'Uh-huh.' He gives me a look like he knows exactly what I'm thinking before he turns around and reaches for a leaflet on the counter behind him. 'This is a local charity I support, for kids in care. If you could find a way to help them, then we have a deal.'

'I definitely can!' I practically rip the leaflet out of his hands. 'I could set up a visit. You going there would get a lot of media attention –'

'No.' He interrupts me. 'I want it to be about the kids, not me. And no gala dinner for a bunch of rich people either. I hate all that shit.'

'*OK*.' I purse my lips. 'It's just . . . The thing about rich people is that they tend to have a lot of money for charitable causes.'

'I know, but I want to do something that draws attention and involves the local community too. The important thing is for these kids to feel like they belong. That means we need local businesses to accept and support them, to offer jobs and apprenticeships, practical things, not just money.'

'That's a good point.' I look down at the leaflet and then back up again. It's like I'm seeing him through new eyes suddenly (or maybe my old eyes, back when he was my favourite driver). I'm not surprised that he wants to do something so altruistic – not when he's so allegedly 'adorable' – I'm just more impressed than I expected to be. Maybe he isn't such a huge asshole, after all. Maybe he's only a medium-sized one . . . A warm glow tries to ignite in my chest before I ruthlessly suppress it.

'So what you're saying is that if I organize some kind of local charity event, you'll set up some social media accounts?' I ask.

'Account. Singular.' He makes a face. 'With the proviso that you have to manage it.'

'Absolutely.' I nod enthusiastically. 'I'd be happy to. And I won't post anything without your approval.'

'I don't care about that. Do what you think is best.'

'OK. I will.' I beam because this is a lot more progress than I expected today. He's agreed to join social media and we're both being polite! I wonder if we ought to shake hands to seal the deal and prove how professional we are, then decide against it because the way his gaze is focused on mine is already making me feel a little hot under my Peter Pan collar. There's a strange look on his face too, though he's probably just wondering what I'm still doing here. Which, now I think about it, is a reasonable question.

'There's one more thing.' I shuffle my feet and clutch my iPad a little tighter. 'I need both you and Corey here next Tuesday for a cookery lesson. Vienna's already agreed it with Bastian.'

'Cookery?' Now it's his turn to look surprised.

'Yes. But it won't be too challenging, I promise. Just a little Belgian cuisine ahead of the Grand Prix there.'

'All right.' He nods. 'I like Belgian food.'

'Great. I'll see you then.'

'And, Ava?' he calls after me as I turn for the door.

'Yes?'

'When can I expect to receive your list of arguments? Twenty-two points, you said, right? It might be useful to have on file in case I'm ever tempted to change my mind.'

'Oh . . .' I clench my jaw. 'Well, today's very busy so . . . tomorrow?'

'Perfect. I'll look forward to it.'

I mutter under my breath and try not to fantasize about committing a random act of violence. So I guess now I have to spend my evening thinking of twenty-two *actual* arguments. And the most annoying thing is that I'm pretty sure Leif knows it.

Contrary to popular opinion, there are several variations on a Belgian waffle, but one thing they all have in common is a distinctive grid pattern. This originated in the fifteenth century and is ideal for filling your waffle full of cream or chocolate or whatever takes your fancy ...

@PatisseriePrincessSimone, 10 June

EIGHT

IT'S A GORGEOUS, SPARKLING summer morning. Even though I arrive too late to get one of the coveted spots in the car park and have to leave my car on the road, I stride towards Rask HQ with a spring in my step and a wide smile on my face. It's been two weeks and working here is even better now than it was on my first day. Firstly, because the fact that it's *real* has finally sunk in. Secondly, because I love everything about my job. I love it *especially* this morning, because after an early morning meeting with Hazel Muir, the director of the care charity Leif wants to support, I've had a brainwave. An actual bona fide, genius-level brainwave, one there's no way he can object to.

'Good morning!' I call out to Sam in reception before scanning my security pass and hurrying upstairs to the communications office. I have another hectic day ahead. As well as producing press packs ahead of the Belgian Grand Prix this weekend, I need to get Leif's opinion on my brainwave and then – fingers crossed – his official go ahead for @RealLeifOlsen. I've got it all planned out. I'm keeping his bio short and on brand (Driver for @RaskRacing) and I've chosen a profile photo of him on the podium in Australia. His hair is damp with sweat and champagne, but he's mid-laugh and his eyes are happy and glowing. That's the vibe I want. 'Adorable' Leif, with his guard down.

But first, waffles.

'Sorry, my meeting ran over,' I say to Emika as I deposit my blazer and bag at my desk. 'Has Simone arrived yet?'

'Ten minutes ago. Yuto's helping her set up.'

'Brilliant. You guys are lifesavers.'

'Just don't forget us if you have any leftovers.'

'Nice try.' I grin at her. 'But you should know I didn't have any breakfast this morning.'

'Spoilsport. Want me to let Leif and Corey know you're here?'

'Please. Tell them I'll meet them in the canteen.'

I grab the camera equipment and head back downstairs for the challenge I've planned to help promote the race at Spa-Francorchamps. It has absolutely nothing to do with cars, but it's a fun segment to showcase our drivers. Based on past performance, I'm expecting easy-going enthusiasm from Corey and pained tolerance from Leif. Whatever. He's making waffles, so he can either like it or (most likely) lump it.

'Hi,' I say as I walk into the canteen to find Yuto and Simone, a Liège-born chef who now lives in London, sitting on opposite tables, chatting. 'I'm so sorry I'm late.'

'No problem.' Yuto leaps to his feet when he sees me. 'I wish I could stay, but I have a meeting with Finance. It was great to meet you, Simone.'

'You too!' Simone, a petite redhead, waves at him before smiling at me. 'You must be Ava?'

'Yes.' I shake her hand. 'Thanks so much for agreeing to do this. I love your videos.'

'*Merci*. I'm happy to be here.'

'Is there anything else you need?' I ask, gesturing to the impressive selection of ingredients and utensils laid out across one of the kitchen counters.

'No.' She scoops her hair into a messy bun and slips on an apron. 'I'm all ready.'

'You're not the only one!' Corey calls out as he barges through the doors like a rock star, closely followed by Leif. 'What are we making?'

'Waffles,' I answer. 'In honour of the Belgian Grand Prix and not remotely because they're my favourite. This is your teacher, Simone de Smet, aka the Patisserie Princess. She has a very successful YouTube channel, as well as two hundred thousand followers on TikTok.'

'Awesome. Are you an F1 fan, Simone?' Corey switches on the charm like a light switch.

'Actually, I don't think I've ever seen a race.' She dips her head apologetically. 'But I'll certainly watch this weekend.'

'Glad to hear it.'

'So, Simone's going to explain what to do,' I say. 'I'll film your attempts and then we'll crown a winner.'

'You mean it's a contest?' Corey's dark eyes twinkle. 'What's the prize?'

'This.' I hold up a T-shirt I asked Merchandising to produce. It has Rask branding and the words 'Waffle King' emblazoned across the front.

'Love it.' His grin spreads even wider. 'Let's do this.'

'Is that OK?' I look nervously past Corey to Leif. He's wearing his usual brooding expression, though he doesn't seem to be dragging his feet. For him, that practically counts as enthusiasm.

'Of course.' He gives me a brief nod before holding a hand out to Simone. 'I'm Leif. Nice to meet you.'

I stifle a flash of annoyance as I fasten the camera on to a tripod. So, apparently it *is* possible for him not to be an asshole when meeting someone new. Good to know.

'Great!' Simone hands them each a chef's apron as they step behind the counter. 'This is where you'll be working.'

'OK.' I give her a thumbs-up. 'Recording now.'

'*Bien.*' She snaps into character, smiling at the camera. '*Bonjour.* I'm the Patisserie Princess, and in honour of this weekend's Belgian Grand Prix I'm in the kitchen with Rask Racing Formula 1 drivers Corey Hammond and Leif Olsen. And because Spa-Francorchamps is only forty kilometres from Liège, we'll be making their version of waffles, which are slightly different to those you find in Brussels, but just as delicious. Crunchy on the outside, but soft on the inside . . .'

I stand to one side as she goes through the steps, combining yeast, milk and water, then whisking it up with flour, pearl sugar, eggs and butter to form a sticky, brioche-like dough.

'That T-shirt is mine.' Corey elbows Leif in the ribs as they compete to see who can knead the hardest. Leif elbows him back, though his expression of concentration doesn't waver.

'So now we need to put the dough aside to rest for about twenty minutes,' Simone says to the camera, which both Corey and Leif seem to have forgotten is there.

'You're both doing great,' I say encouragingly as I hit pause.

'I'm killing it.' Corey slams his dough down hard on the counter. 'Look at that beauty.'

'Not bad.' Simone goes to inspect it.

'Yours looks pretty good too,' I say to Leif. He's still kneading, pressing and stretching his dough with long, strong fingers.

'It's too clumpy.' He sounds dubious. 'I've never made waffles before.'

'Well, don't worry too much. This is just for fun, remember?'

'And a T-shirt.' He gives me a pointed look.

'Wow, competitive much?' I laugh, although this is actually the perfect opening for me to tell him about my brainwave. 'By the way, I had a very productive conversation with Hazel Muir this morning.'

'Already?' He does a double-take.

'Yes.' I clutch my hands together. 'How do you feel about football?'

'OK. Why?'

'Well, I was thinking that we could hold a charity football match as a way to raise money. Hopefully Rask would sponsor the event, then you and Corey could be team captains and some of the older kids at the care home could be players. But we wouldn't announce your participation until the actual day. That way tickets would go to people in the local community rather than just F1 fans.'

'A charity football match?' Leif repeats slowly.

'Yes. What do you think?' His underwhelmed expression makes me wonder if it's really such a brainwave after all. On a scale of one to ten for excitement, he's at one while I'm already at ten. Now nine and plummeting . . .

'I think it's brilliant.'

'You do?' I zip back up to ten. 'That's wonderful! I was

thinking we could set it up for the start of the summer break so it doesn't interfere too much with your schedule. Although we'd need to get Corey's agreement as well.'

'No problem.' He leans sideways, though he doesn't take his eyes from mine. 'Hey, Corey? You in for a charity football match?'

'Just tell me when and where, mate!'

'OK, then.' I smile. For two such different people, their easy camaraderie is actually kind of sweet. 'So . . . do you understand what else this means?'

'I do.' He inclines his head sombrely.

'Great. In that case, I need a photo.'

'Now?' His brow knits as I remove my phone from the tripod.

'Yes. I need to launch your Instagram with some kind of post. This way I can tell people you're "cooking something up" and say to look out for the video later today.' I narrow my eyes when he looks uncertain. 'A deal's a deal.'

'Fine.' He starts to unfasten his apron.

'Leave it. All you have to do is look like you're having fun.' I hand him a whisk. 'Here, hold this if a prop makes you feel more comfortable.'

'I got this.' Corey slides along the counter and drapes an arm around Leif's shoulders. 'Simone, get in here.'

'That looks really good!' I take a couple of shots with them together. 'Now all we have to do is crown a waffle king.'

AN HOUR LATER, AFTER rolling out the dough, cutting it into balls, letting it rest again and then finally tackling a waffle iron, Simone declares Corey the winner.

'Good job, man.' Leif fist-bumps him while shaking his head over his own charred results. 'I think I left mine in too long.'

'That's why I'm the Waffle King.' Corey pulls on his T-shirt and points to the words emblazoned across his chest.

'I'm sure you won't let us forget.' I laugh and end the recording. 'Now if you want to leave me alone with the waffles, you're free to go. The canteen staff are going to want the kitchen back soon.'

'You should put some chocolate sauce on these.' Corey pushes his plate of perfect-looking waffles towards me and kisses his fingers.

'*Non.*' Simone objects. 'Sugar is the best topping.'

'But *everything* tastes better with chocolate sauce!'

'You should probably throw these away.' Leif gestures mournfully towards his waffles.

'Not necessarily.' I snap off a corner that looks a little less burnt than the rest and pop it into my mouth. 'The flavour is still pretty good.'

'Thanks.' He watches as I chew.

'She's just being polite, mate.' Corey slaps him on the back before heading for the door. 'Come on, fun's over. We need to get back to work.'

'Right.' Leif meets my gaze again, his own darker than before. 'Are you sure you don't need any help tidying up?'

'No, don't worry.' Without thinking I lift a hand, wiping away a smudge of flour on his cheek that's been bothering me for the past five minutes. It's only a split second later that I realize how inappropriate I'm being.

'I mean, it's fine.' I clear my throat briskly. 'We've got this.'

'OK.' He hesitates, like he's about to say something, before he turns away. 'Thanks for the lesson, Simone.'

'You're welcome.' She waves goodbye. 'And good luck this weekend!'

'That was so fun. I really appreciate you coming,' I say to her once they've gone. 'I think it went really well.'

'Not so much for Leif.' She laughs good-naturedly. 'But he was distracted.'

'Do you think?' I start to gather up bowls and spoons. Maybe I shouldn't have set up this challenge so close to the Grand Prix. He was probably wanting to get back to the simulator the whole time.

'Ava, didn't you notice the way he kept looking at you?' She gives me a knowing smile.

I'm so surprised I almost drop a waffle iron on to my toes. The idea that Leif might actually choose to look at me, that he might not find me entirely objectionable, is both new and, frankly, unbelievable. If his dislike wasn't blindingly obvious to Simone, it's because he's learning to tolerate me, that's all. Just like I'm learning to tolerate him.

'Oh no,' I protest. 'He was looking at the camera. He's not very comfortable in the spotlight.'

'If you say so.' Her voice is teasing. 'But in my professional opinion, the only reason his waffles are burnt is because he couldn't take his eyes off you.'

With Leif Olsen and Corey Hammond finishing seventh and eleventh at Spa-Francorchamps last weekend, it seems that Rask Racing have finally found their form. They might not be championship contenders yet, but thanks to some new upgrades they're heading in the right direction. Bastian Aalto must be heaving a huge sigh of relief.

@ MotorsportEchoNews, 18 June

NINE

'WE HAVE A PROBLEM!' Vienna announces, marching into the office where Charlotte and I are working on a content plan for the Hungarian GP. We're also trying to liaise with Emika, who's already in Budapest coordinating magazine and TV interviews. Having Hungarian maternal grandparents makes Corey one of the most popular drivers on the grid this weekend, so we decided to take advantage by sending both him and Leif straight there to do press after Belgium.

'If it's that the coffee machine is broken, we already know.' Charlotte lifts her head with a reproachful look.

'Is it? Fuck.' Vienna drops into a chair. 'How are we supposed to run a Formula 1 team when we can't even get a coffee machine to work?'

'One of the engineers is coming to fix it soon,' I reassure her. 'We just have to survive until then.'

'In the meantime, I'm caffeine-deprived.' Charlotte pretends to shudder. 'Somebody should probably send me home before I pass out.'

'Nobody's going home, especially now.' Vienna's tone is ominous. 'Yuto is sick. Gastroenteritis.'

'Ew.' Charlotte cringes. 'Wait, he didn't get it from here, did he?'

'No. He was only in yesterday and he says he didn't go to the canteen. The point is that he's definitely not well enough to come to Hungary with me this afternoon. So which of you is going to be his replacement?'

'One of us?' I sit up straighter.

'Yes. Leif's diary is all set up, so you'd just need to be his minder for the next few days. You know – record everything he says to the press so we can prove if he's misquoted afterwards, and make sure he gets everywhere he needs to go. Emika will be minding Corey and I'll be doing trackside content capture, so you won't be alone.'

I feel my pulse accelerate because it sounds so exciting . . . and if it were any other driver I'd be biting Vienna's hand off to go, but the thought of spending the next four days with a stony-faced Norwegian isn't hugely appealing. Plus I'm still faintly mortified about touching his cheek last week. What if I do something else stupid?

'You should do it,' I say to Charlotte. 'You've been here longer.'

'I would . . .' Her expression wavers. 'Only I have a bridal fitting on Saturday, and if I cancel it'll be months before I can get another appointment.'

'Then I guess it's you.' Vienna swivels towards me. 'Unless you have some kind of urgent dress emergency as well?'

'No.' I'm still hesitant. 'But I thought I was supposed to cover the desk here this weekend?'

'Maya can do it.' She waves a hand when I look around quizzically, like I've missed somebody in the office. 'She's in Merchandising. So?'

I bite the inside of my cheek. It's on the tip of my tongue to suggest that she call Leif to see what he thinks of the idea, but what if he says he doesn't want me? It would only draw attention to the awkwardness between us *and* ruin Charlotte's weekend. And why shouldn't I go? It's an amazing opportunity – a chance to really flex my organizational muscles – not to mention great for my career. Why should I let one man's opinion hold me back, even if that man is a driver with a million-pound contract and I'm just a replaceable nobody?

'I'd love to,' I say eventually. 'What time are we leaving?'

'Two o'clock.'

'But that's –'

'An hour and a half away. I know. Can you get home and back in that time?'

'I think so.'

'Then do it. We'll give you team clothes, but make sure you pack comfy shoes. And sunscreen. It's going to be hot. Be back here as quickly as possible.'

'Right. Are you OK to finish the content plan?' I ask Charlotte.

'Yes, don't worry. You go and enjoy yourself.' She lowers her voice to a whisper as Vienna strides off towards her office. 'And thank you!'

I'm going to Hungary! I text Maisie from a taxi on the way to the airport. The last two hours have been a whirlwind, though as usual my belongings are well-ordered enough that I was able to find everything I needed in record time (passport, underwear, toiletries, shoes).

Ooh! How come? She responds instantly.

Leif's minder has food poisoning so I'm taking over.
That's amazing (but poor him). You'll be doing commentary next!
I wish! Any message for Gio?

I wait while she types. The three little dots are there for so long I'm expecting an epic reply, so it's a surprise when **No** finally appears, quickly followed by **Have fun. I'll look out for you!**

I frown at the screen. I have a sneaking suspicion that she and Gio are having more problems than she's letting on, but I don't want to pry. I'm sure she'll tell me when she's ready, so I send a heart emoji, then drop my phone into my bag and get back to worrying about Leif. Presumably Vienna's told him about Yuto by now, as well as the fact that I'm filling in, but I can't bring myself to ask what he said in response. If he objected, I don't want to know. I'll just have to live with the knot of tension in my stomach.

We land at Budapest airport around 8 p.m., then head straight to our hotel. The Grand Prix at the Hungaroring is one of the longest-standing races in the F1 calendar, set amidst beautiful rolling hills to the north-east of the capital. The crew have been here for two days already, unloading and setting up the garage, team motorhome and race base, which explains the number of exhausted-looking roadies and technicians we pass in the lobby. The amount of planning and coordination that goes into every single race weekend is phenomenal. It's like building, deconstructing and then rebuilding a massive Lego set twenty-four times a year, only one that comes with computers, screens and several miles' worth of cabling.

There are no big social events planned for tonight, only meetings, so Vienna checks us in and then sends me to my room with a stern lecture about getting a good night's sleep.

I'm just emerging from the lift on the fourth floor when my phone pings with a message from Emika.

Hey! Are you at the hotel yet?

Heading to my room now. Do you need any help with anything?

No. I'm still in Budapest, but we're almost done. How's Yuto?

He's been lying on his bathroom floor all day.

!!!

I know!

So I probably shouldn't mention food, but breakfast is at 7.30 in the team motorhome. I'll see you there and don't worry about anything. We'll be fine.

Thanks. I appreciate that!

I open the door to my room. According to the team programme, I'm sharing with Sarah, one of our hospitality ambassadors, but she's on her way out to a meeting with her manager as I come in, so I unpack my bags, grab a bottle of sparkling water, kick my shoes off and curl up on the bed to look over Leif's schedule for the next few days.

I knew race weekends were intense, but I never fully appreciated it until now. Everything is planned, down to the minute, and the timetable needs to be followed exactly, which means I need to be 100 per cent focused. Tomorrow, for example, is Media Day, which means interviews, a press conference, a couple of hours in the Fan Zone and sponsorship activities, all interspersed with time in the garage with the engineers.

There'll be another press conference on Friday, as well as two hour-long practice sessions so the drivers can get accustomed to the track and the team can gather data and make any necessary adjustments to the car set-up. Then on Saturday, there'll be pit-stop practice in the morning, followed by a third practice session, followed by qualifying, followed by yet *another* press conference. Finally, on Sunday, there's a strategy meeting, a drivers' parade and a team briefing, all followed by the *actual* Grand Prix at two o'clock. They've even scheduled nap time.

Just thinking about it is exhausting.

I read through tomorrow's schedule four times, making sure I know it by heart, then reach for my phone. I've never messaged Leif directly before, but it's time I made contact. With any luck, I'll be able to gauge how he feels about me being here.

Hi, it's Ava! See you in the morning. Excited to work with you!

I close my eyes and take a deep, calming breath. I don't expect him to answer quickly, or at all, but at least I've reached out. Now I just need to stay calm and professional and not give him any additional reasons to object to me. Most of all, I need to step up and not waste this opportunity to show Vienna what I'm capable of.

I jump as my phone vibrates in my hand.

See you tomorrow. Leif.

That's it? I stare at the screen for a few seconds, then fall back on to the bed with a groan of frustration. At least he replied, but so much for gauging his reaction. How am I supposed to interpret that?

I guess I'll be waiting a little longer to find out how he feels about me.

Excitement is rising in Hungary and so is the temperature, with forecasters warning it could potentially hit the 40°C mark over the Grand Prix weekend.

@ MotorsportEchoNews, 19 June

TEN

SARAH AND I ARE both up early. With our matching Rask outfits, we look like twins as we head downstairs to take the shuttle bus to the paddock. According to the all-important schedule, Leif's first activity of the day is an hour in the gym, followed by a shower in his private RV motorhome at the track. If everything is going according to plan, that means he should be ready for me to collect him for breakfast right about now.

I tense as I knock on his door. I'm excited to get started, but I'm also still nervous about how he's going to react to me being his minder. My stomach is so tightly clenched I don't know how I'm going to keep any food down, although at least half a dozen people have already warned me to 'get plenty of protein because today's going to be a big day'. Even Yuto, the last person I'd expect to be thinking about food right now, has messaged.

I hear a shout telling me to come in, so I open the door and climb some steps into a compact but cosy-looking lounge area, complete with a kitchen at the far end. I know that Leif prefers to stay here rather than in a hotel, but I didn't expect it to be so well-equipped. It seems kind of unnecessary, considering that drivers also have private rooms in the team motorhome, as well as a catering department ready to prepare anything they want to eat. But I guess this is F1.

'I'm through here!' Leif's voice calls from further inside, so I brace myself and follow it, past a small bathroom and up some more steps into . . .

'Oh!' I come to an abrupt halt in his bedroom. It's smaller than I would have expected, with a low roof and skylight over a narrow bunk, but it's still a room with a bed, which is definitely not an appropriate space for us to meet.

'I'm so sorry. I thought you meant . . .' I gesture behind me. 'I'll wait outside.'

'Don't worry.' Leif stands up from where he's currently bent over, straightening his bedclothes. Like me, he's dressed entirely in Rask merchandise. 'It's my fault. I assumed you were Kelsey.'

'Kelsey?' It must be the name of his girlfriend, though this is the first I've heard of her.

'My performance coach.'

'Oh.' I feel a bump in my chest, one that feels inexplicably like relief, followed by mild shock because he's . . . *not* frowning? Instead he looks almost pleased to see me. It's completely disarming. *What the hell?*

'So, I'm going to be your assistant for the next few days,' I say carefully, because maybe he hasn't been fully apprised of the situation.

'I know.' He folds his arms over his chest, though not in a confrontational way, more like he's unsure what else to do with them in such a confined space. 'Vienna told me. Any news on Yuto?'

'He says he's feeling better.' I give him a suspicious look because *what* is going on? He doesn't seem even remotely bothered about me being here. 'So we're good? Working together, I mean?'

'Of course.'

'OK.' I need another moment to process this. 'Well, that's great. I mean, obviously I'm new to this, but Yuto's sent me a few pointers and if there's anything you need, just let me know and I'll do my best to facilitate it.'

'I'm sure we'll be fine.' He clears his throat as I turn to go. 'Did you sleep well?'

There have been so many surprises in the past minute that I shouldn't be caught out by another, but I'm so taken aback I almost look over my shoulder to see if he's talking to someone else. First he's not frowning, and now he's asking me questions about my well-being? It's like he's had some kind of personality transplant. 'Um . . . yes, thanks. Did you?'

'Yes.'

'Good.' I try to think of something else to say. 'You must be feeling positive after Belgium?'

'I'm working on it.' He pauses. 'It's hard not to worry.'

'That's understandable,' I say, because it is. 'I'm sure the past few months have been really tough, driving a car you couldn't rely on, always waiting for something to break.'

'Yes.' His gaze latches on to mine. 'It was.'

'But all of that's behind you now. The upgrades are working and you're one of the best drivers on the grid. You can't let the past undermine your confidence in the present.' I smile because, as pep talks go, I think I'm doing pretty well. 'Whatever happens, I know you'll drive a great race.'

'Thank you.' He shifts his weight from one foot to the other like he's both pleased and embarrassed by the words. 'I appreciate that.'

'Anyway . . .' It occurs to me suddenly that we're still in his bedroom, standing a little too close for comfort. 'Shall we go to breakfast? Or I can fetch you something to eat here, if you prefer?'

'No. The team motorhome is fine.'

'OK, then.' I swing round and head for the door, so baffled by the 180-degree change in his behaviour I almost bump my head on the frame as I go. As if the past five minutes haven't been weird enough, for a moment I almost forgot the schedule.

COREY AND EMIKA ARE already at a table in the middle of the room when we arrive.

'Hey, guys.' Corey grins as we sit down, me with a plate of toast and scrambled eggs, Leif with a bowl of porridge, piled high with berries and nuts.

'You're in a good mood.' I smile.

'Because I have a good feeling about today.' He leans back, lacing his fingers behind his head. 'The sun is shining, the car is ten times better than it was and a little bird told me some pretty juicy gossip last night.' He glances around and lowers his voice confidentially. 'Noa Shimizu's retiring at the end of the season.'

'Shimizu's leaving Quezada?' I give a startled jolt. I keep an eye on all the gossip forums and this is the first I've heard of it.

'Yep. They're not going to announce anything until the summer break, but it means there's going to be an empty seat at Quezada.'

'Traitor!' Emika hisses at him. 'What about Rask?'

'I didn't say *I* was going anywhere.' Corey holds his hands up. 'I'm just keeping you all informed.'

'How do you know about it?' Leif looks perplexed.

'I have a friend.'

'You mean, a *female* friend?' Emika rolls her eyes. 'You could get her fired by repeating this stuff.'

'Only if you guys tell, which I know you won't. Anyway, the rumours will be flying about soon enough. The driver market will be total chaos. Everyone's going to be delaying their contract negotiations until we know who's going to replace him.'

'Only if they want to move to Quezada.' Leif lifts a shoulder.

'Who wouldn't?' I say, then bite my own tongue as they all turn to look at me. 'I mean, they're a great team.'

'Not as great as Fraser right now.' Corey glances around again. 'The rumour is that Hayden Quaid isn't performing as well as they'd like either. There might be seats at *both* teams.'

'Seriously?' Emika gapes at him. 'Don't tell me you have another "friend" at Fraser?'

'What? I'm a friendly person.'

'Maybe a little *too* much.' She cocks her head to one side. 'How are you feeling, Ava? Ready for the insanity?'

'I think so.' I force down a mouthful of scrambled eggs, trying to ignore the flutter of nerves in my stomach. 'It's the track walk first, right?'

'Yes. Then we move on to the press stuff.' She throws a wary glance at Leif. 'Is that OK?'

'Nope.' He takes a mouthful of porridge. 'But it's in the contract.'

'Message me if you have any problems.' Emika turns back to me. 'The paddock can feel like a maze, but you get used to how things work after a few races.'

'Maybe we should swap?' Corey suggests.

'What?' Leif's head jerks up, his tone a little sharp.

'We could swap minders.' Corey looks between us all. 'Our schedules today are pretty much the same, but Emika and I have both been here before so we know where we're going. It'll take some of the stress away.'

'That's actually not a bad idea.' Emika scrunches her mouth up thoughtfully. 'What do you think, Ava? Just for today?'

'I guess it makes sense . . .' I glance at Leif. Paranoid as it sounds, for a moment I wonder if he's planned this with Corey to get rid of me, only I don't think so. He seems to be frowning at his teammate. Weirdly, I feel a flash of annoyance towards Corey too. Yesterday, I would have been relieved to be paired with him. Now I feel oddly deflated that I don't get to spend the day with Leif, after all.

'Leif?' Corey prompts him.

There's a moment of silence before he nods. 'Whatever you guys want.'

'Great.' Emika drains her orange juice and stands up. 'Let's go.'

'I'M SO GLAD IT'S you and not Charlotte who came,' Emika confides as Leif and Corey walk the track in front of us, discussing the layout with their race engineers. 'I mean, I love her, but I wish she were married already. Sometimes I think if I hear another word about wedding favours I'll tear my hair out.'

'Does that mean you don't want an update?' I tease her. 'Because I have new information about table settings.'

'Don't you dare.' She shudders. 'Speaking of new information, Vienna just made a last-minute addition to the schedule. Now there's a speaking engagement at 6 p.m. in the hospitality centre, but she wants to introduce Leif and Corey separately, so I'll take one in, while you watch the other in the motorhome.'

'You make them sound like puppies.' I laugh at the image. 'Are they likely to wander off?'

'It can happen, especially at the end of a long day. One of the Chiltern drivers went completely AWOL in Miami a couple of years ago. They eventually found him in a hot tub on a yacht; his minder got the boot the next day.'

'OK.' I stop laughing. 'I'll keep an eye on them.'

'Great.' She lifts her phone to her ear. 'I'll just call Vienna and make sure she's not about to spring anything else on us.'

I carry on walking, although the temperature is beginning to feel uncomfortable. I knew it was going to be hot, but I wasn't expecting humidity too, the kind of sticky heat where just breathing makes you sweat – and it's only 9 a.m.

'Ava?'

A voice calls my name and I look over my shoulder to find a middle-aged man in white jeans, white trainers and a blue shirt jogging towards me, looking red-faced and in desperate need of a lie-down. Or possibly even a stretcher. He seems to know who I am, though I don't think I've ever seen him before.

'Hi.' I offer him one of my water bottles since I brought two as a precaution. 'Do you need this? I haven't opened it yet.'

'Thanks.' He grabs it, takes several long gulps and then pours a hefty splash over his shaggy brown hair. 'You're a lifesaver. I can't remember the last time I ran anywhere.'

'Today probably wasn't the best day to start. Can I help you?'

'Yes. I'm Nathan, Leif's manager.'

'It's so nice to meet you.' I smile as we shake hands. 'Although Emika's minding Leif today now.'

'In that case, I'll get to her in a minute. First I want to speak to the woman who persuaded him to join Instagram.' He gives me an appraising look. 'I've been trying to get him online for years. So how did you manage it? Bribery or blackmail?'

'Maybe a tiny bit of bribery,' I concede. 'But really I just explained how useful it could be and we came to a compromise.'

'Hey, Nathan.' Leif drops back to join us. 'What are the two of you talking about?'

'Your recent decision to join the rest of us in the twenty-first century,' Nathan answers pointedly. 'So I hear Emika's your minder today?'

'Yes.'

'Then I'd better go and chat to her as well.' He shakes my hand again. 'It was nice chatting with you, Ava. I owe you a drink.'

'All good?' Leif falls into step beside me as Nathan heads away.

'Fine.' I lift an eyebrow. 'Why wouldn't it be?'

'Nathan can be a little blunt.' He wipes a hand across his brow and his sleeve falls back to reveal a distractingly bulging bicep. 'I'm not sure this walk was a good idea in the heat.'

I seize the excuse to look up at the sky. He has a point. There isn't a cloud in sight, only bright, unrelenting sunshine. Great for a beach holiday, not so much for a GP. 'Do you think it's going to stay this hot all week?'

'Unless there's a storm, which isn't in the forecast.' He grimaces. 'So, probably yes.'

'Ouch.' Just the thought of it makes me sweat even more. Between the engine and power unit, F1 cockpits are hot enough without the weather outside adding to the pressure. Drivers' temperatures can be pushed up to forty degrees, increasing their heart rates and causing impaired judgement, even loss of consciousness. And it's not like they can simply take a layer off to cool down. Everything they wear is essential for safety, which means all they have to combat dehydration is a small drinks pouch. Honestly, it's kind of frightening.

'Time to meet the press.' Corey comes striding over as we arrive back at the paddock, sunshine glinting off his aviators. If he's worried by the heat, he's not showing it. 'You ready, Ava? I feel in a chatty mood.'

'I'm all set.' I get my phone out and then turn back to Leif. 'I've been meaning to say, your interviews ever since Spain have been really good, so thank you and –' I spread my arms out, feeling awkward suddenly – 'you know, just keep doing what you're doing.'

'Full sentences and a smile?' He gives me a long look and then flexes his neck from side to side, though not before I catch a surprising twinkle in his eye. 'OK. Let's get it over with.'

THE PRESS PEN IS packed. I don't think I've ever seen so many journalists in one place. There are cameras and microphones everywhere, though fortunately there's also a barrier so we don't get mobbed. A few other drivers are here already. I can see Zaragoza and Erikkson, the Gold Dart teammates, a few metres away, as well as Gio and Quaid just beyond them. As I look, Gio turns, catches my eye and waves, though I can't help thinking his expression is strained. He looks tired and stressed, like something's weighing on his mind.

'Here we go,' Corey murmurs in my ear as we approach the first camera and I lift my phone to start recording. 'This would make a good drinking game for after the race. How about we down a shot every time someone uses the word "upgrade"?'

Ten minutes later, I'm relieved I didn't get a chance to answer before Corey got into his first interview. The word 'upgrade' has been used twenty-two times, since everyone seems to be asking variations on the same question. What do you think of the new upgrades? How confident are you in the new upgrades? How do you rate your chances of success this weekend with the new upgrades? After a while, I notice that Corey's using the word back at them too, so often that I have to keep my gaze on the ground to stop myself from laughing. Despite that, he still manages to be brilliant, deflecting criticisms, talking up the team and playing down any mention of their former owner, Philip Sawyer.

I'm only half listening, however, because my attention is distracted by Leif. Even though it's not my job to mind him today, I still find myself straining to hear his answers. He's pretty good, though, calm and thoughtful, like he's making a real effort.

*

'AND BREATHE.' COREY GRINS when we finally reach the end of the line. 'How's your wrist?'

'I think it's about to fall off.' I tuck my phone back into my pocket and rub my arm. It's stiff after being held in one position for so long. 'I can't believe you were trying to make me laugh.'

'I've no idea what you're talking about.' He chuckles. 'Come on, it's time for lunch.'

'You know, you were really great back there,' I say as we climb the steps into the team motorhome.

'Don't sound so surprised.'

'It's not that. I just haven't seen that side of you before.'

'Yeah well, I can be serious sometimes. Right now, for example, I'm serious about getting some sushi.'

'Hey.' Emika pushes Leif down into a chair when they join us five minutes later. 'Look after him while I get us some salads, will you? He's talked more in the last hour than he has in the past year.'

'Good job, man.' Corey high-fives him across the table.

'When can we drive?' Leif rests his head in his hands.

'Not long now.' Corey pops a California roll into his mouth. 'Only the press conference and Fan Zone to go.'

'Actually . . .' I put my chopsticks down and look between them apologetically. 'Vienna also needs you to make an appearance in the hospitality centre this evening.'

'What the fuck?' Corey looks accusingly at Emika as she comes back with two plates of chicken salad.

'I told them about the extra event this evening,' I explain.

'Oh.' She slides a plate in front of Leif. 'Yeah, I was going to break the bad news after lunch. I know, it sucks.'

'I'm supposed to be meeting someone tonight.' Corey sounds aggrieved.

'Don't tell me, another friend?'

'Possibly.'

'Where do you get the energy?' Emika waves her fork in the air. 'Look, hopefully it won't take long.'

'It's also a really good sign,' I argue. 'It shows that people want to support Rask. The time to worry is when nobody wants to see you.'

'Ava's right,' Leif interjects. 'One more event isn't so bad.'

Corey turns to him incredulously. 'Who are you, and what have you done with my teammate?'

'I'm making an effort.' Leif glances over his plate at me. 'It's all good for Rask, right?'

FIVE HOURS LATER, EMIKA ushers Leif and Corey into one of the air-conditioned driver lounges at the back of the motorhome and then plants herself in the doorway, hands fixed on either side of the doorframe. 'OK, you two. I'm going to see Vienna while Ava stands here and barricades the door. You're not allowed out of this room, understand?'

'Fine, but tell Vienna no more last-minute events.' Corey throws himself down on to the sofa with a groan. 'I need a shower.'

'You'll be finished after this, I promise.'

'I mean it. I don't care who the sponsor is – nothing else, or I'm refusing to drive this weekend.'

'Yeah, yeah . . .' She gestures for me to follow her. 'You got this?'

'Don't worry.' I raise my voice as we head back out to the corridor. 'I'll sit on them, if necessary.'

'I think Corey might enjoy that a little too much.' She shuts the door as he gives a thumbs-up from his recumbent position. 'I don't blame them for being grumpy, though. This temperature makes everything so tiring. I'm practically asleep on my feet.'

I pluck my shirt away from my skin and stifle a yawn in response. As much as I love Formula 1, she's right; this afternoon has felt like an eternity. I'm exhausted. Maybe it's time I started endurance training with Maisie because I don't know how the drivers manage this, sometimes three long weekends in a row. The press conference wasn't so bad since I got a seat, but the Fan Zone was even busier than the press arena, filled to capacity with hordes of excited supporters. I have a headache from all the noise and heat and all I've done is stand behind a table while Leif and Corey signed hats and pictures and posed for selfies.

They were both incredible. Corey was in his element, but Leif seemed to be enjoying himself too, chatting and smiling and going out of his way to make everyone feel special. He didn't frown once. Obviously he prefers fans to press. I actually got the feeling he would have kept going all night, until they'd seen everyone, but the relentless schedule made that impossible.

'That's Vienna.' Emika glances at her phone as it vibrates in her hand. 'Apparently they've moved the event up. She wants Corey first so I'll take him over now, if you can wait here with Leif?' She opens the door again before I can answer. 'Corey? You're up.'

'Are you kidding? We just started a strike!' Corey is still on the sofa, though now he's sitting upright beside Leif, staring at a screen on the wall, both of them holding PlayStation controllers.

'Complain to Vienna.'

'Like he'd dare,' Leif mutters, swaying sideways as his character on the screen jumps.

'*Destiny?*' I ask, stepping into the room.

'Yes. How do you know that?' Corey sounds surprised.

'Because I play. Here –' I hold my hand out – 'I'll take over. By the look of it, you need some help anyway. Now, hurry up before Vienna comes to fetch you herself.'

'You don't have to play if you don't want to.' Leif shoots me a quick sidelong glance as I slip into Corey's empty space on the sofa.

'I do want to. It'll keep me awake,' I say, taking a moment to get my bearings. According to the top of the screen, we're on Nessus, battling the Vex. Fortunately, I don't need a map or schedule for this.

'So I guess it's you and me tomorrow?' Leif says, as his guardian comes to run alongside mine. 'With you as my minder, I mean.'

'I guess so,' I agree, collecting an orb as I dart ahead of him.

'Fridays are better. Less talking, more driving.'

We don't talk for a while either because we're both too preoccupied, caught up in the adrenaline of the game, twisting and bouncing on the sofa as we fight our way to the end of the strike. He's pretty good, but I'm better. I don't even break a sweat.

'Ha!' I throw the controller down triumphantly.

'That was impressive.' Leif is staring, open-mouthed, at the screen.

'I know.' I can't help sounding smug. 'I used to play a lot with my brother. Plus, I interned at a gaming developer last year.'

'Well, you're way better than Corey.' He turns to look at me. 'We should play again sometime.'

'Maybe.' I twist my face away because I'm suddenly very

aware of how close we're sitting. I'm pretty sure that when we started there was a good foot of air between us. Now there are only a few centimetres. I'm close enough to feel the heat from his body. It's a good thing my feelings are so firmly under control or I might think that my pulse is thumping for some reason other than self-consciousness. I can't move away without making it too obvious either.

I slide my tongue over my lips as I try to think of some non-awkward reason to get up, like maybe I need to stretch? Or get a drink? There's a fridge in the corner. I could get myself another bottle of water.

'Ava . . .?' Leif speaks just as I start to move.

'Ye-es.' I stop halfway out of my seat.

'About my attitude when we met . . . and afterwards. I . . . I'm sorry. It wasn't intentional.'

I drop down again, staring at him in silence for a few moments. It's the first time he's acknowledged any kind of issue between us. A warning voice in my head tells me not to make a big thing of it, that I should just accept his apology and move on, but I'm still buzzing from the game and now that he's brought it up, I don't want to let him off the hook so easily. Intentional or not, his behaviour towards me still hurt. I think I deserve some kind of explanation.

'You know, I was so excited about meeting you in Monaco,' I say finally, aware of my foot tapping. 'You were one of my favourite drivers and you wouldn't even talk to me. You made me feel pretty crappy.'

'*Dritt.*' Ironically, he looks even more horrified now than he did the first time we met. 'Ava, I'm sorry. I didn't realize.'

'Even when I started at Rask, it felt like all you ever did was scowl at me.'

He hangs his head. 'The thing is . . . meeting you was a shock. You reminded me of somebody from my past and . . . it threw me. Then all the social media stuff.' A muscle flexes in his jaw. 'I just don't like talking about myself.'

I bite my lip as I process the words. I was expecting some kind of lame 'I was having a bad day' type of excuse – nothing like *that*. He sounds so sincere I can't help but believe him. 'So you're over it now?'

'Yes. And I'm sorry for how I behaved. Truly.'

'Then, I guess, apology accepted.' I cough because my lungs feel constricted, like there isn't enough air in the room. There's a warm, thrumming sensation in my chest too, one that was supposed to be under control. 'So does this mean we're . . . friends?'

I blink as something flares in his eyes, a flash of emotion, before he opens his mouth and –

'All done!' Corey bursts through the door abruptly. 'How's it going?' He looks at the screen. 'No way! You've finished the strike already?'

'Yes!' I've just leapt so far across the sofa I'm practically perched on the edge. 'But we can do another quick one, if you like?'

'Awesome.' Corey slaps Leif on the shoulder. 'Your turn to perform. Emika's just grabbing a snack from catering.'

'Right. I'll go find her.' Leif hesitates, like there's something else he wants to say to me, before he gets up and heads for the door. 'See you two tomorrow.'

'Bye.' I watch him go as Corey settles down on the sofa beside me. He sits almost as close as Leif just did, only this time I don't feel anything at all.

It's race day. Let's do this!

@ RaskRacing, 22 June

ELEVEN

I WAKE UP WITH my heart pounding, body drenched in sweat and a familiar hollow feeling in the pit of my stomach. Instinctively, I press my palms and the soles of my feet into the mattress and stare hard at the ceiling fan above my head. I know from experience that if I close my eyes my brain will start filling with images from my nightmares again, so I keep them wide open, unblinking. I wish that I could turn the light on as well, but Sarah is fast asleep and I don't want to disturb her.

I don't have this dream very often any more, but I guess all the commotion of the past few days has sent my anxious subconscious into overdrive. Technically, it's not a nightmare so much as a memory, a flashback to the time I felt my most powerless, when the safe, happy world I'd always known became a much darker, scarier place. But it's easier to pretend that it's only a bad dream, a figment of my overactive imagination, and not the worst experience of my life.

When my racing heart calms down, I reach for my phone and burrow under the covers to read the analysis of yesterday's qualifying. It's 4 a.m., but I know I've zero chance of getting back to sleep, at least not without dreaming again, and there's no way I'm going to risk that. On the plus side, it's finally race day, which means I'll be heading home tonight. I just have another fifteen hours to get through.

Scrolling through statistics soothes me. Leif and Corey qualified well again, in P7 and P9, proving that Belgium wasn't a fluke. It might not sound like much – teams like Quezada and Fraser wouldn't exactly be thrilled with those positions – but for Rask Q3 is a major accomplishment and I feel proud to have been a small part of it. The last two days of minding Leif have also been way better than I expected. Ever since he admitted to not hating me, we've been nothing but polite and professional to each other. We haven't revisited the conversation, because we said everything that was necessary. Only . . . as hard as I try to forget it, I can't help wondering what it was he'd been going to say before Corey burst in.

Sarah wakes at 6.30 precisely, stretching her arms wide and smiling like some princess in a fairy tale. I didn't think real people woke up that way – she even looks fresh-faced. Meanwhile, my mirror tells a different story. My skin is puffy and it takes half a stick of concealer to hide the bags under my eyes.

Fortunately, I don't have much to do today. The press mostly leaves the drivers alone before the race, so until then, all I have to do is accompany Leif between the garage and the motorhome, and fetch him anything he needs. Theoretically, it should be easy, except that stepping outside is like walking into a sauna. It's 7.15 a.m. and the temperature is already twenty-five degrees. I'm afraid to think how hot it's going to be when the race finally starts at 2 p.m. At this rate, the asphalt will be melting. I send a quick update to Dan and Maisie, accompanied by a string of hot-face emojis, then climb into the shuttle bus.

AS USUAL, EMIKA IS already at breakfast when I arrive. I'm starting to wonder if she ever sleeps. 'Hey.' She looks up as I collapse into the seat opposite. 'Have you seen the forecast? It's going to be sweltering.'

'It already is.' I gulp down a glass of orange juice and rip open a protein bar. Hopefully it gives me some energy, because right now I'm not sure I can stay awake for the next hour, let alone the whole day.

'Whoa, bad night?' She peers at me over her toast. 'You look exhausted.'

'I didn't sleep well.' I force a smile. 'Nerves, I guess.'

'To be honest, I'm a little nervous about today too. The heat's not ideal.' She sits back and brushes crumbs off her hands. 'Hopefully the ice baths will help.'

'Ice baths?' My eyebrows shoot up.

'Come and see.' She pushes her chair back and stands up. 'We need to get moving anyway.'

I grab an iced coffee to go, and follow her outside, round the back of the motorhome to where an awning has been set up over a pair of dipping tubs filled with ice and . . . two F1 drivers. I clap a hand over my mouth to stop myself from bursting out laughing.

'Morning, gentlemen!' Emika grins down at them. 'Don't mind us. We're just here for the view.'

'Morning.' Corey raises a hand in greeting.

'Hey.' Leif opens one eye and then closes it again.

'Wow.' I get a grip on my laughter. 'That looks *brutal*.'

'Because it is.' Corey dips his head under the surface for a couple of seconds before re-emerging and shaking himself off like a dog. 'My favourite parts are shrivelling. Meanwhile, my crazy teammate is enjoying himself.'

'What? I'm comfortable.' Leif's mouth twitches into a smile. He looks completely relaxed, like most other people are when they're sunbathing.

'Hi, guys.' Leif's performance coach, Kelsey – a five-foot fitness fanatic with a blue pixie haircut who I finally met yesterday – emerges from the back of the motorhome.

'Hey.' Emika waves towards the tubs. 'We've come to get these two out of your hair.'

'It's about time. You should have heard the whining from this one earlier.' She throws a towel at Corey as he heaves himself up. 'Milo had to go for a walk because he couldn't take it any more.'

'*My* performance coach is doing an errand for me,' Corey contradicts her indignantly. 'And not all of us grew up in the Arctic!'

'Technically Trondheim is below the Arctic Circle,' Leif corrects him.

'Just keep reminding them both to drink, will you?' Kelsey's expression turns serious. 'Milo and I have been monitoring their hydration levels and giving them plenty of salts, but these temperatures are dangerous.'

'We will,' I assure her.

'Now get a move on, you two.' Emika taps her watch. 'You need to be in the garage for a strategy meeting in ten minutes.'

'Here.' I pass Leif a towel as he climbs out of the pool, and I get a full, sudden and unobscured view of his dripping body. He's ripped in a way that makes me want to scoop up some of the ice and drop it down the back of my own T-shirt. He's wearing swimming trunks too, and if that's how he looks when he's cold, then . . . I tear my gaze away before anyone notices the direction of my eye-line.

Kelsey's right. These temperatures really are dangerous.

'Thanks.' He takes the towel and wraps it round his waist while I blushingly check my phone.

'Nine minutes!' Emika barks, making shooing motions with her arms. 'Hurry! If we're not where we're supposed to be and there's a random drug test, you'll be the ones in trouble. I'm talking penalties!'

Four minutes later, both drivers reappear from the motorhome dressed in shorts, vests and flip flops.

'No way am I putting on a race suit yet.' Corey shoots Emika a warning look.

'I wouldn't ask you to. Besides, there's no time. Come on.'

We wave goodbye to Kelsey, who's busy putting up a sign offering free dips for anyone in need of cooling off, and make our way towards the garage, Corey and Emika striding ahead while Leif and I walk behind.

I'm trying to think of something to say when I see a familiar figure walking through the paddock towards us. *Jasper Ramirez! Shit!* This trip was so last minute and I've been so busy I somehow forgot he would be here with Quezada. Not that I necessarily expect him to recognize me – I'm just some girl he interviewed six months ago – but if he does, this really isn't a good time for a reunion. One, because it would draw attention to the fact that we know each other, and two because the bags under my eyes don't exactly scream 'Hire me!'.

I drop into a crouch and keep my head down. 'Sorry. I need to retie my laces.'

'Take your time.' Leif's feet stop beside me.

'Um, what?' I hear Emika protest. 'We don't *have* any spare time.'

'I'll just be a sec,' I murmur, waiting until Jasper's shoes pass by. 'There we go.' I spring up again. 'Ready.'

'Good.' Emika is starting to sound panicked. 'Because we have *one* minute!'

'Are you OK?' Leif asks, as we hurry on again.

'Yes.' I give him an innocent look. 'Why?'

'You look tired.'

'Oh.' Apparently my make-up really isn't fooling anyone. 'I didn't sleep well. All the excitement, I guess.'

'Working your first GP is a pretty steep learning curve.' He stops outside the door to the garage, a serious expression on his face. 'But you're doing great.'

'Thanks.' I smile up at him, feeling a warm, fuzzy glow at the words.

'OK, OK, in you go.' Emika ushers him and Corey inside. 'We're off to find Vienna, but we'll be back in a couple of hours. No running away!'

'Yes, boss.' Corey salutes her.

'And don't forget to drink plenty of water!' I call after them.

LEIF'S SCHEDULE SAYS 'Not to be Disturbed 12–12.55' in red capital letters. It's a planned nap time so I wait outside his room in the team motorhome until exactly one hour and five minutes before the race starts, and then knock gently.

'Hello?' I open the door a crack when there's no answer. 'Leif?'

There's still no answer so I push my head through the gap and peer inside. Leif is sitting in an armchair, his feet propped on a small table in front him, snoring softly. After a hectic morning of meetings and discussions, most people would be too wired to sleep, but F1 drivers seem to be able to conk out on command.

'Leif?' I creep forward, keeping my voice low so that I don't startle him. 'It's time to get ready.'

'Mmm.' He moans. 'Ava . . .'

I inhale sharply because he's never said my name like *that* before. Softly, almost tenderly. His eyes are still closed too, like he's dreaming . . . about me?

My stomach flips. Because, despite myself, I *like* the way he said it; part of me wants to hear it again.

'Leif?' I gently press a hand to his shoulder. He's still dressed for the heat, in shorts and a vest, and his skin is smooth and velvety soft beneath my fingertips. It makes me want to slide my hand lower, over his bicep and forearm all the way down to his wrist. I feel a bizarre urge to take hold of his hand, to slip my fingers through his. Only that would be wrong, taking advantage, an invasion of privacy – *completely* unprofessional. I'm not a hand-holder anyway, never have been.

'Ava?'

I jolt my gaze up from his hand to find Leif's eyes wide open and locked on to mine. For a moment, we both stay that way, staring at each other like we're hypnotized. I've always thought his eyes were cold, an icy rather than tropical blue, but right now they're warm and intense and . . . oh crap, *confused*, like he's wondering what I'm doing, bending over him like this.

'You have a race to get to,' I say, as I take a step back and try desperately to pretend that nothing weird just happened. My voice is so tight and high-pitched I hardly recognize it. 'They're waiting for you in the garage.'

'Right.' He rubs his hands over his face. 'I'll get dressed.'

I breathe a sigh of relief. He looks so sleepy he probably thinks he imagined me staring.

'There's just one more thing.' I pull a small plastic box out of my pocket and offer it to him. Inside is a silicon pill containing a micro-thermometer.

'Urgh.' He rolls his eyes, puts the pill in his mouth and then reaches for his water bottle. 'You know, in the past they let drivers just *drive*.'

'It's for your own safety,' I admonish him. 'The team need to monitor your body's levels, especially today.'

I wait outside for him to put on his race suit and then we head to the garage together, dodging photographers and journalists as we go. We don't talk, partly because I'm still feeling embarrassed about the whole staring incident, but mainly because I know he has to mentally prepare for the race ahead.

I really don't envy him today. The Hungaroring is popular with fans, but it's one of the most challenging circuits for drivers, consisting mostly of corners, with barely any straights at all. A lot of people compare it to a karting track, which isn't a huge problem since most drivers start out in karting, but it means that overtaking is tricky and tyres wear out faster than normal. On some circuits, it's possible to get away without any pit-stops at all, but this isn't one of them. It means driver skill and strategy are more important than ever.

Leif goes round the garage, fist-bumping and chatting with his mechanics, while Corey does the same on the opposite side. They put in their earpieces, pulling on their balaclavas and helmets after, so they can listen to the team radio while driving, and climb into their cars. One of the mechanics then does up their seat belts before they pull on their gloves and slowly roll out.

I stand to one side, ready to deal with any media enquiries. The grid is perfectly coordinated chaos, bustling with people and equipment, a sensory overload that makes it impossible to take everything in. Out on the track, meanwhile, Leif does a couple of installation laps before slowing to a stop and waiting for his mechanics, who immediately rush out, raise his car on to trolleys and wheel it to his starting box.

That's my cue to head into the throng, taking a cooling vest, bottle of water and baseball cap with me. It's essential to keep the drivers as chilled and hydrated as possible, even if it's just for a few minutes. In an average race, they can lose up to 3 kilos of sweat, but nothing about today is average. Around me, all the teams are busy setting up fans and dry-ice machines, blowing cool air into cockpits to keep the temperature down.

'Here you go.' I hand Leif the cooling vest. He has already removed his helmet and balaclava, and peeled his race suit down to his waist.

'Thanks.' His cheeks are flushed. 'This is going to be a tough one.'

'You'll be fine,' I say, though I'm not certain which of us I'm trying to reassure. 'Just don't . . .' I start to add and then stop.

'What?' He quirks an eyebrow.

'Nothing.' I suck my bottom lip into my mouth, feeling self-conscious again.

'It was something.' He tilts his head to one side, his eyes crinkling at the corners. 'What was it?'

'Fine. I was just going to say, don't be a hero. If you feel like you're about to pass out, you should stop. Points aren't everything.'

'I'll try to remember that.' His gaze lingers on mine for a long moment before he twists his head, obviously listening to his earpiece. 'Ten minutes until the national anthem. I'd better go and speak to my race engineer.'

'Right.' I step away. 'Good luck.'

I WATCH THE RACE in the motorhome with Vienna and Emika. I don't know if the frontrunners are being extra careful today or they're just feeling drained in the heat, but they're all driving sluggishly. After fifty laps, nothing has changed in the top four other than Shimizu taking third place from Quaid at the first corner. If it weren't for the excitement in the mid field, I'd be fast asleep by now. Both Leif and Corey are driving brilliantly, while our strategy and pit crews have been phenomenal. There was one worrying moment when Corey locked up at turn three and missed the chicane, inadvertently overtaking a Chiltern, but after giving the place back he managed to slip past at the next corner anyway.

The biggest problem is the complete absence of a safety car. Usually, there's at least one during a race, giving the drivers a chance to turn their engines down and harvest power. The majority of teams plan for this eventuality, putting in slightly less petrol than needed for a full race to keep the cars lighter, but despite the heat today no one has retired or even broken down. Which is a good thing, obviously, only it means there's a risk – a small one – of the cars running out of fuel in the last few laps. It's all down to the race engineers to manage the engines.

I hold my breath as the drivers head into the last lap. Leif is in fifth now, Corey in seventh. If they finish where they are, it means sixteen points in total. Sixteen points! I'm so excited at the prospect I barely even notice when Quezada's Jaxon Marr takes first place, closely followed by Gio, then Shimizu and Quaid.

Leif comes round the last corner, heading for the chequered flag. Erikkson is close behind him, aiming for an overtake on the straight. It's close, but then Leif blocks him and . . .

'Yes!' Vienna, who's sat uncharacteristically silent and motionless for the past two hours, springs out of her seat the moment it's over, punching the air like she thinks Philip Sawyer is standing in front of her.

I leap up too, then immediately sway sideways, just catching the back of my chair in time to stop myself from tumbling over. Thankfully Vienna and Emika are too busy celebrating to notice. I feel a little weird, but it's likely only a head-rush from getting up too quickly – that combined with all the excitement. I can't dip out now anyway, not when there are post-race interviews to do.

'Come on!' Emika is already rushing towards the exit. 'We need to get down there.'

I take a moment to pull myself back together and then follow her, running to meet the drivers in the pit lane. Leif and Corey must be completely shattered; their race suits are so drenched in sweat it's like they've just run a marathon. But they're grinning from ear to ear, arms wrapped around each other's shoulders as they stagger towards us.

'Sixteen points, baby!' Corey calls out.

'Hell, yes!' Emika high-fives him.

'You were the best drivers of the day,' I say, my eyes drawn towards Leif as he pushes a hand through his hair. It's so damp it sticks upright. 'Diamandis only scored one point, which means –'

He finishes for me, his eyes lighting up. 'We're in fifth place in the team rankings.'

'We have to do press,' Emika interrupts. 'But afterwards we're celebrating properly, OK?'

'Deal.' Corey lifts his water bottle. 'Lead the way.'

'Leif!' an interviewer calls out, thrusting a microphone into his face the moment we enter the press pen. 'Congratulations on fifth place. This is your best result since Melbourne. How good does that feel?'

'Amazing,' Leif answers, rubbing a forearm across his brow. 'We knew this would be a challenging weekend, thanks to the heat, but it's a great result for the team. Our upgrades have made a huge difference and hopefully we can keep building on that momentum.'

'So you're confident of a good result in Austria in two weeks?'

'We'll do our best.'

I keep my phone raised to record everything, but from the sound of it I don't need to worry. Leif is being engaging and polite and . . . I draw my brows together as I feel myself sway again. Even worse, dots are beginning to swarm in front of my eyes. *Oh no. No, no, no.* I blink rapidly, trying to clear my head, but it's like a blind is being slowly drawn over my vision. The combination of sun, lack of sleep and at least five cups of coffee is too much for me.

I look around for Emika because I need help, someone to take over without drawing too much attention, but I can't see her any more. I can't focus on anyone. The room is spinning and I don't know how much longer I can stay upright. A wave of panic sweeps through me. This is how I felt six years ago, disoriented and frightened, completely out of control and vulnerable.

'Ava? Do you need to sit down?' Leif's voice murmurs in my ear.

'What?' I mumble, turning my head in confusion. I wasn't aware of the interview ending, but it must have because we're facing away from the cameras now. Meanwhile, one of Leif's hands is beneath my elbow, holding me up. I can feel his fingers warm against my skin. 'I . . . don't know. I just need a moment.'

'You need more than that. Come on, I'll take you back to the motorhome.'

'No.' I dig my heels in. 'You have . . . interviews . . . to do.'

'Screw them. You look like you're about to collapse.'

'You have to . . .' I protest. 'They're for the team.'

'You're part of the team too. Here –' he hands me his water bottle – 'drink this. The electrolytes will help.'

'I can't.' I shake my head, but the movement makes me feel even worse. 'Kelsey will kill me.'

'For fuck's sake!' He sounds exasperated. 'Who's going to tell her?'

It's a fair point, so I give in and chug half the bottle in one go. It tastes awful, but it works. My vision starts to clear and I begin to feel steady on my feet again. 'I'm so sorry,' I gasp, wiping a hand across my mouth. 'I feel so unprofessional.'

'Don't. This heat is tough on everyone.'

'You've just driven a two-hour race!'

'I'm used to it. Plus, I had a nice bath to start.'

I snort a laugh, then throw a quick look around. We're still in the press pen but huddled close together, so hopefully it looks like we're discussing a team issue. 'OK, I'm better. I can do this.'

'Are you sure?' He still sounds concerned.

'How much will you be fined if you don't do any more interviews?'

'It depends. Twenty thousand maybe.'

'Pounds?' I almost faint again at the number. 'You're *doing* the interviews.'

'Ava –'

'You can give short answers.'

'All right.' He lets go of my arm slowly, like he's afraid I might fall over without any support. 'But give me a sign if you need to leave. Step on my foot if you have to.'

'Thanks. And, Leif?' I'm the one touching his elbow this time. 'If you don't mind, could we keep this between us? I'd rather nobody else knew.'

'Knew what?' He gives a small smile, walking beside me back to the cameras.

As I re-open my Voice Memos app, it occurs to me that maybe Charlotte was right. Leif might just be 'adorable' after all.

Jaxon Marr may have won in Hungary, but Rask's upgrade success was the talk of the paddock this weekend. A top-ten finish for both their drivers would have been inconceivable just one month ago.

@ MotorsportsEchoNews, 24 June

TWELVE

EMIKA AND I GET Monday off work, so we don't see the rest of the team's reaction to our success until Tuesday, but the moment we set foot back in HQ it's obvious the whole mood at Rask Racing has shifted. The atmosphere in the factory is buoyant and everyone is smiling and positive, more upbeat than I've ever seen them before. Those sixteen points make all the difference and we get to bask in the reflected glory.

Part of me feels guilty about all the attention. Even though my almost-fainting incident wasn't my fault, I still feel like I let the team down. If it hadn't been for Leif, I would probably have collapsed live on television. It could have made headlines – Jasper Ramirez might have seen! Thankfully, after an epic sleep yesterday, I feel almost back to normal again.

'Look at this.' Vienna comes out of her office around midday, brandishing a newspaper. '"Rask in Return to Form"!'

'Really?' I leap up from my chair as she spreads it out over Emika's desk. The fact that we're still making headlines two days after the race is definitely a good sign.

'"After a rocky start to the season, it seems like things are finally turning round for the beleaguered F1 team. With a few new upgrades, Rask is showing detractors how well the company can manage without Philip Sawyer."' She beams triumphantly. 'Good job, everyone.'

'We should follow it up,' I say. 'I'll call their sports editor.'

'Print media?' Charlotte looks appalled.

'Yes, print publicity. Some of us Generation Xers still use it.' Vienna lifts her eyes to the ceiling. 'But there are stories like this online too. Our socials have got more interaction in the past two days than they have all season. It proves our strategy is working. People are starting to support us again.' She darts back into her office and then re-emerges with a large plate of cupcakes, decorated with red, blue and yellow-striped icing. 'That's why I got catering to bake these –'

'Ooh!' Emika jumps up enthusiastically.

'They're giving them out in the canteen so I swiped a few for us.'

'What's the matter?' I'm about to take a bite when I see Charlotte's crestfallen expression.

'Nothing. It's just . . . my wedding dress.'

'You're not getting married until January.' Emika thrusts a cupcake at her. 'Come on, it's a celebration. One little cake isn't going to burst any stitches.'

'OK, just one.' Charlotte take a bite and then closes her eyes with a groan. 'I've missed cake so much.'

'What about you?' Vienna pushes the plate towards Yuto.

'I can't. I'm still scared of food.' He glances at her face and changes his mind. 'But maybe I'll make an exception.'

'Good. By the way, I have a meeting with that frozen yogurt company at one.' Vienna turns to me. 'I want you there too.'

'Why would a frozen yogurt company want to sponsor an F1 team?' Charlotte mumbles through a mouthful of cake.

'It's a Swedish company. Thanks to Leif, we're very popular in Scandinavia now.'

'Fingers crossed it goes well.' Emika reaches for another cupcake. 'But personally I'd rather stick with these.'

'And I have more good news.' Vienna pauses for effect. 'I know this first half of the season has been exhausting, but we only have three more races until the summer break. That's just over a month away. Obviously, we're not prohibited from working, like the factory, but Bastian promises you'll all get a few days off. I'll cover the office, but the rest of you deserve a decent rest.'

'This day gets better and better.' Emika grins at Charlotte.

'I don't mind covering the office too,' I say as Vienna props herself on the edge of my desk. 'Since I only started last month.'

'You've still made a big difference. You're an asset to the team.' She smiles. 'I admit, when Leif first suggested you for the job I was sceptical, but he was right.'

I almost spit out my mouthful of cake. 'It was *Leif* who gave you my name?'

'Shit.' She scrunches her face up. 'I wasn't supposed to tell you that.'

'Why not?'

'I've no idea. He just said not to tell you.' She shrugs. 'Though what does it matter really? You're happy, I'm happy, Leif is *probably* happy. I mean, who can tell most of the time?'

'I don't understand . . .' My mind is whirling as I try to process. I've been so busy I completely forgot to ask Gio if he was the one who recommended me for the job. But if it was Leif, he must have done it right after our first meeting in Monaco, which makes zero sense. We barely spoke that night. He acted like he thought I shouldn't be there. I thought he was an asshole!

'OK, I need a quick chat with Bastian before our meeting.' Vienna slides back off my desk. 'I'll see you in the conference room in half an hour?'

'Right. See you there.' I put the rest of my cupcake down and reach for my phone. I still have my first-day video on it, as well as my first attempt to film my 'accidental' meeting with Leif, the one where he smiled and I forgot my line. Somehow I never got round to deleting it . . . I search for it now and watch again. And again, and then one more time because maybe if I look at Leif for long enough I'll figure out what's going on. First, it turns out he doesn't hate me. And now I find out he actually got me this job that I love. Why? And should I be grateful or just really, really confused?

Because right now I'm both.

BY THE TIME I leave work it's almost 7 p.m., but as afternoons go this one has been hugely productive. Not only does Rask have a new Swedish sponsor, but their investment is bigger than we anticipated. Even better, they want to capitalize on our recent success by launching an advertising campaign as soon as possible.

I head across the car park, swinging my bag with a feeling of satisfaction. Even though it's evening, the air is still warm – though thankfully not as hot as Hungary – the birds are singing and all is well with the world. All except . . . I drop my bag and stare at my car in horror. My rear left tyre is flatter than a pancake.

I close my eyes, tip my head back and take a moment to appreciate the irony. Just when my spirits are inflated, my tyre decides to do the opposite. And here I am, standing outside a building packed full of tyres and tools, none of which are of any use to me because everyone has gone home, meaning my options are to either call a recovery company – an expense I really don't need – or change the tyre myself. I know how to do it – my parents taught me when I first learned to drive. Only ideally I'd be wearing old jeans and a ripped T-shirt instead of a black fitted Khaite dress that I bought on Vinted.

Fuck.

I kick my heels off and change into the ballet flats I use for driving, do a quick google to refresh my memory and then crouch down to loosen and remove the wheel nuts. Next, I heave the spare tyre out of the boot. It's heavier than I expected, especially since I have to hold it away from my body, straining my biceps in a desperate and probably futile attempt to avoid getting dirt on my dress. As soon as I'm able, I drop the tyre on to the ground, then slide the jack under the car, wind it up and sit back on my haunches to admire my handiwork. So far, so good. Now if I can just slide the flat tyre off without losing my balance . . .

'Ava?'

I jerk my head up to find Leif staring down at me, one forearm resting on the open window of his red-and-white sports car. I was concentrating so hard I didn't even hear him pull up.

'Need a hand?' He nods towards my flat tyre.

I open my mouth and then close it again. *Yes*, I want to say. *Yes, I could do with several hands*. But I'm an independent woman and I can change my own tyre. It doesn't help that, after Vienna's slip-up this afternoon, seeing him again so unexpectedly is like a physical shock. I don't know how to react. I haven't had enough time to process.

'No, I'm almost done.' I shake my head, feeling a flush of heat spreading up my neck. 'Thanks anyway.'

'OK.' He stares at me for a few more seconds before shrugging his shoulders and driving on.

What? I stare after him. As much as I appreciate him respecting me as an independent woman, he could have tried a little harder to persuade me!

I turn my attention back to my car, muttering under my breath as I grab the edge of the tyre. Suddenly I don't feel any kind of gratitude towards Leif Olsen. So what if he got me a job? Passing a name on is easy. Low effort. Not like helping somebody to change their tyre. That takes a certain kind of person. A special person, a truly 'adorable' person, which, despite their reputation, is clearly not . . .

'Hey.'

'What the –' I fall backwards, landing on my bum with a yelp, as a pair of feet appears at the edge of my vision.

'Sorry.' Leif holds a hand out. 'I didn't mean to startle you.'

'I thought you –'

'Drove off and left you?' He hoists me back to my feet. 'Ava, even if you don't want me to help, I'm not just going to abandon you. I needed to park, that's all. I can wait in my car if it makes you feel more comfortable, but I'm honestly happy to help otherwise.'

'Oh.' I decide not to look a gift horse in the mouth, no matter how confusing that horse is, especially when his fingers are still wrapped around mine, making my pulse flutter. 'I actually could use some help. I don't want to ruin my dress.'

'It's a nice dress.' His gaze dips to my waist before he releases my hand and crouches down beside the car. 'I've got this.'

'Thanks.' I watch as he removes the old tyre and slots on the emergency one. He's wearing light wash jeans and a grey T-shirt and looks a whole lot fresher than he did the last time I saw him after the Hungarian Grand Prix. I should probably do something more constructive, but I'm too distracted by the way his muscles are bunching under his sleeves.

'You're working late,' he says conversationally as he tightens the wheel nuts.

'Mmm? Oh, I had paperwork to do. We have a new sponsor.'

'I heard. Good job.'

'It was mostly Vienna.' I chew the inside of my cheek. 'What about you? Why haven't you gone home yet?'

'I had a few things to discuss with Bastian. There you go.' He stands up and brushes his hands together. 'That'll do for tonight, but you shouldn't drive far on a temporary tyre and no faster than fifty.'

'I'll take it straight to a garage in the morning,' I say. 'No, wait. I have another meeting first thing. Shit.' I press a hand to my forehead, thinking through the timings. There's no way I'll make it to work on time if I have to find a garage as well. I'll just have to leave my car for another day and figure out some other method of getting here tomorrow. Maybe I can ask Dan for a favour, or I could call Yuto? He lives in Cambridge, too . . . 'Never mind. I'll work something out.'

'No need. I have a friend who owns a garage. I'm sure we can arrange something.' Leif pulls his phone out of his back pocket and quirks an eyebrow at me. 'If that's OK with you?'

'Well . . .' I think about refusing, but, honestly, the sooner I can get my car fixed, the better. 'If you wouldn't mind? If I could drop it off really early that would be perfect.'

'I'll find out.'

Two minutes later, he wanders back to me, tucking his phone away again. 'All sorted. We can go straight there.'

'Now?' I check my watch. It's 7.30 already.

'He's a good friend.' He strides off towards his car. 'Follow me.'

'Wait!' I call after him. 'You can just give me the address. There's no need for you to come too. You've done enough . . .' I stop talking as he closes his car door.

I guess this means we're going together.

After their best result of the season so far, Rask must be keen to hang on to their current line-up – both drivers are on one-year contracts. With rumblings of openings at both Quezada and Fraser, however, Olsen and Hammond may want to wait and see what happens elsewhere before committing to the long term . . .

@ MotorsportEchoNews, 24 June

THIRTEEN

BECAUSE IT'S SUMMER, IT'S still light when we pull up outside a garage in a small town on the coast. It looks ancient. The doors are crying out for a coat of paint and the sign is so faded I can't even tell what it says. As garages go, it's the absolute last place I would have expected an F1 driver to know about, let alone visit, but Leif has already parked and is waving for me to drive straight inside.

'Is here OK?' I ask, winding my window down as two men in overalls emerge from an office.

'Fine.' One of them gives me a thumbs-up.

'Thanks so much for doing this. I'm really grateful,' I say, climbing out and handing him the keys. Despite its battered exterior, the inside of the garage is perfectly neat and tidy.

'No problem.' The man grins at Leif, who's just walked up behind me. 'You owe me a favour, Olsen.'

'Anything you want. How long will you need?'

'To change all four tyres? About an hour. We're not a pit crew.'

'Oh, it's not all four,' I protest quickly. 'It's only the rear left.'

'You can't do one and not the others.' Leif looks remonstratively at me. 'It makes them unbalanced.'

'It's also four times the cost.'

'Do all four.' Leif turns back to the man. 'We'll sort the money out later.'

'Hang on!' I hurry after him as he heads for the door. 'It's my car. I should be the one making the decisions.'

'I know, but I can afford a few new tyres, especially now that Rask have a new sponsor.'

'*Leif*,' I say in my sternest voice.

'Ava.' He stops walking. 'Safety is important. I can't let you drive away on unsafe tyres.'

'That's a massive exaggeration.'

'Maybe, but I'd still feel better if you let me do this. You've done a lot for me recently.' He catches my eye and sighs. 'Look, if you feel that strongly, you can buy dinner to make up for it. There's a decent fish-and-chip shop on the front.'

'Fish and chips?' I squint at him suspiciously. 'Are you allowed to eat fried food?'

'Absolutely not.' His eyes twinkle. 'But what Kelsey doesn't know, she can't yell at me about.'

'Doesn't she do blood tests?'

'Yes, but I have a fast metabolism and a week and a half to burn it off.' He notices my sceptical expression and lifts his eyes skyward. 'Fine, I'll get a small.'

I tap my foot, taking a moment to consider. There's a stubborn set to his jaw that suggests we could be here all night arguing if I don't give in, and anyway he's right – I *have* done a lot for him. I've pretty much single-handedly reinvented his image. I've persuaded him to smile! Also, it occurs to me that I'm hungry. Ravenous even . . . And it's not like we haven't eaten together before. We've had several meals in the team motorhome. This could be like an informal professional meeting, so long as I keep any impure thoughts firmly under control. 'Fine. Fish and chips sounds good.' I stalk past him towards the street. 'But no mushy peas.'

'I can live with that.'

'How do you know this town so well anyway?' I ask as he falls into step beside me. 'First the garage, now the fish-and-chip shop.'

'I'm renting a house here.'

'What?' I almost fall off the kerb in surprise. It's not exactly glamorous. I should know. I grew up in a town just like this.

He shrugs and slips his hands into his pockets. 'I like the sea.'

'Monaco has the sea. I thought all F1 drivers lived there?'

'There or Switzerland. But I like it here.'

'Doesn't that mean paying lots of tax?'

'So Nathan keeps telling me.'

'Huh.' A lightbulb pops to life in my head. 'You know, it would be great if we could do an "At Home with Leif" feature with you. Corey filmed one at his place in Monaco a couple of weeks ago. Here.' I pull up a TikTok, a short video of Corey sipping espresso while giving a tour of his luxury apartment. With his dishevelled bed hair and twinkling brown eyes, it has five hundred thousand likes already. It probably didn't hurt that he decided to go shirtless.

'What do you think?' I look eagerly at Leif.

'I think Corey's better at that stuff than me.' He sounds dubious. 'But I'll think about it.'

'That's all I ask.' I slip my phone back into my bag as we reach the fish-and-chip shop. There's a dining area inside, but it's such a beautiful evening I head for the outdoor counter instead. 'Now you go and find us somewhere to sit while I get dinner.'

Luckily, a couple of fish have just come out of the frier so it's not long before I get to join Leif on one of the picnic benches overlooking the water. There's a scattering of other people about, dog-walkers mostly, as well as a group of kids heading into one of the arcades on the front, but otherwise it's peaceful. All you can hear is the occasional gull and the sound of the waves lapping gently against the sea defences. It still feels pretty surreal, though. I can't believe I'm having fish and chips by the seaside with an F1 driver.

'Here you go. Dinner with a view.' I hand him a cardboard box and point my fork in a generally north-eastwards direction. 'Norway must be over there, right?'

'A little more this way.' He takes my hand and moves it slightly to the left. 'You were pointing at Denmark.'

'Oh. Sorry. My sense of direction isn't the best.' Electricity bolts up my arm at the touch and I pull my hand away under the guise of spearing a chip. 'Thanks for your help tonight, by the way.' I try to sound casual. 'I can't believe you got a garage to reopen for me.'

'It's in my best interests.' He shoots me a sidelong smile. 'If you didn't have transport tomorrow, who'd run my socials?'

'Excuse me?' I splutter. 'Did you just say "run my socials"?'

'I picked it up from Nathan.' He laughs at my stunned expression. 'He says it's all looking good.'

'It is. You've got almost a million followers already. In fact, Rask's overall numbers are on the up. We're getting a ton of engagement.'

'Great.' He looks pleased. 'They deserve it. They're a good team.'

'They are. You know, I thought it was just an image thing at first, but Rask really are like one big, happy family.'

I smile and drop a vinegar-soaked chip into my mouth. It's hot and delicious. Unfortunately, I can't fully enjoy it because now that we're sitting down, facing each other, my head is suddenly brimming with questions, all of which I should probably keep to myself. If Leif doesn't want me to know he was the one who got me the job with Rask, then I probably shouldn't ask him about it. I should keep my mouth firmly shut. Yes. Totally. Only . . .

'Why did you get me this job?' I blurt out before I can stop myself.

As expected, his forehead creases into a frown.

'I found out by accident,' I explain. 'It's not Vienna's fault. I just don't understand. I mean . . . *why*?'

He twists his face away, looking out to sea. 'When we met in Monaco, you said you wanted to work in Formula 1, so I passed your name on. It's no big deal.'

I contradict him. 'It's a huge deal. You didn't have to help me.'

'But I could, so I did. Rask gave me the opportunity to live out my dream. Why wouldn't I help somebody else do the same? It's what anybody else would have done.'

'Actually I'm pretty sure most people wouldn't have bothered. And why all the secrecy?'

'Because if you'd known it was me, you might have thought you owed me something.' He glances back at me briefly, then away again. 'You don't. Besides, it doesn't matter who mentioned your name. Vienna wouldn't have hired you if she'd thought you weren't up to the job.'

'Well, I'm grateful, but I still wish you'd told me. All this time, I thought you didn't like me. Now it turns out you're the one who got me my job *and* you're buying me new tyres.' I tilt my head to one side. 'Is it because of this person I remind you of?'

'No.' He shifts in his seat like he's uncomfortable. 'Honestly, Ava, I just wanted to help.'

I pop another chip into my mouth and chew thoughtfully. I should almost definitely stop asking questions now. We've only recently started getting along and I shouldn't push it, but I'm too curious. 'So, who was she?'

His jaw tightens instantly. 'It's a long story.'

'I have a lot of chips.' I lift my box for emphasis. 'Although, if it's too personal, if she was a girlfriend or something, then –'

'No,' he interrupts. 'It was nothing like that. She was a friend. We were in care together.'

I freeze in my seat. 'You were raised in care?'

'Yes.' His jaw is so tight now I can see the cords of his neck. 'My mother died when I was eight. There was nowhere else to send me.'

'That's . . .' I gulp. 'I'm so sorry. I had no idea.'

'Nobody does. I don't talk about it.' His eyes glint silver in the evening light. 'Usually.'

'If you don't want to now . . .'

'It's OK.' He puts his fork down. 'Ask whatever you like.'

'Really?' He's such a mystery that my mind is bursting with questions. 'Well . . . what about your father?'

'I never met him.'

'A foster family?'

'I had a few.' His voice falters. 'But I was so messed up and angry I refused to let anyone help me. Eventually, I ended up in a facility for difficult children. It felt like a kind of family. One of the girls, Britta, had red hair, green eyes . . .'

'Ah.' I let out a breath. 'How long were you there?'

'Only a year, in the end. Then I met the Falsens. They were my sixth foster family.'

'And it was different?'

'Not at first. Then they took me ice karting.' He braces his hands against the table. 'Remember how you asked me what I would have done if I hadn't been a driver? The truth is, I don't think it would have been a good path. But ice karting was a turning point, maybe even saved my life. I'd never been good at anything before, but being behind a wheel . . . That was different. It made me feel alive, but calm too. It helped me channel my feelings, and all of my pain and anger just faded away. People said I was talented, so my foster parents took me go-karting next. I was old for a beginner, but I worked hard and gradually moved up the rankings. Being a driver became all I wanted.'

I listen in wonder. This must be the most words I've ever heard him say in one go. I feel honoured and touched and . . . confused. Why is he telling *me* this? But I still have questions.

'And Britta?'

His face falls in a way that makes me regret asking. 'She wasn't so lucky. When I was fifteen, she came to one of my races. I was pleased to see her, but I could tell something was wrong too. She was so thin and jittery. We arranged to meet afterwards, but then something came up and I bailed. A little while later I heard she'd got mixed up with a bad crowd. Eventually she ran away.' His voice is laced with pain. 'They said it was a heroin overdose.'

'Leif, I'm so sorry.' I reach a hand out, though I don't touch him, just place it on the table beside his own. 'That's tragic, but it wasn't your fault.'

'Maybe not, but I still let her down. I broke my word. If I'd met her when I said I would, then maybe I could have helped.'

'You were only fifteen.'

'Old enough to know better.' A look of surprise crosses his face. 'I've never told anyone that before.'

'I won't repeat it. I promise.'

'I know.'

'So . . .' I pull my hand away, feeling self-conscious again. 'Do I look that much like her?'

'No. There was a similarity at first, but now . . . you're Ava.' His gaze settles on my face again. 'And personality-wise, you're about as far from Britta as you could get. She was lost, but you're more focused than anybody I've ever met. You must be one of the hardest-working people in the whole team.'

'Present company excepted.'

'Obviously.' His lips curve before he clears his throat. 'So maybe we could go out for dinner again sometime?'

'It's OK.' I shake my head sympathetically. 'You don't have to feel guilty about me. We had a rough start, but now you've told me about Britta, I understand. We're good.'

A furrow appears between his brows. 'I'm asking because I like spending time with you. Not because you remind me of Britta. But because you're *you*.' He puts extra emphasis on the word.

'You mean . . . like a date?' My stomach is alive with butterflies suddenly. Very surprised, very confused, very excited butterflies. 'But I called you monosyllabic!'

'I know. It was pretty funny.'

I stiffen indignantly. 'I thought you were going to get me fired.'

'Please.' He makes a scoffing sound. 'You should hear what they call me in the workshop.'

'What do they call you in the workshop?'

'That's need to know only. By the way, I listened to your podcast.'

'Really?' A quiver of pleasure rolls its way down my spine. 'Which episode?'

'All of them.'

'*All?*' I open my eyes wide. I didn't think anyone had listened to all of them, not even my mum. 'But I've been doing it for four years. That's more than sixty episodes.'

'I know, but I enjoyed them. I thought your analysis was very perceptive.'

'Oh . . . thank you.'

I'm not sure what else to say. I've only recently got my head round the idea that he doesn't hate me. The switch from that to him asking me on a date is making my head spin. A week ago, before Hungary, I thought he was a grumpy asshole. Yes, I might have fantasized a little over how hot he is, I may even have had a couple more spicy dreams, but I would never seriously have considered him as anything other than a colleague. Now I can feel my heart speeding up, beating a staccato rhythm in my chest.

'Ava?' He rubs a hand around the back of his neck. 'What do you think?'

I lick my lips but still don't answer. I must seem like the most indecisive woman on the planet, but it's just . . . I don't date. I'm not a relationship person. I'm too uptight. I *know* that. Look at what happened with Oliver. *But Leif isn't Oliver*, a voice at the back of my mind tells me. Everything about him is different. Even sitting here opposite him right now feels different. It's like my whole body is covered in goosebumps. This must be what chemistry feels like. Would it – *could it* – be different?

Maybe.

I gulp. The truth is, I only went out with Oliver because I thought that I should, because I wanted to try dating again, despite what happened the last time. With Leif, there's no should. There are several very big shouldn'ts. It would be too complicated. We're colleagues. It could interfere with my job. I should say no.

So why am I hesitating?

Instead of an answer, a question finds its way past my lips. 'Would it be allowed?'

'Allowed?' He sounds confused.

'Yes. Rask might have a non-fraternization policy or something. I mean, eating fish and chips together is one thing, but an actual date . . .'

'There's no policy,' he answers. 'Not that I'm aware of anyway.'

I mentally scan my own contract of employment. I don't remember such a clause, but maybe I glossed over that part because I simply assumed it wouldn't apply to me.

'Think about it.' He lifts a shoulder. 'If you'd like to, you know where to find me.'

Our eyes lock and a flare of something new and powerful

flashes between us. I feel like I've woken up from a long sleep to find the world around me looks different. It's so striking, I find myself opening my lips to say – something, I'm not even sure what – just as the wind catches a lock of hair that's escaped from my ponytail and blows it straight across my face, blinding me.

'Here.' Leif lifts a hand to my cheek and tucks the loose strands behind my ear. The moment his fingers brush against my skin it's like they've stolen my breath away.

We lean closer, obeying a pull neither of us can resist. Closer . . . closer . . . our lips are almost touching when a loud dinging sound erupts from the arcade on the street behind us. Somebody has obviously won something, but it's just about the least romantic sound you could ever imagine, enough to bring me back to my senses.

'That must be an hour.' I jolt backwards, gulping down cool mouthfuls of air. 'We'd better get back to the garage.'

Leif, answer your phone. We have things to discuss...

Nathan Wallis, voicemail to Leif Olsen, 1 July

FOURTEEN

'DID YOU EVER GET an answer from Leif about Ashley Hart?' Yuto puts his phone down and swivels his chair round to face me.

'Mmm?' I lift my head from the promotional packs I'm putting together for Austria. 'Oops . . . No. Sorry, I completely forgot.'

'Me too, but her people have been in contact with Nathan again. They think the premiere of her new F1 movie next month would be a good opportunity for a date, but they need an answer asap.'

My stomach lurches in a way I'm not prepared for. I haven't spoken to Leif in a week, not since our almost kiss on the seafront. Once my new tyres were done, we parted ways and I haven't had any promotional stuff for him to do in the meantime. Or at least I haven't asked him to do any. Also, I've been busy helping Vienna charm another potential sponsor, a finance company with a long acronym name that I keep forgetting.

It's not like I've been avoiding him exactly. I've just been . . . working.

'Leif's not seeing anyone, is he?' Yuto asks.

'I don't know.' I try to sound nonchalant. 'But it's only a publicity thing, isn't it?'

'I think so, but who knows? Maybe celebrities have a hard time meeting people. Anyway, Nathan wants someone to go and find out what Leif thinks.'

'Well, I can't right now.' I drop my gaze because I have a horrible feeling I know where this is going. 'I have these packs to finish.'

'Yeah, the thing is, he says Leif's turned his phone off and Kelsey's not answering hers, which means they're probably in the gym, and I have a Teams meeting in about two minutes, so . . .'

'If Leif's not answering his phone, maybe that means he doesn't want to be disturbed, and I really have so much to do –'

'I'll help you with your packs after my meeting.' Yuto's expression turns pleading. 'All Nathan needs is a yes or no. It won't take long. Just text me when you get an answer and I'll pass it on.'

'Yuto . . .'

'Please, please, please.'

'*Urgh.*' I can't think of any more excuses. 'Fine, but you owe me.'

'Yes, I do. You're my favourite co-worker!'

I stomp out of the office, down the stairs and along a series of winding corridors, slamming doors into walls as I go. The gym is on the other side of the building, beside the canteen, which still isn't far enough because I arrive before I have any idea what I'm going to say. I mean, what *can* I say? *Hi, Leif, so I know we almost kissed and I still haven't given you an answer about a date yet, but hey, how would you like to go to a movie premiere with some gorgeous actress instead?*

It's not that I haven't thought about his invitation, because I have. A lot. I've also relived the feeling of his hand on my cheek several hundred times. I just haven't decided yet because everything seems to have happened so quickly, and I'm torn. I've also checked my contract, and while dating isn't forbidden, it's strongly discouraged. HR would need to be informed, Vienna too – and what would she think? I want to impress her and this could look *so* unprofessional. Basically, everything about this idea has the potential to send all my future plans spinning off course. Which is why I should say no – *absolutely no* – to a date.

The problem is I can't help remembering the feeling of connection between us that evening by the sea; and how, for the first time, I didn't stiffen up and panic at the idea of being kissed. Maybe it was a fluke or maybe I'm just finally ready to date again, but what if it means something more? It makes me wonder whether us being together might actually . . . work?

Unless Leif wants to date Ashley Hart instead.

There are too many people about for me to loiter outside the gym, so I go straight in and hover by the door. The music is so loud there's no way anybody could have heard me knock, although both Leif and Kelsey are so engrossed in his workout they probably wouldn't have noticed anyway. He's sitting on a balance ball a few metres away, holding a large weight in front of him, tipping it slowly from side to side like he's turning a steering wheel. His muscles are straining so hard I can see his veins bulging and there are actual beads of sweat trickling over his arms, making his skin glisten. As I watch, he grunts, and I feel it deep inside, a hot agitated feeling that would be deeply inappropriate if he hadn't already asked me on a date . . .

Suddenly I really want to say yes.

'Ava?' He sees me first, his face registering surprise and then something else I can't identify, before he puts the weight down and gets up.

'Sorry to interrupt.' I order myself to get a grip as he turns the music down. 'But Nathan has an important question to ask you and he says you've turned your phone off.'

'That won't stop him.' Leif glances at Kelsey. 'We're almost done anyway, right?'

'Nice try.' She laughs. 'We can stop for now, but I want to see you back here this afternoon.'

'Two workouts a day?' I look quizzically between them.

'I only train five days a week, so I need to do extra on three of those days,' he explains. 'It means I get weekends to relax.'

'Within reason.' Kelsey hands him a towel. 'Here. You two chat while I clean the machines.'

'So what's so urgent?' Leif asks, standing up and rubbing his face.

'Right. So, like I said, sorry to intrude . . .' I avert my eyes from his pecs as he moves closer, fixing my gaze at a point just beyond his shoulder. 'It's about that F1 film premiere next month.'

'OK?'

'The thing is . . .' I stop and take a deep breath. I'm so uncomfortable right now it aches. 'Nathan wonders how you'd feel about going to see it with Ashley Hart.'

He looks baffled. 'I don't know anyone called that.'

'She's an actress, in the film. Her people have been in touch, and she'd like to go with you.' For Kelsey's sake, I try to inject some enthusiasm into my voice. 'If you're photographed together, it would be good PR for Rask. She has a huge online following.'

'That's a great idea.' Kelsey comes back over to join us. 'She's incredibly talented. I'd love to meet her.'

'Right.' I nod vigorously. 'So?' I force myself to look Leif in the eye. 'What do you think?'

He stares back at me for several seconds before folding his arms. 'No.'

'Why not?' Kelsey sounds offended on Ashley's behalf. 'It could be fun.'

'I'm not going on a date with a complete stranger.'

'You might hit it off!' She rolls her eyes. 'You know, it wouldn't hurt you to have a life beyond cars.'

'I have a life beyond cars.' He glowers at her.

'Oh, really? How many cars do you own?'

'Six.'

'And how many girlfriends have you had since I've known you?'

'You've only known me a year.' His jaw clenches. 'I've been busy. Driving.'

'Uh-huh. All I'm saying is that maybe you should start making time for a personal life. *Look*.' She pulls up a picture on her phone and shows it to us. Crap. Ashley Hart is even more gorgeous than I remember. Toned, tanned and glowy.

'I said no.' Leif's voice hardens.

'But . . .'

'*No*.'

'Fine.' Kelsey throws her arms out. 'I'm going to get a smoothie.'

I bite the inside of my lip as she storms away. I shouldn't be happy about Leif's answer, but I can't help it. A warm, fuzzy feeling has just suffused my whole body and I want to hug him. I actually start to lift my arms before stopping myself. I can't, not when I still haven't made a decision about 'us', so instead I wait until Kelsey flings the door open before turning to follow her. 'I should probably go too.'

'Wait.' Leif tosses his towel aside and takes a step closer, gripping the machine next to me with one hand. 'Is this what you want, for me to go on a date with an actress?'

'It doesn't matter what I want.' I thrust my chin out because I don't like his tone. It sounds accusatory, like he thinks I actually *enjoy* asking him any of this. 'Speaking on behalf of the communications department, it would be good for the team.'

'What about speaking as you?'

'I –'

I pause because now that he's standing right in front of me, the musky scent of him filling my senses, I'm finding it harder to focus. There's an intimacy about our position, making everything feel heightened; my pulse is thumping and I have a sudden, overwhelming desire to be half-naked and sweaty too. Or possibly all naked, pressed up against him . . .

'Ava?' His eyes search mine, ice and fire combined.

'Speaking as me –' my voice catches – 'I don't like the idea.'

'Why not?'

I swallow as he moves incrementally closer. Or maybe I'm moving towards him?

'Because I don't want you to date anyone else.' I press a hand to my mouth in surprise as the words emerge, honest and unfiltered. Standing this close, only a couple of inches apart, his bicep right next to my face, all my defences come tumbling down. I can't help but tell the truth, even if it's one I'm not entirely comfortable with. This could be a terrible idea, but right now I can't bring myself to care. I'm in the grip of something more powerful, something I want – *need* – to explore.

'Neither do I.' He lifts a hand, gently pulling my fingers away from my mouth.

'But the thing is,' I say quickly, 'I'm not good at this.'

'This?'

'Dating. Relationships. *This*.'

One of his eyebrows lifts. 'What makes you think that?'

'It's just not something I do. And when I've tried it . . . it goes wrong.' I take an unsteady breath. 'I find it hard to relax. I guess I'm too uptight.'

'Ava . . .' His brow furrows slightly as he lets go of my hand. 'If you don't want to date me, just say so and I'll respect that. But if all that's stopping you is some idea that you're uptight . . .' He shakes his head. 'I don't think that's true. I like you. I think we could have something really special.'

My heart skips a beat because I want to believe that, so badly. But he doesn't understand. 'You'd be better off with Ashley Hart.' I make one last attempt at being sensible. 'She'd be good for your brand.'

His lips quirk at the corners. 'There's a limit to what I'm prepared to do for my brand.'

'Leif . . .'

'Ava . . .' He leans forward before I can argue any more, bringing his lips to within a hair's breadth of mine and then stopping. The implication is obvious. This has to be my move – my choice. So I make it. I close the distance between us, kissing him tentatively and catching my breath as I wait for my body to stiffen. But like before, it doesn't. Instead I melt. Our noses nudge together and my lips cling to his like they never want to let go. I fall into the moment because for the first time in six years I *want* to be kissed.

Leif's mouth is warm and his breath soft. He's a good kisser – not that I thought he wouldn't be, I just didn't think I was the sort of person who could appreciate good kissing. But I appreciate this *so* much; I'm already slipping my hands over his shoulders, digging my fingers into his vest so that I can pull us even closer together. I don't let my lack of experience stop me. I want this too much to feel self-conscious.

Desire blooms in me, like a flower unfurling its petals in sunshine, spreading its tendrils along every nerve until my whole body is vibrating with sensation. I kiss him fiercely, like I'm channelling all this pent-up emotion into one moment. Now that I've let my guard down, I can't seem to put it back up again. I want to throw him down on one of the gym mats and do things I've never wanted to do with anyone before. My knees are weak and I can feel my pulse everywhere . . . in my wrists, my elbows, my throat.

I'm out of control . . . and I *love* it.

'Ava . . .' Leif breaks the kiss finally, his breathing more ragged than when he was working out. 'Kelsey will be back any moment.'

I step away from him, panting just as heavily. He's right, this isn't the time or place. I need to pull myself together.

He looks at the door and then back at me. 'Meet me later?'

I grimace. 'I have to work.'

'Afterwards.'

'We can't.' I hate to say it, but one of us has to be sensible. 'You're leaving for Austria tomorrow. You need to rest.'

'Shit.' He throws one last glance towards the door and then snakes a hand around my waist, hauling me back against him. Amazingly, this kiss is even hotter than the last. He slips his tongue past my lips and I wrap mine around it, pulling him deeper. We're embracing so tightly I can feel his erection pressing against me.

'*Fuck.*' He murmurs against my mouth because I can't resist rubbing against him. 'That feels so good.'

'I know.' I give a low moan. I might not have had sex before, but that doesn't mean I'm inexperienced. I know what I like and, while I don't need a man to make me feel good, I can't deny this feels amazing.

'When I get back . . .' he murmurs between kisses.

I nod, then jump back because I can hear voices outside the door, not just Kelsey's but Yuto's as well. I exchange a panicked look with Leif. He's already sitting down again, his towel in his lap, though he grins when he sees me notice.

'So we'll talk about it with Vienna?' he says the moment they enter the room.

'Vienna?' I'm so shaken by our kiss it takes me a moment to comprehend what he's doing. 'Oh . . . yes. I'll tell her.'

'Hi!' Yuto comes towards us, lowering his phone from his ear. 'My meeting didn't take as long as I expected. Here –' he passes the phone to Leif – 'it's Nathan.'

'Tell him I'm not here.'

'Too late.'

'Fuck.'

'He said no, right?' Yuto murmurs to me as Leif takes the phone.

'He said no,' I agree.

'Called it. Hey, are you OK?' He does a double-take. 'You look really flushed.'

'Do I?' I press a hand to my cheek, like I have no idea my body is still a raging torrent.

'Yeah. Sorry if I caused another argument between the two of you.'

'Oh . . . um, right. Don't worry about it.' I wave towards the door. 'I should probably get back to my press packs anyway.'

'I'll come and help as soon as I get my phone back.'

'Thanks.' I turn and hurry away. Behind me I can hear Leif telling Nathan to 'mind his own fucking business', and I can't help but smile.

With Marr on pole and Bauer in P2, it looks like the Red Bull Ring is going to be another battle between Quezada and Fraser! But in the middle of the grid, all eyes will be focused on Rask to see whether they can keep building on their recent momentum ...

@ MotorsportsEchoNews, 6 July

FIFTEEN

'THANK YOU SO MUCH for bringing me,' Maisie says, munching on a protein bar as we drive through the Cambridgeshire countryside. 'Have I told you how good a friend you are?'

'Once or twice.' I laugh because this is the fifth time. 'So how are you feeling about today? Positive?'

'Pretty good. I've been training really hard since my exams ended, so I'm hoping to be in the top three.' She scrunches her wrapper up and stuffs it into the door pocket. 'But don't feel you have to watch. It's so typical that my event coincides with the Austrian GP.'

'Of course I'm going to watch you,' I protest. 'I'll be the one cheering at the front. I'll just be watching the Grand Prix on my iPad the rest of the time.'

'Thanks.' She sounds pleased. 'Dad wanted to come, but it's his and Briony's wedding anniversary so I told him not to. Daisy says I'm a terrible stepsister for leaving her with them, because they're being all romantic and icky. But it's nice to have somebody here supporting me.'

I give her a sidelong look. I get the feeling 'somebody'

refers to a specific person, currently 900 miles away. 'How was Gio when he left?' I ask tactfully.

'Trying to be supportive. Just like I was trying to be supportive of him, but our schedules, you know . . .' She clucks her tongue. 'Some things were a lot easier when we were fake-dating.'

'You're still having problems?'

'Mmm. One of them is really pretty too.'

I give a jolt. 'There's another woman?'

'Not exactly.' She sighs. 'I trust Gio. It's just that he's mentoring Fraser's new reserve driver, and we can barely get through an hour without him mentioning her.'

'You mean Quinn Sommers?'

'Yes, and she's so annoyingly talented. He says he really admires her "racing intelligence". Meanwhile, I still haven't passed my driving test.' She makes a growling sound. 'But parallel parking is so hard!'

'Gio loves you for you, not your driving abilities.' I try to sound reassuring. 'You should talk to him about it, tell him how you feel.'

'No. Because I hate the way I sound right now, like some insecure, jealous girlfriend.' She heaves another, even heavier sigh. 'It's just something I need to get past. Anyway, I don't want to bring the mood down, not when we should be celebrating our exam results!' She twists her head to grin at me. 'Who was it who got a first again? I can't remember . . .'

'Mmm . . .' I purse my lips. 'Was it me?'

'Yes!' She clicks her fingers. 'But I knew you would. You can do anything you set your mind to, even turn around a failing Formula 1 team. It can't be a coincidence that Rask only started improving once you arrived.'

'I think the mechanical upgrades might have had a little more to do with it.'

'Nope, it was all you. That's my theory and I'm sticking to it.' She points to one side suddenly. 'There's the sign for the event.'

'Thanks.'

'So how are things going at Rask?' she says, once we're off the road and driving through a bumpy, gravelled area that apparently counts as a car park. 'Any nice guys there?'

'Maybe.'

'What?' I can see her gaping at me out of the corner of my eye. 'Really? Who?'

'Just . . . someone.'

'I need details!'

'It's too soon.'

'OK, don't tell me. I'll guess. It's the team principal, isn't it? What's his name?'

'Bastian Aalto, and he's *married*. He's been with his wife for thirty years.' I frown as we turn down the third row of parked cars. 'Wow, this place is really busy. Tell me if you see any spaces.'

'Only if you tell me who the guy is.'

'You know we're here for you to race, right? That means we need to park first.'

'Fine. There's one.'

'Perfect!'

'So? Who is it?' She's practically bouncing with excitement. 'Come on, we tell each other everything.'

'Ahem.' I turn the engine off before turning to face her. 'Remember how you lied to me about your fake relationship with Gio?'

Her face falls. 'Ye-es, but in my defence I *wanted* to tell you.'

'How long was it?' I tap my finger against my chin. 'Three months?'

'Again, *not* my decision. And you were the very first person I told in the end.'

'OK fine, but you have to promise not to tell anyone. Gio included.'

'I promise. Wait! That must mean it really *is* somebody important.' She inhales sharply. 'It's a driver, isn't it? Corey? No way! Although he is pretty gorgeous. And funny. And his accent . . .'

'It's not Corey.' I give her a meaningful look.

'Not . . . Leif?' Her jaw drops. 'I thought you said he hated you?'

'I thought he did.' I lift my shoulders. 'Only it turns out . . . he doesn't.'

'No way! This is perfect!' Maisie breaks into a huge smile. 'We'll both be dating drivers.'

'Slow down.' I push my door open, gripped by a sudden urge to escape. 'We haven't even been on a date yet. It was only a kiss.'

'You kissed?' Maisie leaps out of her side. 'What happened? Tell me everything. Who initiated it?'

'It was kind of . . . both of us.' I feel a tug in my chest at the memory. 'Although technically, I guess I kissed him first.'

'Love it! And?'

'And . . . it was *really* good,' I admit. 'But don't get carried away. It probably won't come to anything.'

'Why not?'

'Because it's complicated,' I say, drawing my brows together. No matter how good our kiss was, I still don't know if us being together would be a smart idea.

'Ava.' She gives me a serious look as she starts to unhook her bike from the rack on my boot. 'I know things didn't work out with Oliver, but that doesn't mean you should never try again.'

I smile tightly. She sounds just like my brother. I wish I could tell her the truth, about why the very concept of dating, of opening myself up to somebody, is so difficult for me to get my head around, but I work too hard at *not* thinking about the past to let those barriers down easily. I've almost told her what happened several times, but somehow I've never found the right words, and today is definitely *not* the day for it, not when she has a big event. I don't want to ruin her frame of mind – or mine, for that matter.

'Maybe,' I say. 'But it could make things weird in the team. I have my professional reputation to think about. And what if . . .' I stop because I don't like what I'm about to say.

'What if what?' She heaves her bike to the ground.

I fold my arms defensively. 'What if Jasper Ramirez were to find out? F1 is a small world. He might disapprove and refuse to interview me in December.'

'I guess . . .' She grips her handlebars. 'But maybe it's time you stopped letting Quezada dictate all your life choices?'

'I don't let them dictate *all* my choices,' I answer indignantly. 'In fact, since I've been at Rask, I've barely had a chance to think about them. I just have a plan and I don't want to jeopardize it.' I grab our bags off the back seat and slam the door. 'Especially because of a man.'

'Then maybe it's your turn to keep a secret. Don't tell anyone you and Leif are dating. Trust me, keeping a low profile can be a good thing. I learned that the hard way.'

I decide not to mention my contract. Perhaps she's right, and Leif and I *could* date in secret. I don't like the idea of going behind Vienna's back, but until I know whether this thing between us is serious or not, it might be the only solution. I'm sure it wouldn't be hard to convince him. He's so private he might even be relieved. And it's not like *he'd* get into trouble if we were caught. He's too important to the team. As for me . . . I don't know whether a secret relationship would constitute gross misconduct, so we'd have to be careful, but I'd rather take the risk than ruin my chances of a future with Quezada. Only there's one more question nagging at the back of my mind.

'Do you think I should tell *him* about my interview in December?' I blurt out.

'You could. Or you could just relax and go on a date first.' Maisie wheels her bike in the direction of the registration tent. 'See how things go before you start worrying about the future.'

'But what if we get along really well and it turns into a relationship and then I get the job at Quezada?' My thoughts are spiralling. 'We'd end up working for rival teams.'

'So?'

'So we'd have conflicting loyalties! I don't know if that could work.'

'No offence, but now it sounds like you're looking for obstacles. Anyway, isn't there a chance Leif will be switching teams too?' Maisie sounds thoughtful. 'Gio says he hasn't signed another contract with Rask yet, and there's been so much buzz about the driver market recently. His name has been linked to lots of different teams.'

'Has it?' I look at her in surprise. I've been so busy recently I haven't been paying my usual amount of attention to F1 gossip. I just assumed Rask would be re-signing Leif. Nobody's so much as hinted at anything else. Although, now I think of it, if that was the case, why hasn't he signed already?

'All I'm saying is, why tell him about your future plans when his are still up in the air?' She winks at me. 'And hey, maybe he'll be moving to Quezada too? Everyone says he's talented enough, and it's an open secret that Shimizu's retiring at the end of the year. That could be the perfect situation for both of you, right?'

I catch my breath because actually . . . yes. If things work out between us, then it really could be. I wouldn't have to change my own plans at all. And if they don't work out . . . Well, I'm sure we could both still behave professionally.

'OK, that's enough relationship advice for one day. I need to register.' Maisie reaches for her bag. 'Wish me luck?'

'Good luck.' I smile. 'Don't break anything.'

'I'll do my best.'

I wave her goodbye before walking over to a picnic area and spreading my blanket out on the grass. I feel like a weight has been lifted. I can't believe I didn't consider the possibility of Leif switching teams before! Because, of course, Quezada will want him. He's one of the most talented drivers on the grid, and now that they've seen what he can do with the new upgrades, they'd be mad not to try to poach him. It's a shame for Rask, but he has to do what's best for his career. Just like I do. Maisie's right. There's no need for me to tell him my plans yet, especially when he hasn't mentioned his to me.

I pull my iPad out and log into my TV account, just in time to catch the Austrian national anthem. As if on cue, the camera pans past Leif. He's standing with his hands clasped behind his back, his chin in the air and a look in his eye that says he's ready to race. The thought of him in yellow Quezada overalls makes my temperature soar.

I come to a decision. I'm going to go on a date with Leif Olsen. I'm going to explain my need for secrecy and then I'm going to explore this connection between us, whatever it is. I'm not giving up on my life plan – I'm only embellishing it slightly. I'm going to take a chance, for the first time in six years.

Because really, how much harm can it do?

Interviewer: Bastian, as team principal, you must be thrilled with this weekend's result.
Bastian: I'm extremely happy with the performance of our drivers and the team overall.
Interviewer: What does this mean for the future? Have Corey or Leif signed for next year yet?
Bastian: We're still in negotiations, but we're keen for them both to stay.

Post-race interview with Bastian Aalto, 7 July

SIXTEEN

'I BOUGHT A HOUSE.'

I'm so engrossed in my laptop, trying to arrange liability insurance for a charity football match, I almost jump out of my chair at the words. It doesn't help that my heart leaps at the same time, leaving me completely disorientated. Hearing Leif's voice again so suddenly makes me realize just how much I've missed him.

'Hi!' I look up to find him standing right in front of me, hands braced on the edge of my desk.

'Hi.' The corners of his eyes crinkle with amusement. 'Sorry if I scared you.'

'You didn't.' I throw a quick look around the office, but we're alone. Emika and Yuto have the day off after Austria, and Charlotte's in a meeting. 'What are you doing here? Aren't you supposed to be resting?'

'Technically, yes, but it's Montreal next weekend so my official excuse is that I'm getting a head start.' He leans closer, his voice deepening. 'Unofficially, I wanted to see you. Yuto's a good minder, but he sucks at playing *Destiny*.'

'Poor Yuto.' A thrum of warmth ripples through me at

the words. Leif missed me too! And we're alone. Maybe I could show him how pleased I am to see him again? If I'm quick . . . *very* quick. I push myself upwards, lifting my lips to meet his, just as Charlotte comes through the door.

'So I've been looking at your socials,' I say loudly, dropping back down into my chair with a thump. 'You're at two million followers on Instagram.'

'What?' Leif looks briefly confused before he catches on, straightening up and rubbing his chin like he's processing this information. 'Is that good?'

'In less than a month, absolutely. Your fanbase is growing.'

'You know they're calling you the Arctic Fox?' Charlotte comes over to join us. 'Congratulations for yesterday, by the way. The way you held off Quaid for the last ten laps was amazing. I was on the edge of my seat.'

'Thanks.'

'Hang on.' I give a start as the first words he said finally sink into my brain. 'Did you say you've *bought* a house?'

'Yes.' His face splits into a grin. 'I've been looking for a while and the deal went through last week. I moved in right before Austria.' He pauses, glancing at Charlotte and then back to me. 'So I thought we could do that video you talked about, the "at home" one?'

'That's a great idea! We've got to keep your new fans happy.' Charlotte beams.

'Um . . . Of course.' I start fiddling with some papers on my desk because I have a horrible feeling my cheeks are burning. On the plus side, I haven't even spoken to Leif about the need for secrecy yet and he's already covering for us. This might be easier than I thought. 'Why don't you give me the address and I'll pop by on my way home.'

'Sounds good.' He places his phone next to mine, airdropping the details across. 'So I'll see you later?'

'Yes.' I nod briskly. 'Later.'

'OK. I'd better get going.' He smiles at Charlotte. 'Say hi to Andre for me.'

'I will.' She takes his place in front of my desk as he walks out. 'Honestly, you two.'

'What do you mean?' I hoist my eyebrows, ready to make an excuse for anything she might be about to accuse me of.

'Both of you are such workaholics. I can't believe he came in to discuss social media on his day off.'

I feel my cheeks flush all over again. I'll have to stop wearing blusher to work because this is getting ridiculous. 'I guess we both just love Formula 1.'

'Corey loves Formula 1 and he's only here half the time.' She shrugs. 'Then again, we're only twenty-eight points behind Chiltern in the Constructors' table now. I guess hard work really does pay off.'

MY STOMACH TWISTS WITH nerves as I approach Leif's new house. It's almost 8 p.m., two hours later than I intended to arrive because Vienna called me in for an impromptu progress meeting at five thirty, but I refuse to reschedule. I'm excited and anxious and I don't know if tonight is a smart move or not, but I know that I have to see Leif. If nothing else, I need to set out some ground rules before things go any further. *If* they go any further.

After twenty minutes of driving through countryside, Waze takes me through a pair of open gates, then along a tree-lined road that leads to a small lake and a beautiful wildflower-filled meadow. Beside it, the land slopes up towards a house made of pale grey stone and wood. It has a living roof and blends seamlessly into the landscape, like a cross between a cave and a log cabin, with a wide terrace, accessed by some steps beside a basement-level triple garage. Above that is a balcony that runs the entire width of the house, with glass doors glittering in the evening sunshine. Somehow it manages to be rustic and modern and traditional and innovative at the same time.

I step out of my car and take a moment to compose myself. It's easier than I expected because the atmosphere here is so peaceful. I can't hear anything other than the sounds of nature – the rustle of leaves, the thrum of insects and the calls of at least six different types of bird.

I'm still taking in the view when Leif emerges through a steel door and comes down the steps to greet me, dressed in cargos and an Amiri T-shirt.

'Your house is stunning,' I tell him.

He smiles, like he's pleased by my reaction. 'I knew it was the one the moment I set eyes on it. Come on in.'

His hand twitches, like he's about to reach out to me and then changes his mind. I totally understand. It's been a week since our kiss and it's clear we're both feeling self-conscious.

I follow him into the house and look around. The front door opens into a large, open-plan kitchen-living area, with pale wooden floors, high beamed ceilings and giant windows overlooking the lake and meadow below.

'No furniture yet.' Leif sounds faintly apologetic.

'It doesn't matter.' I twirl around in a patch of sunshine. 'It's perfect as it is.'

'I'm glad you like it.' He watches me from the kitchen. The counters are all a shade of duck-egg green and presumably contain appliances underneath, but there's no sign of them. Everything is smooth and sleek and shiny. 'Can I get you anything? Are you hungry? Thirsty?'

'No, thanks.' I smile over my shoulder at him. 'I had a wrap just before I left.'

He looks anxious suddenly. 'You know I only mentioned that video as a way to get you here, right?'

'I had my suspicions.'

'So we don't really have to film anything, do we?'

'We probably should.' I bite my lip to stop myself from laughing at his horrified expression. 'Charlotte might wonder otherwise.'

'You could tell her I looked so grumpy you had to shelve it.'

'That seems kind of harsh.'

'Yet believable.' He moves round the edge of the counter towards me. 'Do you want to see the rest of the house? This isn't the best part.'

'There's something better than this?' I open my eyes wide incredulously.

'Trust me.' He leads the way through a door and along a corridor towards a glass wall. Behind it I can see a long, narrow pool, clearly designed for doing laps, and in the far corner another room made of wood.

'A sauna?' I laugh. 'That is *such* a cliché.'

'I know.' He grins unrepentantly. 'I'm thinking of adding a plunge pool too. But this still isn't the best part.'

'Wait, upstairs?' I falter as he takes me back to the main staircase. 'You want to show me the bedrooms?'

'No. We have to go through one, but that's not what I want to show you.'

'*OK* . . .' I go ahead. There's a landing at the top, with four doors leading off it. Leif goes to the first, opening it to reveal a large bedroom with a mat and sleeping bag on the floor.

'Are you camping?' I blink in surprise.

'Kind of.' He sounds sheepish. 'It's a temporary arrangement until I order a bed, but it's actually quite comfortable.' He walks across the room, opening some more doors leading on to a large wooden balcony and . . .

I stop and stare in amazement. From here, we can see above the tops of the trees and out over the fens. It's breathtakingly beautiful.

'Wow . . .' I whisper.

'I'm hoping, on a good day, I might be able to see Scandinavia.' He rests his forearms on the railing beside me.

'So you've actually bought this place?' It's a genuine effort to tear my eyes from the view.

'Yes.'

'It's pretty close to Rask.' A tendril of worry steals down my spine. 'I guess this means you're fully committed to the team?'

'I try not to plan too far ahead. But for now, yes, I'm 100 per cent committed to Rask. If that changes . . .' He tilts his head towards mine. 'I can always keep this place as a getaway.'

'Meaning, if you move to a different team?' I ask, in as casual a tone as I can manage. Given what he told me about his childhood, I guess I can understand his attitude to planning, even if it's the complete antithesis of mine.

'I suppose so. The driver's market is kind of up in the air at the moment.' He gives me an apologetic look. 'I can't really talk about it.'

'That's fine.' Relief floods through me. If he doesn't want

to talk about the future, then there's no obligation for me to either. 'You don't have to tell me anything. It's completely your business.'

'Not that I *want* to leave Rask –'

'But opportunities crop up,' I finish. 'You have to do what's best for your career. I understand that. If you want to be a world champion, you'd have a better chance with a team like . . .' I pause like I'm actually considering the answer. 'Quezada, for example.'

'That's true.' His brows draw together. 'And I do want to be a world champion one day, but Rask gave me an opportunity this year when other teams wouldn't. Bastian and the Jokkinens took a chance on me when it looked like I was going to be stuck as a reserve driver for another year. I feel a sense of loyalty to them for that.'

I drop my gaze because his words hit a little too close to home. Rask took a chance on me too, yet here I am, fully intending to interview with Quezada in December.

'I'm sure they'd understand,' I argue. 'F1 is a business, after all. And it's not like you haven't been delivering results for them this year. You've got eighteen points in the last two Grands Prix.'

'I guess so.' He clears his throat. 'But that's enough about work.' He slides one hand along the railing until it's touching mine. 'Thank you for coming.'

'Thanks for inviting me.' I lift my little finger so that it's overlapping his.

'I couldn't wait to see you any longer. Kelsey keeps asking what's wrong with me. Every time I work out, my mind starts wandering.' He gives a wry smile. 'Suddenly I find gyms very distracting.'

My face heats at the words. The last time I went jogging, I found myself distracted too. The way my heart was pounding reminded me so much of the last time we were together. It's starting to flutter now. If I'm not careful, I'm going to forget what I came here to say.

'Leif.' I pull my hand away and turn towards him. 'Before we . . . do anything, there are some things I'd like to discuss.'

'Of course.' He nods. 'Go ahead.'

'First of all, what I said about not being good at relationships . . .' I take a deep breath. 'I meant it. So I think, if we do this . . . I'd need to take it slow.'

'Whatever you want.'

'Oh.' I'm taken aback by the ease of his answer. He didn't even hesitate. 'OK. In that case, I also think we should keep it a secret, for a while anyway.'

'A secret?' This time he looks confused.

'Yes. At work, I mean. Contractually, I ought to inform HR, but I don't want people there to start seeing me as *Leif Olsen's girlfriend.*'

'You think they'd treat you differently?'

'Possibly. They might think they have to mind what they say around me. And it could make things awkward, especially if I have to ask you questions on subjects like your perfect woman again.'

'If you ask me that, I'll tell you the truth.' His gaze roams over my face. 'She has hair like cinnamon, eyes like summer grass and seven freckles on her nose.'

Desire flares in my stomach. To my knowledge, nobody has ever counted my freckles before. Or called me their perfect woman . . .

'I also don't want anyone to think I'm getting preferential treatment.' I try to stay on point. 'I mean, what if I was offered another chance to be your minder? People might assume it was because we were together, rather than because I was good at my job.'

'You're phenomenal at your job. Everyone knows that.' He smiles softly. 'But if it bothers you then fine, we won't tell anyone.'

'You'd really be all right with that?'

'Yes.'

'Thank you.' I repress a pang of guilt. I mean, I'm not lying. I do want to keep things professional and for nobody at work to treat me any differently. I'm just not telling him the whole truth – that I don't want Quezada to hear any gossip about me either.

'Is there anything else?' Leif cocks his head.

'No.' I exhale heavily. I almost can't believe how easy that was. 'That's everything.'

'Good. Because I still haven't shown you the best bit of this house.'

I gesture at the view. 'What could be better than this?'

'One more room, but –' he smooths a hand across his jaw – 'it's kind of personal.'

I peer at him dubiously. 'It's not some kind of sex dungeon, is it?'

'No, that hasn't been installed yet.' His eyes twinkle. 'But you might find this just as stimulating.'

'Show me.' I push myself off the railing. 'Whatever it is, I'm sure I can handle it.'

'I'm sure of that too.' His lips curve again. 'This way.'

The tense atmosphere from before is gone because this

time, when he holds a hand out, I take it, threading our fingers together as we walk back through his bedroom-campsite and across the landing.

'Don't say I didn't warn you.' He opens a door slowly.

'No. Way.' My mouth drops open.

He squeezes my fingers.

'Leif . . .' I turn to look at him.

'Yep.'

'This is . . .'

'Uh-huh.'

'I mean . . .' I gulp. 'Can we play?'

'I was hoping you'd say that.' He gestures towards the two black gaming chairs set in front of three large screens. 'Choose a station.'

I move like I'm in a dream. Sitting down is like sinking into a soft leather cloud.

'Which game do you want?' He turns the system on. 'Pick anything you like.'

I suck in my cheeks, mentally reviewing my options, before wriggling my shoulders and getting my game face on. 'Personally, I'm in the mood to race.'

I have a brilliant plan! Come to Canada with me this weekend! You said you weren't working. All expenses paid for. What do you say?!

Maisie Evans to Ava Yearwood, 8 July

SEVENTEEN

I WAKE UP FIRST, though it takes me a few moments to process where I am, in a curtain-less room with a view of trees and Leif asleep beside me, one arm flung above his head as his chest rises and falls in a smooth, steady rhythm.

This wasn't supposed to happen. I had zero intention of staying the night, but we got carried away playing video games. Then, once we realized it was past midnight, he offered me a sleeping bag and mat to place alongside his. He was a total gentleman, presenting me with a brand-new toothbrush, towel and oversized T-shirt to sleep in. He didn't even try to kiss me goodnight, although he did offer me s'mores and a hot chocolate, both of which I declined because, as it turned out, once I put my controller down, I was really tired.

Now it's daylight again, I prop myself up on one elbow to look at him. Ironically, this is the closest I've ever come to sleeping with a man, although there's still a good metre of space between us. Leif's features are completely relaxed in sleep and the lower half of his face is covered in a thick layer of stubble. He looks so rumpled and dishevelled. I feel a powerful urge to wriggle out of my sleeping bag and slide into his. The morning air is cool and it would be so cosy to snuggle into the circle of his arms.

Instead, I get up and pad barefoot across the room, putting some distance between us before I can do anything stupid. We haven't even been on an official date yet. There won't be any snuggling for a while, not until I'm 100 per cent certain I can trust him, although incredibly I feel like I'm already almost there, like I've known him for longer than just over a month. It's hard to believe how much has changed between us in that short time. Part of my brain is still yelling that this could be a huge mistake, but it doesn't feel like one. It feels pretty great.

The morning is a bright electric blue, so I slide the balcony door open and slip outside. The view is just as impressive as it was yesterday evening, with the tops of the trees swaying gently in the breeze, while the rivers of the fens are like ribbons of silver in the distance. I feel like a bird, surveying the world around me, letting all my worries float away.

'You're up early.'

I look over my shoulder to find Leif standing in the doorway, dressed in a white T-shirt and boxers.

'Am I?' I realize I have absolutely no idea what time it is. 'Sorry. I didn't mean to wake you.'

'It doesn't matter.' He comes to stand behind me, placing his hands on the railing on either side of my waist. 'You look good first thing in the morning.'

'So do you.' I smile as he props his chin on my shoulder. His breath is warm and he smells musky in a good way. One that makes me want to sink back against him. Or turn around and carry on where we left off in the gym . . . My blood heats at the idea.

'What are you thinking about?' His voice vibrates against my skin.

I open my mouth and then close it again because I get the feeling he knows exactly what effect he's having. 'Only that this would be a great shot for your Instagram.'

'It would.' His lips skim the side of my neck, a feather-light touch that shoots lightning straight to my core. 'But it's not happening.'

'Why not?'

'Because some things are too personal to share. I want to keep this just for us.'

I can't resist any more. I turn and slide my hands up and around his neck so that I'm pressed flush up against him. The communications officer in me wants to object to his answer. The rest of me thinks it's the most romantic thing I've ever heard. Now that he's said it, I want to keep this just for us too.

There's a moment of stillness when our eyes meet. Then he lowers his head, tilting it slightly as I push myself up on my toes.

Part of me was afraid our second kiss couldn't possibly live up to the first, and yet it's even better. We go from zero to a hundred in under a second, our tongues tangling and clashing as we each try to get more of the other. A pulse thumps between my legs as my back meets the railing. I kiss him passionately, rifling my hands through his hair while his sweep upwards, gripping the sides of my ribcage and then curving around my breasts, bringing my nipples to points. It feels so good, I can't resist pushing myself even closer against him . . .

'Ava . . .' He murmurs, and then pulls back abruptly, twisting his face to one side for a few seconds. 'Are you hungry?'

'What?' My breath catches in my throat. I'm so disorientated, I can't process the question.

'Are you ready for breakfast?'

'Breakfast?' I stare at him blankly. 'Leif, what just happened?'

'Nothing.' He moves closer again, pressing his forehead to mine. 'But if you want to take this slowly, then we need to do something else right now.'

'Oh.' I swallow, then consult my stomach and smile. 'In that case, breakfast sounds good. Can I help?'

'No, but you can watch. Come on.' He reaches for my hand, tugging me after him back into the house. 'I'll cook, you relax.'

'That sounds even better.'

'How about waffles?' he asks, when we reach the kitchen.

'Um . . .' I make a face, remembering his last attempt.

'Hey! I've been practising.'

'Well, in that case I'd love some.' I glance at the clock on the wall. It's 6.15 a.m. 'But I'd better get going soon. I need to go home and change before work, and I don't want to be late.'

'I could always tell Vienna I need you here.' He waggles his eyebrows at me.

'She's smarter than that.' I slide myself up on to one of the counters. 'OK if I sit here?'

His gaze slips down from my face to my exposed thigh, his pupils dilating before he looks away and coughs. 'It's perfect. Orange juice?'

'Please.'

'Coming up.' He opens the fridge door and pulls out a tub of what looks like batter, along with a carton of juice.

'You made dough in advance?' I look between him and the tub in surprise.

'I've been practising a *lot*. And I remembered how much you liked them, so I thought . . . Just in case.' He smiles sheepishly as he plugs in a waffle iron and then hands me the juice. 'Here. You first.'

'Thanks.' I take a few gulps before handing it back and running my tongue along my bottom lip. 'Your turn.'

He keeps his eyes on mine as he drinks. It feels weirdly intimate to drink from the same carton, kind of gross too, but I'm into it. It's like I've woken up a completely different, more relaxed person, because I experience a sudden urge to wrap my legs around him and pull him towards me, to feel him between my thighs, to use this counter in ways it definitely wasn't designed for . . . But we're taking this slow, I remind myself. That's what I want, what I asked for. I just have to remember that.

'Can I ask you a question?' I say to distract myself.

'Go ahead.' He puts a ball of dough into the iron.

'It's kind of personal.'

'Are you planning to put the answer on the internet?' He glances up at me.

'No.'

'Then I don't mind.'

'OK.' I tip my head to one side. 'How are you single? I mean, you're gorgeous, rich, talented and apparently you can now make waffles. You're basically the whole package.'

'Thank you.' He throws me an amused look. 'I had a couple of girlfriends back in Norway before I got on the Chiltern training programme, but nothing serious. Mostly I've been focused on my career. I still would be, only . . .' His gaze flickers. 'I guess I didn't expect to meet anyone I had this kind of connection with.'

'Oh.' My throat turns dry because I feel the same way.

'Now tell me about you.' He picks up one of my hands and turns it over, pressing his lips to the inside of my wrist. 'I want to know everything.'

'There's not much to tell.' I shake my head. 'I grew up in a village near King's Lynn, then I moved to Cambridge to do Media Studies. That's pretty much my full bio.'

'What about your family?'

'My parents are abroad right now, travelling, and my brother Dan also lives in Cambridge.' I smile. 'They're all pretty great, other than not caring enough about motorsports.'

'Nobody's perfect.' He chuckles. 'So if your family don't like F1, what got you into it?'

I squirm beneath his gaze. It strikes me suddenly how hypocritical I've been, asking Leif about his past when I'm so uncomfortable talking about parts of my own. Only there are some things I still want to keep hidden.

'It's hard to explain. I had to miss a few months of school when I was fifteen, the Grand Prix was on TV and I got hooked – that's all.'

'Huh.' He looks surprised, though thankfully he doesn't pursue the subject. Instead, he tips the waffles on to two plates and slides one across to me. 'There you go. Breakfast is served.'

'Thank you.' I sprinkle some sugar on top as Simone instructed and take a bite. 'Oh wow. That's delicious.'

'If at first you don't succeed . . .' He drizzles syrup on to his. 'Obviously, we'll be keeping this a secret from Kelsey too?'

'I presumed. Hey, do you mind if I check my messages quickly?' I mumble through a second mouthful of waffle, as I reach across the counter for my bag. I can't believe I left it down here last night and didn't even notice. I'm normally glued to my phone.

'Of course not.' He flicks on a coffee machine. 'Any crises at Rask?'

'No.' I glance up. 'But there's an interesting message from Maisie. She's invited me to go with her to Canada this weekend.'

He gives me a stern look. 'To enjoy *Fraser* hospitality?'

'Yes, but I'd still be cheering for you.'

'What about after the race?' He looks thoughtful. 'Will Maisie need you then?'

'I doubt it. Not if she's with Gio.'

'Then why don't we hang out? I've heard that Montreal is a beautiful city. We could be tourists together.'

I take another large bite of waffle, considering the idea while I chew. It sounds risky, but kind of exciting too. 'Will there be time?'

'We'll make time. I like to see more than a track in the places I visit. When I was a kid, I never expected to leave Norway, so now I never waste an opportunity to explore.' He leans forward, touching a syrupy kiss to my lips. 'Nobody else needs to know what we're up to.'

'You mean like a *secret* sightseeing tour?' I feel a rush of adrenaline at the idea. 'I'd love that.'

Welcome to Montreal, where the weather is balmy, the fans are enthusiastic and the drivers are raring to go. It's an unusual week because we have a different team on pole for once. Hugo Zaragoza set an incredible qualifying time in the Gold Dart, putting both Fraser and Quezada in the shade. Meanwhile Rask continue storming up the league table, both their drivers getting into Q3 for the third race in a row. If they keep up this pressure, it should be an exciting race.

@ MotorsportEchoNews, 13 July

EIGHTEEN

'DO YOU REMEMBER THE first time we did this, at Silverstone?' I ask Maisie as we make our way along a crowded grid, dodging cars, pundits, mechanics and visitors. As a VIP guest of Fraser, rather than a Rask employee, I have nothing to do today except soak up the atmosphere, which is pretty incredible, although I'd enjoy it more if my loyalties weren't so all over the place. As if being torn between Rask and Quezada wasn't bad enough, now I feel duty bound to support Fraser too, for this race anyway. It's so confusing that I had to ransack my entire wardrobe to find a neutral outfit, eventually settling on a white broderie summer dress with silver sandals.

'How could I forget? I had no idea what was going on and I was completely terrified.' Maisie slips a hand around my arm. 'Isn't it funny how I knew nothing about F1 back then and now I'm basically an expert?'

'Umm . . .'

'Compared to most people.' She sees my expression and laughs. 'But you have to admit, I've learned a lot.'

'You really have.' I look at her quizzically. 'You're in a

good mood today. Does this mean things are better between you and Gio?'

'*Much.*' She beams. 'I talked to him, like you suggested, and afterwards he introduced me to Quinn and it turns out she's really nice and I've been completely over-reacting. There's a reason they've been spending so much time together, only I'm not allowed to talk about it.'

'And you're certain he's not gaslighting you?'

'Completely. *And* . . . I've come to a decision.' She stops walking abruptly, to the annoyance of a camera crew following close behind. 'I've decided to defer my MA. I'm going to concentrate on biking this year. After that, we'll see.'

'Are you sure?' I ask her seriously. 'That's a big deal.'

'I know, but I just can't manage a sports career, an MA *and* a relationship all at once.'

'I guess that makes sense.' I squeeze her arm. 'You know I support you whatever you choose. And I'm so pleased you and Gio have worked things out.'

'So am I. The past couple of months have been tough, but we're going to stay with his family in Italy over the summer break and I can't wait. We're both desperate for a holiday.' She lowers her voice. 'What about you and Leif? It's such a shame you can't invite him to your graduation on Thursday.'

'Mmm,' I answer noncommittally. To be honest, I'm relieved my graduation clashes with a promotional event in London ahead of the British Grand Prix. Bringing a Formula 1 driver to a university ceremony would have provoked way too much attention, not least from my grandmother, who's coming with Dan. My parents have repeatedly offered to come home from New Zealand – where they're spending the next two months with my aunt Janice – to attend, but I've told them not to because it would cost far too much. They can always stream it online anyway.

'You're still meeting him after the race today, though, right?' Maisie asks.

'Yes. If you're sure that's OK?'

'Of course! I'll cover for you and bring your bags to the airport. Just go and have fun.'

'Thanks.' I feel a spring in my step as we continue along the grid. I'm so excited about today, and not just because of my sightseeing tour with Leif this evening. We also had a team meeting at HQ on Tuesday and everyone was in an optimistic mood. Bastian's certain we'll get points, and my imagination is already conjuring up social media posts to celebrate our imminent achievement. Maybe a photo of Leif on the podium, holding the trophy above his head, the sunlight glinting off his golden hair . . . *Or*, if the podium is a little far-fetched, Leif celebrating fifth or sixth place again. In which case, a photo of him afterwards, striding through the paddock or maybe leaning against a wall, looking sexy in sunglasses and a racing suit rolled down to his waist . . .

Or Corey could do it, I remind myself. Because we have two drivers. *Two*. I need to remember that before anybody notices our social media is getting a little one-sided. In fact, no matter what happens today, my next project will be all about Corey.

'Who's that with Leif?'

'Mmm?' I follow Maisie's gaze to where my secret date for the evening is standing beside his car, talking to a woman with impossibly long balayage hair to match her impossibly long legs to complement her impossibly tiny waist. I recognize her instantly, although despite my surprise I don't feel even the tiniest bit jealous. I guess I really do trust Leif.

'She looks familiar.' Maisie purses her brow.

'Ava!' Yuto waves us over. 'You can't keep away from me, can you?'

'I guess not.' I laugh. 'Yuto, this is my friend Maisie. Maisie, this is Yuto from the office.'

'Good to meet you.' He lifts a hand to high-five her. 'I've heard lots of positive things.'

'Ditto. Ava's always saying how much she loves her job.'

'So . . .' I clear my throat. 'Ashley Hart?'

'Yeah.' Yuto lifts his eyes skyward. 'Nathan invited her despite what Leif said. She's a guest of Rask's today.'

'That's who it is!' Maisie clicks her fingers. 'Hey, why don't we say hi? Leif!' she calls out. 'Hello again.'

'Maisie.' He turns his attention away from Ashley.

'P7.' She grins. 'Congratulations.'

'Thanks.' His gaze shifts to me, intensifying like he's trying to convey some message. 'Hi, Ava.'

'Hi.' I give him a professional nod and then turn to Ashley. 'Sorry to interrupt. I'm Ava, a communications officer for Rask, although I'm off-duty today.'

'What an amazing job. I'm keeping everything crossed for you guys.' She smiles between us. 'I've told all my followers to support you.'

'That's great.' As a communications officer, my heart lifts. As *me*, I actually kind of like her too. I get the feeling we could probably have a decent conversation about Formula 1.

'Oh no, you're Gio Bauer's girlfriend, aren't you?' Ashley's eyes widen as she notices Maisie. 'I'm so sorry. I totally love Fraser too.'

'That's OK.' Maisie laughs, for once not objecting to the description. 'Rask are my second favourite.'

'It's not a date,' Leif murmurs to me as Ashley and Maisie fall into conversation. 'I had no idea she was coming.'

'I know.' I give him a reassuring look. 'Yuto told me.'

'I'm going to wring Nathan's neck.'

'Don't.' I swing my arm so that it nudges gently against his. 'He's only doing his job and we have more important things to think about. Like our first official date tonight. I'm going to catch one of the shuttles into the city when the fans start leaving.'

'Are you sure? I could arrange a driver.'

'There'll be literally thousands of people around. I'll be fine.' I'm touched by his concern. 'You can come and meet me once you've finished debriefing.'

'I'll let you know as soon as I can get away.' He throws a quick look around and then moves a step closer. 'Is there anywhere you particularly want to visit?'

'I don't know yet. I meant to do some research, but I ran out of time.'

'Good.' His lips curve. 'In that case, meet me in the Esplanade Place Ville Marie. It's downtown.'

'Esplanade Place Ville Marie,' I repeat. 'Any particular reason?'

'You'll see.'

'I can't wait.' I can't resist nudging his arm again. 'And good luck today.'

'Thanks.' His gaze drops to my mouth. 'You've no idea how much I want to kiss you right now.'

My body floods with heat because I want to kiss him too. Standing so close to him, I tingle all over, like my blood is rushing a little faster through my veins. But we couldn't exactly be any more public. There are at least two camera crews heading in our direction right now.

'Later.' I force myself to step away from him. 'Just concentrate on driving for now.'

'I'll try.' He gives me an intense look a split second before one of the camera crew steps between us.

'Wow, you *really* like him, don't you?' Maisie whispers as we move away.

'What do you mean?' I swing towards her in panic. 'Is it obvious?'

'Only to me. I've never seen you look at anyone like that before.'

'I've no idea what you're talking about.' I toss my hair and smile as we carry on towards the front of the grid. For once there's a Gold Dart in pole, but Jaxon's Quezada car is next, followed by Gio's for Team Fraser. Maisie hurries off to wish him luck, but I stop because out of the corner of my eye I've just caught a glimpse of a familiar face. It's Leif's manager, Nathan, and, from the look of it, he's deep in discussion with Emiliano Romero, team principal of Quezada. If I'm not mistaken, he's also gesturing in Leif's direction.

This day is getting better and better.

INCREDIBLE. I TIP MY head back, staring up at the thirty-metre-wide, stainless-steel ring that hangs suspended between two buildings. I guess this is what Leif wanted me to see. According to the travel guide on my phone it represents the past, present and future of the city, as well as its connection with visitors, all unified into a symbolic whole. There's something pure and powerful about its simplicity. I love it.

I've been wandering around downtown for a while because there's no sign of Leif yet. He messaged a little over an hour ago to say he was finished with meetings, but I told him to stay and enjoy the party for as long as he wanted because after coming fifth, with a spectacular overtake on lap twenty-three, he deserves to celebrate. I'm also happy to be on my own for a while, listening to all the different street musicians, eating poutine and admiring the architecture.

Having fun? I look down at my phone to find a message from Dan.

Yes! Montreal is my new favourite city.

Good. Just so you know, I've made a lunch reservation for after your graduation. Anything you'd like as a present?

You fixing my light fitting.

Shit. I forgot. I'll come by one evening soon. I promise.

Thank you!

'Sorry I kept you waiting,' a voice calls the moment I tuck my phone away.

I spin around and laugh. The man standing next to me looks like a tourist trying to evade arrest, with a giant Canada baseball cap, a pair of oversized sunglasses, even though it's getting dark, and a lightweight jacket with the collar turned up. 'Leif?'

'Shhh.' He lifts a finger to his mouth. 'This place is crawling with F1 fans. I want to spend an evening with you, not them.'

'Oops.' I bite my lip. 'So this is your clever disguise?'

'Yes. Tonight you can call me Axel.' He lowers his sunglasses, just enough to peer over the top. 'It's a popular name in Norway.'

'OK.' I grin because I want to play too, only I don't have

a disguise ready. Not unless . . . I reach behind me and pull my hair out of its band, then shake my head so that it falls around my shoulders. I almost never wear it down, even in bed, so this should make me look different enough. Leif obviously thinks so because he's staring like he doesn't recognize me at all.

'What's a popular girl's name in Norway?' I ask.

'Ingrid.' His gaze roams over my hair. 'It means beautiful.'

'Then I like it.' I get my phone out again and pull up a map. 'I've been looking up things to see. Did you know Montreal has the largest underground city in the world? It's so that people can still shop and visit restaurants in bad weather. There are even stations down there, so we could take the RESO to the old port.'

'Sounds great.' He raises a hand, gently stroking the hair now hanging by my face. 'What time is your flight in the morning?'

'I need to be at the airport by seven.' I tip my head into his hand. 'I'm already packed so Maisie's bringing my bag.'

'So we have all night?'

'We do.' I smile because I already know his flight is at 8 a.m. 'Unless you're too tired?'

'I'll sleep on the way home. First, Axel and Ingrid have some sightseeing to do. After that, there's a boat waiting for us in the harbour. I thought you might like a dinner cruise.'

'What about being recognized?'

'Not a problem. I rented the whole boat.' He rubs his thumb across my chin. 'There are a few perks to being a racing driver.'

'Come on then, Axel.' I slip an arm around his waist, pulling him forward because a guy a few metres away is looking at us a little too intently for comfort. 'Let's go.'

Rask's inexorable rise up the Constructors' table has other teams and a few bookies worried. Who would have thought at the start of the season that they would be fighting Chiltern and Gold Dart for third place? Philip Sawyer must be regretting his life choices.

@ MotorsportEchoNews, 21 July

NINETEEN

I REST MY CHIN on my hand and gaze lovingly at the miniature moose figurine on my desk. Leif bought it for me in Montreal, in a shop 20 metres below ground, after I bought him an arctic fox souvenir. His 'n' hers figurines, definitely not something I thought I'd ever be interested in, and yet each time I look at it, a warm glow fills my chest and spreads through my body. It's been a week and the effect is still pretty powerful . . .

'Ava?'

'Mmm?' I look up to find Emika standing in front of my desk with a concerned expression. 'Sorry. Did you say something?'

'Yes. Your name. Three times.' She folds her arms. 'Why are you smiling like that?'

'Like what?' I check my computer screen to hide my expression. 'This is how I smile.'

'No, it's not. You look all . . . dreamy.'

'Maybe I'm just pleased with our follower numbers.' I feign innocence. 'And the report from Merchandising this morning. Our sales have quadrupled in the past month.'

'Uh-huh.' She looks doubtful. 'Anyway, Vienna needs you.'
'Now? I thought she was busy with the photoshoot?'
'She is, but there's some kind of problem.'
'OK.' I grab my phone, glad to get away. That was close. I'm making my feelings far too obvious, but hiding them is harder than I expected. Luckily, most people are too preoccupied to notice. With three Grands Prix this month, we've been so busy I actually considered skipping my own graduation last week, but Vienna insisted I go.

Today's photoshoot is for another new sponsor, a bespoke men's tailoring company, because now our racing fortunes are on the rise, we seem to be on a roll. It's good news for the team, if mildly inconvenient when the sponsor asks to use the factory as a backdrop for their photoshoot concept.

I open the factory door and slip inside. Usually, it's dazzlingly bright in here, but right now it's like stepping into a cave, one where Frank Sinatra is playing in the background. The main lights are off, but there are two huge spotlights on the floor directed at one of the racing cars in the centre of the room. Leif and Corey are standing on either side wearing . . . Oh my. I feel the hairs rise on the nape of my neck.

Both of them are dressed in three-piece, single-breasted suits, Corey in navy with a matching tie, Leif in a pale grey tweed with a powder-blue tie. While Corey's jacket is fastened, so that his hands hang loosely at his sides, Leif's is open, revealing a matching waistcoat as he poses with a hand in one pocket. I don't know much about men's tailoring, but I know this is how suits are *supposed* to fit. They must have been made to measure because there isn't a dimple or crease in sight. Everything is seamless and sartorial and . . . hot.

I take a couple of seconds to cool down. Since Canada, Leif and I have stolen a few moments together in his 'office', but mostly we've kept things professional and only seen each other outside of work. It's going well, better than I expected. I feel like I'm living in some kind of parallel universe, one where I'm a person without any issues or hang-ups, doing completely normal things, like hanging out with her new boyfriend, enjoying his company, swimming in his pool, sweating in his sauna, approving (or not) his furniture purchases and constantly thinking about sex.

Leif's being a complete gentleman about it – the ball is in my court to make the first move. Which I will. Soon, because I want it too. I trust him, only . . . part of me *is* still afraid of what might happen, that I might freeze up.

And if things are going to go wrong, I want to enjoy the way they are for a while longer yet.

'Emika says you need me?' I murmur to Vienna. She's standing to one side, watching with a hand pressed to her forehead as a man in dark jeans and a black jacket shouts instructions.

'Fuck, yes.' She sounds like a woman at the end of her tether. 'We need to do something about Leif.'

'What's the matter with him?' I twist my head in his direction. Personally I can't see anything wrong – he looks incredibly hot.

'The director wants them to look casually elegant. *That* isn't casual.'

'Oh.' Now that she mentions it, his expression does look a little . . . strained. Angry, in fact, like he's channelling his Viking forebears and thinking about wrapping his tie around the director's neck. The more the man talks, the deeper the furrow between his brows is becoming. Yep, somebody really needs to step in before there's actual bloodshed.

'I've tried talking to him, but it's no use.' Vienna jerks her thumb. 'You have a go.'

I jolt. 'Why me?'

'Because you're the one who persuaded him to do social media. Clearly you have a knack.' Her eyes narrow with a vengeful gleam. 'Plus I need to tell Corey to stop smirking.'

'Oh.' I try not to sound too relieved. 'OK, I'll try.'

'Good. Edward?' she calls out to the director. 'Why don't we take a break?'

Everyone downs tools and heads for the refreshments table set up at the side of the room, while I head in the opposite direction, sidling past a giant silver reflector screen on my way to intercept Leif. He's still glowering, though his expression softens as he sees me.

'Are you all right?' I take the opportunity to inspect his suit at close quarters. The grey tweed really brings out the blue in his eyes and it fits to perfection, defining every contour of his body. I have to fight the urge to reach out and stroke the fabric.

'I don't wear suits.' He flexes his shoulders and the suit flexes with him.

'You look good. Honestly.'

'They keep telling me I look tense.'

'Well . . .' I scrunch my mouth up. 'You do look a little uncomfortable.'

'Because they also keep telling me to relax.' His face darkens again. 'Do you know how *not* to get somebody to relax? Tell them they look tense.'

'So ignore them. Ignore this.' I gesture to the suit, allowing my fingers to brush lightly across the front of his waistcoat.

Damn, it's soft. 'Think of something else. You told me you feel calm when you're driving, right? So imagine you're doing that. In a race suit.'

His expression wavers. 'I could do that.'

'Great!' I sway closer. 'And for the record, I think you should wear suits more often.'

He looks surprised. 'Do you think I should keep it?'

'I wouldn't object.' I make an impulsive decision. 'Maybe you could wear it tonight? Come to my flat and I'll make us dinner.' I pause as my hand touches against his, sending a shockwave of electricity through me. 'Then maybe I could wear something you like too?'

He doesn't even pause to think. 'Do you still have what you wore in Monaco?'

'My black jumpsuit?'

'Yes.' His pupils swell. 'I know I behaved badly that night, but I still thought you were the most gorgeous woman I'd ever seen.'

'Hey, man.' Corey interrupts before I can respond. 'Vienna's trying to talk them into a more dramatic concept. Then we can both look furious.'

'It's fine. I know what to do now.' Leif flexes his neck from side to side, squares his shoulders, and then slides one hand into a pocket as his eyes take on a far-off expression. He looks instantly more relaxed.

'I'll leave you to it.' I walk slowly backwards, ignoring Corey's incredulous look. 'Just remember, you're on the last lap, you're feeling completely calm and in control, all you're thinking about is your car . . .' I cough. 'And that other detail we mentioned is definitely a go. I'll text you with timings and . . . stuff.'

'OK!' The director claps his hands. 'Everybody back into positions. Leif, can you . . .?' He stops mid-sentence. There's one horrible moment when I think he's about to say something critical, but even I can tell that Leif's expression is perfect. 'Um . . . stay just like that.'

'What did you say to him?' Vienna whispers fiercely, as I rejoin her.

'I told him to imagine he's in a car,' I whisper back.

'Why didn't I think of that?' She smacks her head and then lifts her voice. 'Hey, forget the music. Can somebody rev an engine in here?'

TONIGHT IS THE NIGHT, I tell myself, as I peer into my bathroom mirror and sweep setting powder across my cheekbones. I'm going to seduce Leif.

The only problem is that I've never seduced anyone before, never even considered it, so I'm not totally sure what I'm doing, but I've made a checklist to help. I've bathed and shaved and exfoliated and moisturized and put on my laciest underwear under my jumpsuit, and I think I look pretty good.

I've also planned every last detail of the meal. I've made a healthy chicken salad, bought an expensive bottle of wine, lit at least a dozen candles and put on some ambient music. Not bad, considering I only left work an hour and a half ago.

I'm actually glad I haven't had much time to prepare because it's keeping my nerves at bay. Most of them anyway. The important thing is that Leif doesn't guess I've never done this before. I'm not embarrassed by my lack of experience, I just don't want him to suspect there's any kind of story behind it. I don't want to answer any awkward questions.

Right on time, I hear a knock on the door. There's something familiar about the pattern – three short raps – but I'm too excited to process what it means.

Which, as it turns out, is a big mistake.

'Dan?' I stare at my brother in horror.

'Whoa.' He looks me up and down. 'You look nice. Are you going somewhere?'

I'm horribly aware of my cheeks flooding with colour. 'I have a date.'

'No way. That's great.'

'I know.' I try to shoo him away. 'So you have to go.'

'You said you wanted me to fix your light fitting.'

'I do, but not *now*.' I put my hands on the door frame, blocking the way as I peer past him into the corridor. There's no sign of Leif yet, but he could arrive at any minute and the last thing I want is for my big brother to be here when he does.

'It'll take me ten minutes, tops.' Dan's brow contracts. 'What's wrong with me meeting your date anyway?'

'There's nothing wrong.' I toss my hair. 'But we haven't been dating for long and I don't need you acting all protective.'

'I won't.' He picks up his toolbox and barges past me. 'I won't do anything to embarrass you, I promise, but I'm here now. I might as well get the job done.'

'Wait.' I try to run past him.

'You'll hardly know I'm here.' He takes a couple of steps into the lounge and freezes. 'This is . . . um . . . atmospheric.'

'I was going for cosy,' I mutter stiffly, as I turn the music off and start blowing out candles, though it's obvious what kind of evening I was actually planning. There's no way this could get any more embarrassing.

'What can I do to help?' I ask in an attempt to rush him along.

'Make me a cup of tea?'

'You said you'd only be ten minutes!'

'Fine, no tea, but I need a ladder.'

'Right.' I scurry to the cupboard and pull out my steps. 'Here you go.'

'Hold it steady for me?'

Fifteen minutes of foot-tapping later, I'm ready to tear my hair out. Next time I need work doing, I'm just going to hire somebody and pay a premium. How can Dan not see how awkward this is? And how long can it possibly take to install a light fitting? Thankfully Leif seems to be running late. With any luck he's stuck in a mile-long tailback that will take half an hour to clear . . .

'There.' Dan finally brushes his hands together. 'What do you think?'

'Perfect. Thank you.'

'I'll send you a bill.'

'Haha.' Now that he's leaving, I feel marginally more grateful. 'Sorry about not making you a cup of tea. Next time I'll cook dinner as a thank you.'

'I'll remember that.' He stops in the hallway and looks seriously at me. 'I'm glad you're dating again, Ava.'

'Me too.' I reach for the door handle. 'So thanks again and . . .'

I freeze as there's a knock on the other side of the door. It's Leif. I know it. And now Dan is lifting an eyebrow at me, so I have no choice but to open up and introduce them to each other.

Crap.

I close my eyes and drag in a breath. This is going to be mortifying . . .

'Hi.' I open the door.

'Hi.' Leif's gaze heats as he takes in my jumpsuit, which I don't mind because I'm ogling him too. He's still wearing his suit, as requested, and looks even hotter than he did earlier, possibly because there aren't a dozen people bustling around us. Unfortunately, my appreciation is spoiled by the presence of my big brother, who decides to step into view right at this moment.

I clear my throat as Leif's gaze shifts sideways. 'This is my brother, Dan. He came, *unannounced*, to fix a light fitting for me.'

'Hey.' Leif holds a hand out. 'Good to meet you.'

'Dan is just leaving,' I say after they've shaken.

'Actually, I didn't catch your name.' Dan's expression is quizzical.

'It's Leif.' A faint look of surprise crosses Leif's face. 'Olsen.'

'Leif Olsen . . .' Dan rubs his chin. 'I feel like I've heard that name before.'

'I've probably mentioned it,' I answer, because it hits me suddenly that, despite watching the Spanish Grand Prix with me and Maisie, he's clearly forgotten who Leif is. If I weren't so annoyed with him for ruining my evening, it would be funny. But I still want him to leave before he puts two and two together.

'Do you work at Rask too, Leif?' Dan folds his arms like he's settling in for a long discussion. 'Are you in the technical or administrative side?'

'Ah . . . Technical.' Somehow Leif manages to keep a straight face.

'And the two of you are seeing each other?'

'We're *trying* to.' I tap my foot impatiently.

'Since when? Is it serious?'

'*Dan!*' I hiss, because now he's going too far. 'That's none of your business.'

'You're my sister.'

'Your twenty-one-year-old sister!'

'It's still my job to look out for you.'

'It's OK,' Leif interjects. 'Dan, I promise you, I'm not messing around here. I'm serious about Ava.'

'*There.*' I swivel to Dan. 'Satisfied?'

'Actually . . .' Dan gives Leif an appraising look. 'Yes. Nice to meet you, Leif. Enjoy your dinner.'

'I'm so sorry.' I cringe as I close the door behind him. 'He normally behaves like a sane person.'

'He's just looking out for you.' Leif smiles. 'Has he always been so protective?'

I hesitate because the answer to that is complicated. 'Not always, but I guess with our parents being abroad, he thinks he needs to act like my dad now.'

'Then I'm glad I passed his test. You look beautiful, by the way.'

'Thanks.' I try to smile back, but my muscles feel stiff with tension. 'Are you hungry? I made dinner.'

'Famished.' He follows me through to the lounge/kitchen where my new light is much too bright and I'm too embarrassed to start the music again. As romantic settings go . . . it's really not. Suddenly I kind of wish we could cancel tonight.

'I'm sorry I was late,' Leif says as I take a bottle of white wine out of the fridge. 'Bastian wanted to talk about contracts. Then Nathan joined in on Teams. I thought I was never going to get out of there.'

The pop of the cork sounds much too loud. 'You mean, another contract with Rask?'

'Yes. Bastian's keen to sign me for next year, but there are other options.'

'I guess you still can't talk about it?' I leave the question hanging.

'I wish I could, but it's confidential. There are just so many factors to think about. Like us.' He moves closer, coming to stand by my shoulder as I pour the wine. 'Ava, I meant what I said to your brother. Even if I moved to a different team, it wouldn't change how I feel about you.' He pauses. 'If it meant being based in a different country, I'd still come back here all the time. We could still be together.'

I smile, some of my tension ebbing away at both the words *and* the implication behind them. Personally, I think he's being overly optimistic. I don't see how a couple can work for competitors and maintain a relationship, but it looks like that won't matter. The majority of teams are based in the UK. If Leif is hinting about moving abroad, he *must* mean Quezada. All I need to do is ace my interview and we can carry on as we are.

'I'm not worried about that,' I say. 'Besides, there might be other opportunities for me too, away from Rask. I'm still only there on a trial basis.'

'But Vienna's definitely going to want to keep you. She's always telling people how amazing you are.'

I feel a rush of professional pride, closely followed by guilt. 'All I'm saying is that we both have our careers to think about.

And I'm sure neither of us would want to hold each other back, so . . . don't let me influence your decision.'

'Maybe I want to let you influence me a little.' He takes hold of one of my hands, caressing the palm with his thumb. 'But that's enough work talk. Tonight is about me and you.'

'Right.' I agree, though I can feel my body stiffening again. It's not him, it's just that this evening isn't going remotely as I planned, and being out of control is making me spiral. 'Actually, Leif . . . I'm sorry, but I can't do this.' I pull my hand away. 'I had everything ready, but then my brother turned up and I'm not in the right place any more.'

'Hey.' Leif's gaze turns very intense suddenly. 'It's OK. I'm not expecting anything here. I'm just happy to spend time with you. We can eat dinner and talk and watch old races, whatever you want.'

'You'd be OK with that?' I tilt my head suspiciously.

'Totally. I don't want you to do anything you're not ready for.'

I rise up on my toes, straighten his tie and kiss him. 'Thank you.'

Rask are excited to announce that our team captains for today's football match are none other than Leif Olsen and Corey Hammond! Grandstand tickets are sold out, but we still have a limited number of standing places available. If you're in the Huntingdon area, why not stop by?

@ RaskRacing, 2 August

TWENTY

THE F1 SUMMER BREAK started a few days ago, after Silverstone, meaning no work is allowed to be done on car development or analysis for at least a whole fortnight. The technical side of Rask has shut down completely and the factory is eerily silent. Communications, however, is a different story. Between keeping on top of my day job and organizing a charity event, I've never worked harder or talked more.

Fortunately, today is finally kick-off. To help me, I've made the to-do list to end all to-do lists. I'd call it a thing of beauty, but I'm too stressed. It's not that I think I've actually forgotten anything; it's just that today means so much to Leif – and me too, now I've learned more about what the charity does. I had no idea how many challenges there were facing the care system – young people being sent long distances away from their families, then being expected to stand on their own two feet the very day they turn eighteen – but Hazel Muir and her staff go above and beyond to help them. Because of that, I want this to be the best charity football match in the history of charity football matches.

That's why I'm here at 8 a.m., wearing a neon vest over

my denim capris and pastel-blue crop top, even though the gates don't open until 1 p.m. I have a lot to supervise if I'm going to turn the local amateur football club, which consists of a field and clubhouse surrounded by six-foot-tall hedges, into a large-scale event. Fifty Portaloos have just arrived, along with two temporary grandstands that are currently being erected on each side of the pitch. The weather looks like it's going to stay fine (meaning I can scrap my wet-weather contingency plan), and I have the football kits – blue for Leif's team, red for Corey's, in a subtle nod to the Rask colours – and a trophy safe in my car. The giant marquee should also arrive soon, followed by the food vans and charity stalls for people who don't like football but still want to enjoy the festival atmosphere. Emika and Charlotte have offered to scan tickets at the gates, and Yuto and a few other volunteers will be running a stall of Rask merchandise that Vienna has agreed to donate. After that, we'll just need our players and a referee (the club volunteered one of theirs), as well as some spectators.

We sold out of advance purchase tickets within a week, which means we'll fill the grandstands, and there'll be some standing room tickets available at the gate. Security has been a little expensive, but now that I've posted about Leif and Corey playing today, I don't want there to be a sudden stampede of F1 fans. That minor worry aside, however, it's all looking good. We're on target to make several thousand pounds for the charity, and we'll hopefully create a lot of goodwill in the local community.

I'm looking towards the gates, wondering whether it's time to put up the entrance banner I've made, when a familiar red-and-white sports car turns into the field.

'Hey!' I hurry over to meet Leif. 'I told you not to bother coming until noon.'

'I thought you might need an extra pair of hands setting up.' He hands me a coffee as he gets out, dressed in grey shorts and a white Pangaia T-shirt.

'That's sweet, but you should be resting. You have a game to play this afternoon.'

'I've had plenty of rest, trust me.' He throws a quick look about and then wraps his arms around me, smoothing his hands from my shoulder blades down to the small of my back. 'You've been working so hard on this. I want to help.'

'Well, the moral support is nice. And I appreciate the coffee.' I can't resist pressing myself against him.

'It's the least I could do. When I suggested doing something for charity, I never imagined anything like this. I can't believe you've pulled it together so quickly. You're incredible, Ava.'

'Thank you.' I feel a warm glow in my chest, one that has nothing to do with the temperature of my coffee. 'Just don't get hurt! If you twist an ankle or break a leg, Vienna will never forgive me.'

'I won't.' His eyes spark. 'I mean, how risky can it be, playing football with a group of teenagers?'

'Don't say that!' I stiffen in panic. 'Promise me you won't get competitive – and stay away from tackles.'

'Don't worry. Corey and I are only here to support the kids.'

'Have you told Corey that?'

'Good point. I'll remind him it's for charity.'

'We'll *both* remind him.' I glance round at the sound of another engine, just in time to see a shiny blue Maserati drive through the gates.

'I guess I'm not the only F1 driver who's come to help out this morning.' Leif grins.

'I guess not . . .' Instinctively, I start to pull away from him, before changing my mind and curling an arm around his waist instead, as we head over to greet Maisie and Gio. 'Hey! I thought you guys were flying to Italy this morning?'

'We decided it could wait a day.' Maisie springs out of the car. 'Hi, Leif.'

'Hi, Maisie, Gio.' He tightens his hold on my waist.

'We're here to help.' Gio rubs his hands together. 'Just tell us what to do.'

'Amazing, thank you! Well, we have a banner to put up, but you could start getting chairs out for me.' I gesture in the direction of the clubhouse. 'There are two hundred stacked up inside. They can go in the marquee when it arrives.'

'Sounds good.' Maisie nods. 'But no slacking off to gaze into each other's eyes. I saw you when we drove in.'

'Let them gaze,' Gio objects. 'It's romantic.'

She winks at me and then reaches for his hand. '*Andiamo, caro.*'

'*Molte grazie!*' I call after them.

'OK, no more gazing.' Leif turns his head, pressing a kiss into my hair. 'Let's get to work.'

'THANKS SO MUCH FOR doing this.' I give Corey a hug when he arrives just after noon.

'No worries!' His face splits into a wide smile. 'It's good to have a chance of beating Leif for a change.'

I smile back, although I can't help thinking there's an edge to his words. It's one thing being outperformed by drivers in different cars, but being consistently beaten by your teammate, even when it's only by seconds, must be tough, even for someone as easy-going as Corey.

'Well, your team are waiting in the clubhouse,' I say, gesturing for him to follow. 'Come on, I'll introduce you.'

Forty minutes later, when every last item on my list is ticked, I take a deep breath, cross my fingers for luck and text Emika to say it's time to open the gates. Then I take up position with Maisie beside the grandstands, ready to help anyone with mobility issues or those who can't find their seat.

Kick-off is right on time. Leif and Corey shake hands, the spectators cheer, the whistle blows and . . . it's total madness. There are four goals in the first ten minutes, two to each team, and the crowd goes wild every time. It's more exciting than I'd expected, not to mention nerve-wracking. Now that the possibility of an injury has occurred to me, it's all I can think about. Leif and Corey are passing the ball to the kids every chance they get, but I have to keep moving, checking on the stalls, on security, on the arrangement of chairs in the marquee, to control my nerves.

'There you are.' I hear Dan's voice during one of my stationary moments. There are only ten minutes left and I've finally ventured back to the side of the pitch. 'You're a hard person to find.'

'Hey.' I wave to him without moving my eyes from the field. 'I didn't know you were coming.'

'Of course I came. I knew you'd do an amazing job.' He coughs. 'So you can stop worrying about things going wrong.'

I shoot him a glare. Sometimes it's annoying how well he knows me.

'Not until it's over. I thought race days were stressful, but this is a whole new level.'

'It serves you right for not telling me who your date was last week.'

'Like I said in my text the next day, you deserved that.' I smirk. 'How long *did* it take you to figure it out, by the way?'

'About an hour. I googled him as soon as I got home.'

'You what?' I spin towards him. 'Dan, I appreciate you looking out for me, but –'

'I should butt out and mind my own business? Yeah.' He looks embarrassed. 'That occurred to me too. I guess, after what happened back in school, I got a little over-protective of you. But you're right. I can't encourage you to date and then try to micromanage when you do. It's your life.'

I give him a double look. 'So you're saying that maybe I'm not the only control freak in the family?'

'I guess so.' He laughs. 'And about last week . . . I should have taken the hint and left when you asked me to. It's just . . . Hailey's flight to Australia was that day.'

'Oh, Dan.' I press my lips together. 'You should have said.'

'No, I shouldn't. I messed your night up enough. Sorry about that.'

'Don't worry about it. Us control freaks need to stick together.'

'Thanks.' He jerks his head towards the pitch. 'You know, your boyfriend isn't such a bad player.'

'Shhh,' I hiss at him. 'Don't call him that. It's a secret.'

'What is?'

'That he's my –' my tongue trips over the word – 'what you just called him.'

'Boyfriend?'

'Yes! It could make things awkward at work.'

'I thought he said you two were serious?'

'We are, but it's easier this way for now.' I give him a sharp look. 'It's my decision, so don't tell anyone.'

'OK, but –'

Fortunately, Hazel Muir chooses this moment to interrupt, her dark-blonde curls scooped up into a gigantic bun on the top of her head. 'Ava, I can't thank you enough. This whole event has been wonderful. The kids look like they're having loads of fun too.'

'They definitely are,' Dan agrees. 'Some of them are pretty talented. What's the score now?'

'Fourteen–twelve to the reds.' Hazel lowers her voice confidentially. 'Although I have to admit, I'm secretly rooting for the blues. Leif has been so generous with his time and money. He's such a lovely guy.'

'He is.' I smile sentimentally. 'But I don't think there's time left for his team to catch up. It's almost over.'

'That's it!' Dan confirms as the final whistle blows. 'Corey's won.'

'And nobody got injured.' I press a hand to my chest and exhale. 'I can start enjoying myself now.'

'Good. You deserve to.' Hazel puts a hand on my shoulder. 'I guess this means it's time for the trophy?'

'The trophy!' I yelp. 'It's still in my car!'

'On it.' Dan holds a hand out for my keys. 'Where are you parked?'

'Next to the clubhouse.'

'Give me five minutes.'

'Don't worry, I'll stall with a speech.' Hazel chuckles at my panic-stricken expression. 'Now, let's go and congratulate them.'

*

THE TROPHY-GIVING CEREMONY INVOLVES almost as much running around as the game. Hazel awards the cup to Corey, who celebrates like he's just won the world championship, handing out bottles of fizzy water to the kids, who charge about, spraying them all over the crowd.

Leif, the gallant loser, is on his way over to me when a local TV crew intercepts him so I move to one side and post a few shots to his Instagram account instead. The video I posted at half-time already has four-figure likes, which is great for the charity and good publicity for Rask too, but that's not why we're here.

By the time I look up again, he's finished with the TV crew and is crouching down for a picture with his teammates. Opposite him, Corey is doing the same thing, before they all gather together for one big group photo.

I'm so busy watching I don't notice the person coming towards me until he's only a metre away, and then I'm so surprised I have to blink a few times to make sure I'm not hallucinating.

'Mr Ramirez?'

'Hello again, Ava.' Jasper smiles at me.

'Hi.' I have to shake my head to clear it. 'Sorry, I just didn't expect to see you here.'

'Leif's manager told me you were organizing a game so I thought I'd come and offer my support.' He gestures around the pitch. 'I hear this is all your work.'

'Not entirely. I mean, the charity helped out too, so it's really been a team effort, all for a good cause.'

'It's certainly that. Speaking of which . . .' He reaches into his jacket and pulls out a cheque. 'This is on behalf of Quezada. I hope it helps with your fundraising.'

I look down and gasp at the amount. Ten thousand pounds. 'Thank you! I'll be sure to mention you in the press release.'

'I appreciate that.' His smile widens. 'You know, Ava, I've been paying attention to your work for Rask and I think after today I can safely say you've already aced the interview. In fact, you might want to start brushing up on your Spanish. One of my content managers in our other office in Barcelona is leaving at the end of the season and I'm looking for a replacement.' He tips his head towards mine. 'I'll be in touch closer to the time to formalize things, but I look forward to working together next year.'

My mouth is still hanging open as he turns and walks away. I can't believe he just offered me a job at Quezada. Just like that, without any interview! It's incredible – phenomenal – everything I've ever wanted. I might actually achieve all of life my goals before I turn twenty-two. At this rate I'm going to have to set some new ones or I'll peak before I'm thirty.

But looking around the pitch, at Emika and Yuto and Charlotte, my enthusiasm dims slightly. Part of me doesn't want to leave Rask. I love the people and I love working there. But if Leif is going to Quezada too . . . Well, maybe Spain could be even better?

A huge thank you to Ava Yearwood, who arranged today's event with charity director Hazel Muir. I don't know what Rask would do without her!

@ RealLeifOlsen, 2 August

TWENTY-ONE

'DID YOU POST THIS?' I look up from my phone in surprise as Leif drives me back through Cambridge. I was so exhausted by the end of the day I decided to leave my car at the football club overnight. By the time all the equipment had been collected and the field was back to normal, only Leif, Hazel and I were left. She was the one who took this photo of us, standing side by side in front of the clubhouse.

'Yes. It's the first thing I've posted myself.' He looks proud of himself and then worried. 'Does it bother you? I wanted to say thank you somehow, but if you want me to take it down –'

'I don't want you to take it down,' I say quickly. I probably should, but it's a nice photo. We both look happy and relaxed, and it's not like we're holding hands or anything incriminating. People at Rask will just take it at face value.

'Good.' He throws me a smile. 'I feel like I owe you a holiday for all your hard work.'

'No time.' I yawn. 'Communications don't get an official summer break. Although Vienna's promised we can all have a few days off.'

'Then maybe we can spend some time together?'

'I'd like that.' I sit up straighter as we turn on to my street. Despite my exhaustion, I don't want today to be over quite yet. I don't want Leif to drop me off and leave either. 'Maybe we could start with you staying here tonight?'

He doesn't answer at first, manoeuvring into a parking space and turning the engine off before twisting in his seat to look at me. 'Are you sure?' His voice sounds husky.

'Yes.' My foot starts to tap, but I force it to stop. I'm not going to spiral. I want this – I want Leif – and I'm not going to let my past ruin my present. 'If you'd like to, that is?'

'I'd like to.' He glances down. 'But I'm kind of sweaty.'

'So am I.'

'I've been running about a pitch.'

'And I've been walking around in the heat since 8 a.m. I think we're equally gross.' I lift a hand to the side of his face, sweeping my thumb gently across his cheek before leaning closer and inhaling. 'I like the smell of you anyway.'

He catches my hand and presses a trail of kisses all the way from the inside of my wrist to the crook of my elbow. It makes me shiver so hard I can't hide it. I can't speak any more either. All I can do is nod silently, then open my car door and wait for him to do the same.

The distance to my flat seems like miles. I want to be there already, touching him, kissing him, moving together. There's a pulse low down in my body, strong and insistent, and if I don't do something about it soon, I'm going to scream because I'm wound so tight. I'm aware of Leif walking beside me, but I daren't even look in his direction until we're inside and I've taken off my coat, deposited my bag on the floor and – yes, OK – done a quick check of my appearance in the hall mirror. My skin is a little shinier than I'd like and some of my hair has escaped from my crown braid, but considering how crazy busy I've been all day I'm relieved it's not worse.

By the time I turn around, Leif has closed the front door and is leaning back against it, watching me. He must be equally tired and yet he looks wide awake, his gaze dark and hungry.

'Ava?' He takes a step forward like he can't wait either, so I reach out and weave my fingers through his, pulling him after me into my bedroom.

I stop by the side of the bed, turn on the lamp, then hook my hands around his neck and draw his face down to mine. It feels different to all the other times we've kissed, deeper and hotter and more urgent. My whole body lights up in response, like my blood is racing to the surface of my skin.

Between kisses, I wrench my crop top over my head and drop it on to the floor. I could definitely use a spritz of perfume right now, but Leif doesn't seem to care because he's already dragging his lips along my collarbone and sliding his tongue down to the dip between my breasts. His stubble scratches my skin, but somehow that only makes the ache between my legs even more intense. I feel him unhook my bra, so I grab at the hem of his shirt and then we're pulling the rest of our clothes off, hands everywhere like we can't get enough of each other.

We topple sideways on to the bed, arms and legs entwined. It feels so right, I don't even care about freshly laundered, vanilla-scented sheets. My body feels relaxed and all I want is this. Him. Us together. As soon as possible.

'You feel so good.' He groans as he bites into my shoulder.

I spread my fingers out over his chest, tracing patterns over his skin. He's so toned. I want to explore every part of him.

'If I do anything you don't like . . .' He slides lower,

drawing one of my nipples into his mouth in a way that makes me want to combust.

'I'll tell you.' I pant.

'Good.' One of his hands slips between my thighs. 'Now, tell me what you like.'

What I like? I freeze. How am I supposed to answer that?

'Ava?' He lifts his head and takes his hand away immediately. 'What's the matter?'

'Nothing.' I try to sound casual, but I can feel my body tensing up. 'I'd just rather do it than talk about it.'

'I didn't mean . . .' He looks confused. 'Ava?'

'OK, fine. I haven't done this before.' I pull away from him, hoisting myself up to a sitting position. 'I can't tell you what I like because I don't know.' I fold my arms defensively. 'It's no big deal.'

'I know that.' He crawls up the bed. 'If it helps, I haven't done it for a while.'

'Really?' I narrow my eyes.

He nods. 'But that's no big deal either, right?'

'Right.' I unfold my arms as I hold on to his gaze. His sincere expression is so powerfully, fucking sexy, I feel myself start to melt again. 'You're right. Let's keep going.'

'You're certain?' He leans forward, pressing his lips to the side of my neck.

'Absolutely.' I feel like I'm being caressed all over. 'I want this.'

'So we'll take it slowly and if you want me to stop, just tell me.'

'I will.' I smooth my hands over his biceps. 'And don't worry. It might be my first time with someone else, but I've had plenty of solo practice.'

His brow furrows like he doesn't understand.

'Look under the bed.' I smile teasingly.

I prop myself on one elbow as he rolls on to his stomach and peers over the side. I hear the sound of a box being pulled out, followed by a sharply indrawn breath.

'Whoa.' He looks over his shoulder. 'That's a lot to live up to.'

'You can always back out if it's too intimidating.'

'Never. You just made this a competition.'

'Well, in that case . . .' I roll on to my back as he climbs on top of me. 'Let's see what you can do.'

'I'll try my best.' He grins as he takes hold of both my hands and pins them over my head with just one of his. Then he captures my mouth again, his hand still pinning my wrists to the mattress, but the other moving to between my legs, and . . .

I moan, arching my body upwards because it's impossible not to.

'You're so wet.' Leif presses his forehead against mine.

'I know.' I writhe against him.

'Where do you keep your protection?'

'I'm on the pill.' I wrap my arms around his waist, as he starts to move away. 'I thought, once we started dating, I should be prepared.'

I see his throat bob as he lowers himself again. 'I have medicals every month. Lots of blood tests, so –'

'So we're both healthy.' I hold on to his gaze. 'That means we can . . .'

I don't finish the sentence because I can feel his erection pressing against me and I'm too busy catching my breath and clutching hold of his shoulders to think of words. We're pressed together so tightly that if either one of us pushes even a little . . .

I'm not sure which of us moves first. Maybe me, maybe him, maybe both of us at the same time. All I know is that one moment we're staring into each other's eyes, the next he's inside me and all feeling is suddenly centred at my core. It feels strange and tight and a little painful, but it's all right because I feel completely in control and safe.

'Ava . . .' Leif's voice is a rasp. 'I need to —'

'Yes. I'm OK.' I roll my hips tentatively and he thrusts deeper.

'Fuck.' He gives a low growl in his throat. 'You feel incredible.'

'So do you.' I flex my hips again.

'Wait.' He pauses after we've moved together for a little while, bracing his hands on the bed either side of my head. 'Just give me a moment or your toys are going to win this contest before I've even begun.'

I smile and hook my ankles over his legs because he's so wrong. He's already won. The discomfort has gone and I can feel the pulse in my stomach again. It's like a drum beat, vibrating along every nerve, making my whole body ache with desire. I want more, but I can wait too. For a little while.

'OK.' Leif lifts his head again. 'I can do this.'

'You know, we have all night.' I trace a pattern on his back with my fingernails. 'We could call this one a sprint race. We'll get to the main event later.'

He arches an eyebrow, his expression interested, before he shakes his head. 'No. This is your first time. I want it to be special.'

'It already is.' I push myself up against him.

'Ava —' He clenches his teeth.

'Let me take charge,' I say, pushing him over gently, so that he's lying on his back and I'm sitting astride him. 'I'm the organized one, remember?'

'Whatever you want.' He moans, curling his fingers around my hips as I rock gently back and forth, sliding my body against his. I try to go slowly, to make every movement long and drawn-out, but it's not long before my desire takes over. He's so deep inside me, the friction is mind-blowing. I'm riding him so hard but I can't bring myself to stop because I can feel myself getting closer and closer . . .

'*Fuck.*' Leif bucks, tightening his grip on my hips.

'Almost.' I slip my fingers between us.

'Ava –' He surges upright, wrapping his arms around me as he shudders, but I don't mind because I'm almost there too. I can already feel myself tightening.

I fling my head back and cry out, my whole body convulsing as I shake. My orgasm bursts through me, more intense than any I've ever felt before. It's like my whole body is contracting to a single point and then bursting apart, making the room reel around me. It's so amazing I keep on rocking against him because I want to draw out every last drop of feeling.

A few minutes later I'm wrapped in Leif's arms, lying against his chest. We're so sweaty we're practically glued together. I probably look a total mess, but I don't care. I feel safer and more relaxed than I have in a long time.

I close my eyes and let sleep overtake me. *Wow.* If that was a sprint race, then I can't wait for the main event.

We're halfway through the summer break and for those who wonder what F1 drivers get up to during their holidays, we're reliably informed that at least five of them are busy enjoying romantic getaways. Jaxon Marr, Giovanni Bauer, Noa Shimizu, Idris Llewelyn and Hugo Zaragoza are all soaking up the sun with their other halves.

Meanwhile, committed bachelors Corey Hammond, Matti Erikkson and Hayden Quaid have been enjoying the party scene in Monaco. As for Leif Olsen, he's being as elusive as ever ...

@ MotorsportEchoNews, 8 August

TWENTY-TWO

'YOU MISSED A BIT.' I wave my paintbrush across the living area at Leif. 'On the left. I told you, if you concentrate on three-foot sections at a time –'

'– then I won't miss anything.' He chuckles and runs his roller over the area I'm indicating. 'Not all of us are so ruthlessly organized.'

'You'll thank me later.'

'I'll thank you for a lot of things.' He puts his paint tray down and comes over to my ladder, holding it steady as I stretch upwards. 'Be careful.'

'I'm almost finished. *There*.' I survey my own section of wall with satisfaction. 'That looks pretty good.'

'Very professional.' He strokes a hand down my leg. 'You know, you look sexy in my old race overalls.'

I throw him a playful look. The overalls are from a couple of seasons ago, but they're soft and comfortable and smell like oil and rubber. Maybe some people wouldn't find that a turn-on, but I've had goosebumps all morning. I'm also completely naked underneath, but that's something I want Leif to discover for himself.

'So which room do we paint next?' I ask.

'None of them.' He squeezes my calves. 'I can do the rest myself. You should be enjoying your time off, not helping me decorate.'

'I like to keep busy.'

'I've noticed.' He steps up close behind me, his voice deepening. 'But I can think of other activities for us, trust me.'

Trust me . . . I feel a stutter in my chest. I've had a couple of these moments since we slept together – nothing major, just times when I've had to stop and take a few breaths. I *do* trust Leif, only sometimes the thought of it overwhelms me, making me feel like I can't get enough oxygen. Luckily, I'm relaxed enough today that I can calm the panic quickly.

'Is that so?' I twist around, handing him my painting tools to put aside before stepping down a few rungs. 'What exactly did you have in mind?'

'A little rest and recuperation, that's all.' He grasps the ladder on either side of me, making a cage of his body.

'I suppose I am feeling a little hungry.' I toy with the zip of my overalls. 'Could you make me some more waffles?'

'Didn't you have enough for breakfast?'

'I don't think enough is ever going to be enough.' I draw my tongue slowly over my lips. 'You're getting *so* good at them . . .'

'Then I'll make some. Later.' He presses against me in a way that makes me purr with pleasure. 'First, we need to work up more of an appetite.'

'We've been painting all morning!'

'I still have energy.'

'That's because you're a high-performance athlete.' I lean forward, digging my teeth gently into his earlobe. 'Some of us tire more easily.'

His breath hisses. 'I'll do all the hard work, I promise.'

'I should hope so . . .' I dart my tongue out, my imagination already running riot. 'How sturdy do you think this ladder is?'

I watch his face as he starts to slowly unzip my overalls. It's been a week since the football match and I've had three of those days off as leave, all of which we've spent together. We're still taking things slowly – or slow-*ish* anyway – getting to know each other, hanging out, buying furniture, testing out his new super-king-sized bed. And his new sofa. And, on one memorable occasion, a gaming chair. Aside from a few panicky blips, it's been a lot of fun. He hasn't asked me any awkward questions and I'm starting to feel like the past is finally behind me.

'Shit.' Leif pulls away as his pocket starts buzzing. Just as my overalls were about to get interesting too.

'Somebody really wants to get hold of you,' I say as he looks at his phone and then tosses it aside. This must be the fourth time in an hour that it's rung and he's refused to answer.

'It's Bastian.' He rubs a hand over his face. 'I'm not ready to talk to him yet.'

'So why don't you turn your phone off?'

'I would, but I'm expecting a call from somebody else too. It's complicated. And –'

'Confidential,' I finish, though I'm desperate to know what's going on. The online rumours about which team he's going to sign for next year have reached a fever pitch, and if he's dodging calls from Bastian that's a pretty good sign of where his mind is. But I don't want to push him. It's surely only a matter of time before he signs with Quezada, and I want him to tell me the news when he's ready. Then, when he does, I can tell him about Jasper's offer. If he feels guilty about his decision, maybe it will help him to know that I'm leaving Rask too.

'Well, then . . .' I pull my zip the rest of the way down and let my overalls slide to the floor, curving my lips in a provocative smile. 'Although we should really clean the paint brushes.'

Leif's jaw drops. 'They can fucking wait.' He takes two steps towards me and cups his hands under my bottom, lifting me up against the ladder. 'This can't.'

'Good.' I wrap my arms and legs around him. 'Because –' I freeze at the sound of an engine. 'Wait, is that a car?'

We both crane our necks towards the giant windows. A white Porsche 911 GT3 is speeding its way down the drive. Like *really* speeding, stirring up a cloud of dust in its wake. Whoever's driving will be here in less than a minute and I'm stark naked, practically spread-eagled, in full view of the front door.

'Shit, shit, shit!' I jump out of Leif's arms.

'It's OK, it's only Nathan.' He sounds annoyed rather than alarmed.

'He still shouldn't see me – especially like this!' I make a run for the stairs, then stop and swing round. 'My car! He'll know I'm here.'

'He'll know somebody's here, that's all.' Leif heads towards the door. 'Don't worry. I'll make this quick.'

'But how will you explain it?'

'I'll tell him the truth – that my girlfriend is upstairs.' He looks back at me and lifts an eyebrow. 'If that's OK with you?'

I blink because we haven't discussed our relationship status yet and now definitely isn't a good time, but I don't feel like contradicting him either. Instead I throw a quick glance at the window, then dart back across the room, kissing him full on the lips before running away again. 'OK with me!' I call over my shoulder.

I bound up the stairs, sprint across the landing and launch myself into the bedroom, landing on the bed at the same moment as I hear the front door open below. It occurs to me that maybe I'm over-reacting. Maybe it wouldn't matter now, if Nathan were to find out about me and Leif (just preferably when we were all fully clothed). He's a neutral party in all this. And maybe it wouldn't even matter if *anyone* found out . . .

I fling my arms above my head and gaze up at the ceiling. Maybe it's time for us to go public with our relationship. I don't want Vienna to find out by accident and I hate lying to Emika, Charlotte and Yuto because they're more than colleagues now. They're friends. As for Quezada, Jasper as good as offered me a job, and he's unlikely to alienate their new driver by reneging. There wouldn't need to be any more secrets or sneaking around . . .

But I don't want to make an impulsive decision; maybe after the summer break would be the perfect time to tell everyone. It was probably naive of me to think I could keep our relationship a secret all the way until December anyway.

I twist my head sharply as I hear the word 'Quezada' downstairs. Nathan's timing might suck, but if he's here to get Leif to hurry up and sign a contract, then I'm grateful. Briefly, I consider the ethics of creeping to the top of the staircase and eavesdropping, but I can't do that to Leif. As of five minutes ago, we're officially a couple and that means trusting each other.

I let out a deep sigh of contentment. My life, my future and my emotions are completely under control because everything is going exactly according to plan.

According to the regulations, there are certain discrepancies with Rask's car this year ...

Philip Sawyer, *London Echo*, 14 August

TWENTY-THREE

I'M TRYING HARD NOT to smile. I mean, really hard. Emika is on the other side of the room and if she catches me at it again, she'll want to know the reason why. Fortunately, Yuto and Charlotte are working from home today and there are no other witnesses, so if she does ask then I can probably get away with pretending I don't know what she's talking about. But, ironically, this time I actually want to tell her the truth, that I'm daydreaming about all the time I've spent with Leif recently. Now that I've (almost) decided to come clean about our relationship, the words are on the tip of my tongue, but I haven't discussed it with him yet and we should really make the decision together. Then, once we've got our story straight, our first stop needs to be HR.

And afterwards – I really do smile this time – maybe I'll send out a memo.

I reach into my desk for some Post-Its, realize I'm humming to myself and quickly turn it into a cough. It's just so hard to hide my good mood. I'm high on endorphins and my body is all relaxed, like I'm floating in a hot, foamy bubble bath. I have to constantly battle the urge to dance around the room like some kind of loved-up cliché. I'm so distracted I don't even register the fact that I've answered my phone until Vienna's voice at the other end startles me.

'Ava!' Her tone is sharper than usual.

'What's up?'

'Fucking Philip Sawyer is what's up.'

'Oh no.' My stomach twists. 'What has he done?'

'The bastard wrote a newspaper article implying our upgrades breach current regulations.'

'He's accusing us of cheating?' I gasp, putting my phone on speaker. 'Isn't that libelous?'

'Unfortunately not. Our lawyers are looking into it, but he knew what he was doing. He stayed just the right side of getting sued.'

'Is there any truth to it?' I exchange a look with Emika as she comes over to listen. 'I mean, *does* the car breach regulations?'

'No!' Vienna sounds outraged by the question. 'But now that he's raised it as a potential issue, there'll probably be a formal investigation, meaning a heap of bad PR for us, which he knows, the underhand, conniving piece of human excrement.'

'What can we do?' I ask, feeling a rush of anger towards Philip Sawyer.

'Damage limitation. When you're asked, which you will be in about five minutes, say that we have complete confidence in our cars, our engineers and our team principal. Then start calling our sponsors. Tell them this is all just a formality and there's nothing to worry about. Get Yuto and Charlotte on it too.'

'Right. Do Leif and Corey know yet?'

'No, but I'm calling them next. They're going to be pretty pissed off. Whatever way this plays out, it's going to be hanging over us when the season resumes next week.' She makes a sound somewhere between a sigh and a scream. 'I'm in London now and I'm meeting Bastian, Mika and Nova in an hour. We're going to try and get this resolved as soon as possible. In the meantime, good luck over there. It's going to be a long day.'

'OK. Let us know how it goes.' I press *end call*.

'Shit.' Emika looks like she needs a stiff drink. 'This is bad.'

'Yep.' I feel like I could do with some gin myself. 'We just have to stay calm, right?'

'Right. There's no need to panic.'

The words are barely out of her mouth before the phones start ringing. And ringing. And then ringing some more. We're both so busy fielding calls, it's over an hour before I get a free moment to text Leif.

Hey. Did Vienna call you?

Yes, he responds straight away. **It's total bullshit. There's nothing wrong with the car.**

It's crazy here. I'm probably going to be working late.

Do you need me to come in and help?

Thanks, but we've got this.

OK. Message me when you're finished. I could bring dinner to your place?

Sounds perfect x

BY THE END OF the day my throat is sore from talking to journalists and my head is aching from repeating the same lines over and over. *Total confidence, just a formality, a difference of opinion* . . . I've said variations on the same thing so many times I'm pretty sure I'll be saying them in my sleep. I only hope I'm telling the truth, because if I'm not then we'll be back near the bottom of the Standings and it won't be long before Philip Sawyer gets exactly what he wants. I clench my fists at the thought. The idea of Rask going under, of being beaten by a backstabber like Sawyer ... We can't let that happen. This team is too special.

'Here.' Emika places a mug of tea and a napkin containing a pink doughnut on the desk in front of me. 'You look like you need this.'

'Thanks.'

'Actually, that's a lie.' She pulls up a chair. 'I need it, but I'll feel better about the calories if you have one too. Although we must have burned enough just picking up phones today.'

'Definitely.' I sink my teeth into the gooey dough. 'You're right – this does help.'

'Have you heard any more from Vienna?'

'Not yet.' I wipe my mouth and glance at the clock on the wall. 'I don't know if that's a good or a bad sign.'

'It has to be good.' Emika sounds like she's trying to convince herself. 'I mean, Bastian is a stickler for the rules. There's no way he would have breached them.'

'Unless it's some kind of technicality? That's happened before ...' Suddenly I wish I didn't know quite so much about the history of F1. I don't want to think about those other instances.

'At least one good thing's come out of all this.' Emika taps at her phone and then hands it to me. 'Take a look.'

I find myself staring at an online article about Philip Sawyer. According to the byline, it was written by one of the friendlier journalists I spoke to this morning and the headline makes me splutter with laughter.

'"Sawyer Grapes"?'

'It basically accuses him of trying to stir up trouble for his own ends.'

'Wow.' I skim-read the article. 'It really goes for him.'

'There are others too, and it's all over X, so at least popular opinion is on our side.' She looks thoughtful. 'You know, if his claims are dismissed, in a weird way this could actually end up being good for the team. And if he realizes he's destroying his own reputation, he might finally stop trying to ruin us.'

'I hope so.' I quickly swallow a mouthful of doughnut as my phone lights up with Vienna's name.

'Hello?' I put it straight to speaker.

'No case to answer!' Vienna sounds triumphant.

'Already?' I jump to my feet. 'How did you manage to get it dismissed so quickly?'

'It turns out, Nova can be very persuasive.'

'That's such a relief.' I practically hurl myself across the desk to hug Emika. 'So what now?'

'Now we need to put out a press release telling the world we're back in business. Then we need to get everything ready for Monza. We're going to *own* the second half of this season! We're going to be faster and better and we're going to show the whole world exactly what we think of Philip fucking Sawyer!' She sounds ferocious. 'Are you with me? With Rask?'

'Oh, we're so with you,' Emika answers. 'One hundred per cent.'

'Um . . . yes.' Guilt makes my voice a lot smaller. 'We're with you.'

*

'HI! WHAT ARE YOU doing here?' I ask, smiling at the sight of Leif leaning against the wall outside my flat, dressed in baggy jeans and a vintage hoodie. I texted him when I was leaving work, but I told him not to worry about dinner because it was so late.

'I brought you this.' He holds up a bag. 'Beef and black bean, your favourite, just in case you were hungry after all. And I wanted to make sure you were all right. It sounded like a rough day.'

'It was. You know, when I joined Rask I wanted a challenge, but I never expected anything like this.' I reach up and kiss him. 'Thanks for the food.'

'You're welcome. At least it all worked out for the best.'

'It did.' Somehow I manage to sigh and yawn at the same time. 'We're in the clear and you're free to go back out and win races.'

'I'll try.' He steps aside so I can unlock my door. 'Now I'd better get going. I don't want to intrude and you look like you need some sleep.'

'I do, but you're not intruding. I want you to stay.' I reach a hand out, curling my fingers around his and tugging him after me through the door. 'Once the season starts again, I'll hardly see you for almost two months. I want to get as much of you now as I can.'

'Then I'm all yours.' He closes the door behind us. 'You have no idea how much I'm going to miss you.'

'Oh, I think I do.' I drop my blazer to the floor and walk into his arms. The next race after Monza is Singapore. After that, it'll be São Paulo, then Mexico City, Austin and Las Vegas. With such a punishing schedule, the plan is for Leif to stay mostly in the Americas so he won't get too jet-lagged.

It's another reason why I want to tell Vienna about our relationship. I'm hoping she'll take pity on me and find me something to do at one of the races.

'Ava . . .' Leif's tender expression turns serious all of a sudden. 'I know this isn't the best time to talk, but there's actually something I need to tell you and I don't want you to hear it from anybody else.'

'Is it about your career?' I feel a flutter of excitement.

'Yes. I've felt conflicted about what to do for a while, whether to sign with a bigger team or stay where I am, but today clarified things for me. So I've finally made a decision.' He tightens his arms around me. 'I'm signing a new contract with Rask.'

'What?' I stiffen because I must have misheard.

'I'm signing a two-year contract. I've decided to stay.'

My mind is reeling. 'What about your other options?'

'I like Rask.'

'But they –' I pause to correct myself – '*we* can't win a championship, not yet anyway.'

'I know, but we will one day. Bastian has a vision and I want to help him achieve it.'

'What if he's wrong?' I press my face into his neck to hide my expression. I feel like I'm close to hyperventilating. My heartbeat is getting faster and heavier with every word he utters. 'You could be jeopardizing your whole career. What does Nathan say?'

'A lot. He's stalling. He'll probably drag it out for a while, arguing about details, but it's not his decision. It's mine. And as far as I'm concerned, it's a done deal. I spoke to Bastian on the phone this evening and I gave him my word.'

'Is this because of us?' Maybe it sounds egotistical to ask, but I have to know. Despite all my hinting, he obviously thinks

I'm staying at Rask too. 'I mean, are you staying because of me?'

'No. I wouldn't want to put that kind of pressure on you. It would be nice to keep working together, but this is a career decision and if it's the wrong one then that's on me. *Just* me.' He presses a kiss into my hair. 'Although I guess it's a little because of you.'

'What do you mean?' My voice is so high-pitched it actually hurts my throat.

'I remembered what you said a few weeks ago, about how Rask are like a family. What happened today made me realize just how much Bastian and this team mean to me, and how much I owe them for that. I feel like I've finally found a place I belong.'

I resist the temptation to wrench myself out of his arms. I can't believe they felt so good around me a few moments ago and now they're like shackles, holding me in place. My mind is reeling out of control – I thought he was going to Quezada! I was so completely sure of it! I assumed we'd be going there together. Now I feel like I've been tricked, because if he's staying at Rask then what about my plans? What about me?

'Hey,' he murmurs into my hair. 'Are you OK?'

'Yeah, I'm . . .' I curl my toes into the floor. 'I'm just . . . tired.'

'Sorry. I shouldn't have sprung this on you now. We'll talk in the morning. I just wanted you to be the first to know.' He smoothes his hands over my back. 'Come on, your dinner's getting cold.'

'Actually . . . could you give me a couple of minutes?' I take a step towards my bedroom. 'I need to . . . get changed.'

'Sure.' He takes a step towards the kitchen and then stops. 'There's one other thing.'

My stomach twists with dread. *What now?*

'I was thinking that once I've signed the contract maybe we could tell people about us?' He rubs the back of his neck like he's nervous. 'I know you have reasons for wanting to keep our relationship a secret, but I can't imagine anyone treating you differently. They all know how great you are at your job.' He smiles shyly. 'I want everyone to know how much I care about you.'

I gulp. It's too horribly ironic. An hour ago I would have told him I wanted the same thing and then launched myself back into his arms. Now my head is spinning so hard I can barely process the words, let alone come up with a coherent response. All I can think of is to stall.

'That's . . . a big step,' I finally manage. 'Can I think about it?'

'Of course.' A flicker of disappointment passes over his face. 'I just want you to know I'm ready to take this to the next level. Whenever you are.'

'Right . . . Thank you.'

I go into my bedroom, push the door to and open my mouth wide in a silent scream. Now that he's told me his plans for the future, it's only fair I tell him mine too, but at this point, instead of it being good news, it's like I've been keeping a huge, treacherous secret. *It's so unfair!* I want to yell the words after him. I'm the one who's had the ground pulled out from under her feet. There's no way I would *ever* have let myself get so close to him if I'd thought we'd be heading in different directions at the end of the season! Because, despite what he claims, I don't see how it's possible to maintain a relationship while working for competing teams. Even if Jasper hadn't specifically offered me a job 900 miles away, we'd have different loyalties. It's unworkable. Impractical. Impossible! Which means that now I have to choose between my career and the man I –

I stop the thought in its tracks. I refuse to let it go any further. The situation is bad enough without bringing feelings into it. Feelings are what got me into this mess in the first place. But this isn't Leif's fault, I remind myself. He never told me that he was going to Quezada. If anything, he kept telling me how conflicted he felt. I'm the one who didn't tell him about Jasper's offer. Because I thought it wasn't necessary. Because Quezada was the obvious, *best* career choice for him. Everyone expected him to go there. *Everyone!* How was I supposed to know he'd put loyalty ahead of ambition?

Except . . . My heart plummets because maybe I should have. After everything he told me about his past and about Bastian and the Jokkinens giving him a chance . . . Those should have been big clues. I was just too fixated on Quezada to see it.

So maybe I should stay at Rask too?

I'm so shocked by the thought I almost forget to breathe. I like working at Rask, I truly do. When I thought Philip Sawyer was trying to destroy us, I felt genuinely angry. We really are like a family.

But . . . but . . . My brain stutters.

Quezada are the team that got me into F1, the one that saved me when I was depressed. And Jasper's offer is my dream job, everything I've worked and planned so hard for. How can I give up on that? And what if I stay at Rask and things go wrong between me and Leif? Then where will I be?

I'll have lost control of my life all over again, all for a man. The prospect of that terrifies me. I can't do it – can't take the risk of spiralling a second time. It's not possible.

But I care about Leif too . . .

I have no idea what to do, not yet. I need breathing space. So the moment I hear his footsteps heading towards my room, I climb into bed and pretend that I've fallen asleep.

Hey. I just tried calling again. We keep missing each other.
Voicemail from Leif Olsen to Ava Yearwood, 22 August

Is something wrong? Can we talk?
Voicemail from Leif Olsen to Ava Yearwood, 10 September

Ava?
Voicemail from Leif Olsen to Ava Yearwood, 30 September

Despite persistent yet unsubstantiated rumours that Quezada were on the verge of signing Leif Olsen, the big announcement this week is that rookie driver, twenty-year-old Alessio Valenti is joining the team as Jaxon Marr's teammate next year. The big question now is, what about Leif?

@ MotorsportEchoNews, 13 October

TWENTY-FOUR

I'M IN THE RASK canteen, absently moving salad around my plate with a fork, when my phone vibrates with a WhatsApp from Maisie.

Hey. I just heard the news about Quezada. Are you OK?

I take a steeling breath. Maisie knows everything, since I called her pretty much the second she got back from Italy. It helped to talk, even if I'm still as conflicted now as I was then. When I saw the announcement about Valenti this morning, I felt like my heart had just shrunk several sizes. I hadn't realized how much I'd been hoping Leif would change his mind about Quezada.

Not really.

I'm so sorry. Have you spoken to Leif yet?

My stomach twists with guilt. No, I haven't spoken to Leif. I've successfully avoided him for two months, ever since the night he told me his decision, first on the morning afterwards when I snuck out of bed at 4 a.m., leaving a spare key to post through the letterbox and a note about an imaginary early meeting, then during the build-up to Monza, when I had a real, if slightly exaggerated, pile of paperwork to get through.

I've been dodging his calls ever since, pleading my workload and an urgent need to spend time with my 'heartbroken brother', although I've been neglecting Dan too. I even managed to arrange meetings in London on the couple of occasions Leif has flown back to Rask's UK headquarters for some simulator time. As for social media content . . . that's been heavily focused on Corey and other members of the team recently.

But I know I can't keep this up. It's Monday morning and the Las Vegas Grand Prix, the last race in the Americas, is on Saturday night Pacific Time, which means next week he'll be home and I'll need to make up my mind one way or the other.

Rask or Quezada. Leif or . . . no Leif.

I'll talk to him when he gets back.

Does that mean you've made a decision?

No. But I will.

OK. Call me if you need to talk x

I abandon what's left of my salad and get up, winding my way through the canteen. Charlotte leaps up from a different table to walk back with me, but I'm too preoccupied to do more than smile and nod as she tells me about some new wedding detail. I've been like this for weeks now, operating on autopilot. I must be putting on a good act too, since no one's accused me of behaving any differently, but inside I'm an emotionally drained mess. I just feel incapable of making a decision. I've dreamed of working for Quezada for so long that walking away seems impossible, and yet the thought of breaking up with Leif makes my heart ache in a way I've never felt before. I want both of them and I resent being placed in this position because it was never supposed to be a choice. My plan was straightforward, a linear step-by-step progression towards a clearly defined end. Leif is the one who's thrown a spanner into everything. And even though I know it's not fair to blame him, I can't help it.

Then again, maybe it doesn't matter what I decide any more. My last voicemail from Leif was two weeks ago. For all I know, he's already decided we're over. But if he hasn't . . . I still don't know what to do. The question is whirling around my mind all the time, like a persistent headache that won't leave me alone. It's almost a relief when we walk into the office to find Emika and Yuto huddled together with anxious expressions.

'Something's wrong,' Emika announces. 'We're in big trouble.'

'Again?' I can't even bring myself to feel alarmed. 'Everything was fine when we went to lunch.'

'Well, it's not now.' She jerks a hand towards the conference room. 'Vienna and Bastian have been holed up in there for forty minutes! Then Mika and Nova arrived ten minutes ago.'

'So?' Charlotte and I exchange glances. Emika's been working late a lot recently, maybe too much.

'So they must have flown in this morning.' She glares at us like she's reading our minds. 'I am *not* over-reacting.'

'She's not.' Yuto sounds gloomy. 'Something's definitely wrong. Take a look at their expressions and you'll see what we mean.'

'How?' The conference room has a glass window, but we can hardly just go and peer in.

'Walk past. Emika has. Four times.'

'I'll go.' Charlotte picks up a pile of papers and heads towards the photocopier, casually twisting her head like she's just flicking her hair as she goes. The moment she gets to the other side, however, she swings around with a horrified look on her face.

'You see!' Emika practically crumples into a chair. 'We're finished. We must have run out of money and they're selling the team back to Sawyer.'

'I'm sure that's not it.' I try to sound soothing. 'We've got fifty-two points over the past three races.'

'They're talking to somebody on a laptop,' Charlotte says in a loud whisper.

'Lawyers probably.' Emika scrapes her palms over her cheeks. 'And I just put down a deposit on a flat. Sawyer's bound to fire us.'

'If things were that bad, we would have heard rumours, wouldn't we?' I look around for support.

'That's true, actually.' Yuto looks brighter again. 'I saw Jay in Finance yesterday and he didn't seem stressed.'

'Exactly. So we're not going to lose our jobs.' I squeeze Emika's arm reassuringly. 'Congratulations on the flat, by the way.'

'Thanks. It's taken me so long to find somewhere even remotely affordable –'

She stops talking as the door to the conference room swings open abruptly and Bastian, Mika and Nova file out and walk past, their expressions all tense. A second later, Vienna appears in the doorway, her arms folded.

'Good, you're all here. I guess you're wondering what this is about.' Her tone is ominous. 'I have news.'

'It's over, isn't it?' Charlotte's the one over-reacting now, her mouth trembling. 'We're all going to lose our jobs.'

'What? No. Why would you think –' Vienna stops and mutters under her breath. 'Never mind. It's nothing to do with your jobs. It's about Corey. Apparently he decided to go rock climbing somewhere near the Grand Canyon yesterday.'

'Oh no.' Emika presses a hand to her mouth.

'Oh yes. He broke his leg in three places.'

'So we're down a driver?' Charlotte squeaks through the chorus of gasps.

'Worse. We're down a driver who was supposed to meet us in Las Vegas *tomorrow*.' Vienna places a hand to her chest. 'Obviously I'd like to take the first flight to Corey's hospital bed and stamp on his other leg, but –' she closes her eyes – 'I'm trying to stay calm.'

'One of the reserve drivers can take over, though, can't they?' I say. As a customer team to Fraser, we share their reserves.

'That's what we've just been discussing. It's the only bit of good news I've had today. She'll be meeting us in Las Vegas tomorrow.'

'She? You mean Quinn Sommers?' Emika stands up straighter. 'That's so cool!'

'I think so too.' Vienna opens her eyes again. 'Or it would be if she had more than three days to learn everything she needs to know about the car. That's enough pressure without being nineteen years old and the first woman driver in Formula 1 for decades.'

'Has she driven the car at all?' Yuto sounds worried.

'She's had a little time in the simulator, but not much.' Vienna takes a deep breath and exhales loudly. 'But if Fraser think she's up to the challenge, then we'll just have to trust them. Bastian's telling the engineers right now, and Mika and Nova are briefing the rest of the staff. We, however, need to put out a press release asap. After that, the phones are going to be ringing off the hook. Remember when Sawyer accused us of cheating? It's going to be like that times ten. All media attention is going to be on us for the next few days, so everyone cancel any plans you have for the week.' She looks at me. 'And I'll need you to come to Las Vegas too.'

'Me?' I put a hand out to grasp the back of a chair. The Las Vegas GP is a huge deal, but it also means seeing Leif again and I'm nowhere near ready for that. 'But I thought I was minding the office this weekend?'

'That was then. Now it's action stations. I'll need someone to help me field media enquiries stateside, and Emika and Yuto are going to be too busy with the drivers. Emika, you'll be minding Quinn, by the way.'

'No problem.'

'And Charlotte?' Vienna narrows her eyes. 'Don't even think about telling me you have a dress fitting this weekend.'

'I don't.' Charlotte shakes her head quickly. 'I'll mind the office.'

'Are you sure?' I ask her. 'Because if you'd rather go to Vegas, I can stay here. I mean, I went to Hungary, so really it's your turn.'

'Actually, I don't have a passport right now because I'm getting it renewed for my honeymoon.'

'Then that settles it.' Vienna pulls herself up to her full height. 'Charlotte, you'll be on your own for the rest of the week, so if you need any help, go to Merchandising and tell them I said you could borrow their interns. If anyone argues, call me.' She looks around each of us in turn. 'We have to view this as an opportunity. If it goes well, we'll be trailblazers and it'll look great for the team. In other words, it has to fucking go well. Failure isn't an option.'

'Yes, boss!' Emika, Charlotte and Yuto all grin.

'Good. So forget about sleep until next week and let's get started.'

I force a smile along with everyone else, but inside I'm screaming.

Hot on the heels of Quezada's announcement is the news that fan favourite Australian driver Corey Hammond will be missing the rest of the season due to injury. Meanwhile, his replacement is the nineteen-year-old racing prodigy from Aberdeen, Quinn Sommers.

@ MotorsportEchoNews, 14 October

TWENTY-FIVE

BY THE TIME WE reach Las Vegas late on Tuesday afternoon, my mental panic is under control, but I'm physically the most tense I've ever been in my life. Every muscle in my body is twitching and I haven't been able to eat anything since we left Cambridge. It doesn't help that Pacific Time is eight hours behind the UK, and I was too wound up to sleep on the flight, so I'm both exhausted *and* edgy. I'm making a conscious effort to sit still and not fidget as I sit in the back of a Lincoln Navigator, driving along The Strip towards our hotel.

Now that we're here, surrounded by an infinite array of neon signs and illuminated billboards, it's obvious why they decided to hold the Grand Prix at night. Aside from the nightmare logistics of shutting down so much of the traffic infrastructure during the day, it's not called the City of Lights for nothing. The whole place is thrumming with energy and excitement. I only wish I could relax and enjoy it.

'I can't believe they're going to turn this street into the race track,' Yuto murmurs beside me. 'It's incredible.'

'What's incredible is the number of messages on my

phone.' Emika groans. 'It's going to take me all night to deal with every one.'

'Just do your best.' Vienna glances up from her laptop. 'Your priority is Quinn. Anything you can't handle, forward to Ava.' She shoots me a look. 'Sorry.'

'It's fine. That's why I'm here.' I smile at Emika, then look out of the window again, at a red, white and blue medieval-style castle, closely followed by the Statue of Liberty, the Eiffel Tower and the spectacular Fountains of Bellagio. Everywhere I look is another world-famous high-rise hotel or casino. It feels surreal, like driving through a Hollywood set.

'We should have brought Charlotte and Andre.' Yuto nudges me. 'They could have got married in the Little White Chapel and we'd never have to hear another word about wedding planning ever again.'

'No one's getting married,' Vienna interjects. 'I don't care if you meet the loves of your lives, there's not going to be time for anything but F1. Thousands of fans, not to mention sponsors, are descending on this city right now and I want all of them to leave in five days thinking what an incredible team we are. This is going to be intense.' She looks down at her phone and then immediately back up again. 'And one more thing. Everyone keep an eye on Leif. I don't know what happened to him over the summer break, but he's been in a bad mood ever since Monza. It wasn't so obvious when he had Corey beside him to charm everyone, but this week we need him to step up and represent the team in as positive a light as possible. If he starts scowling, let me know.'

'Vienna's right. He's been like a bear with a sore head for the last four GPs,' Yuto grumbles. 'It makes no sense when he's driving so well.'

I squirm in my seat because I'm pretty sure Leif's recent behaviour is my fault. I've been so wrapped up in my own thoughts, I haven't allowed myself to wonder about how my sudden silent treatment might have affected him. Or, whenever I have, I've nipped it in the bud straight away because I have enough to deal with, without adding guilt into the mix.

As cowardly as it sounds, I've also decided the best thing to do this week is to keep on avoiding him. I know I need to tell him about my job offer from Quezada, but I can't do it here, especially not just before the race. I'll tell him as soon as we get home and then maybe . . . Maybe talking about it will help me make a decision.

'OK, this is our hotel.' Vienna slams her laptop shut. 'We'll drop our bags off and then head straight to the Media Centre. I want to make sure everything's ready for Media Day.'

'I wonder what Quinn is like,' Emika muses, as we enter a huge, dimly lit lobby, decorated in shades of scarlet and gold. 'Your friend Gio must know her pretty well. Have you met her?'

'No.' I purse my lips. Personally, I have mixed feelings about meeting Quinn. I find it hard to forget how she almost came between Maisie and Gio earlier this year, even if it did turn out to be innocent. 'But I've heard she's nice,' I add, to be fair.

'I'd better find out what room she's in, so I can go and introduce myself.'

'Good idea,' I say, as my anxiety skyrockets. The drivers' personal motorhomes are for European races only. That means Leif and Quinn are probably staying in this hotel too. They – he – could appear at any moment.

'Look!' Emika's hand on my arm almost makes me jump out of my skin. 'It's our pop-up store!'

She doesn't wait for a response, tugging me across the lobby to where a temporary Rask store has been set up beside the entrance to the casino. It's decked out in chequered flags and there's even a replica of this year's car, along with cardboard cut-outs of Leif, Corey and Quinn, for people to take selfies with. Even better, they seem to be doing a thriving trade in baseball caps and T-shirts. I take a couple of quick pictures and post them online. We want as many people as possible to know we're here.

'You two are roomies.' Vienna comes over to hand us our key cards. 'Drop your bags off and then get back down here asap. We have a lot to get done before the gala tonight.' She strides off towards the lifts.

I stare after her. 'What gala?'

'For our sponsors. It's in the schedule.' Emika gives me a strange look. 'Are you OK? No offence, but you seem kind of jittery.'

I clamp a hand to my stomach as it starts churning. No, I'm not OK. If there's a gala for the sponsors, Leif will definitely be there. How could I not have known about it? How could I not have even looked at the schedule? I love schedules! It's like I don't know who I am any more . . .

'Jet lag.' I push the words out.

'Ah.' Emika nods sagely. 'You get used to it. Come on, we'd better hurry up and do what Vienna says.'

TWO HOURS OF FRENETIC activity later, I've tried everything I can think of to get out of the gala. I've suggested I skip it to get more work done. That I could help run the pop-up store so some of the merchandising team can go instead. I've even offered to help install wiring in the motorhome, not that I have any idea about electrics. Short of feigning a sudden illness – not that I've entirely discounted the idea – I'm all out of options. I'm going to the gala.

Fuckity fuck fuck.

'What do you think?' Emika emerges from the bathroom looking like Rita Hayworth, or some other 1950s Hollywood siren. Her hair is set in short, glamorous waves and she's wearing a plunging red dress with a slit all the way up her thigh.

'You look stunning,' I tell her.

'Thanks.' Her flawlessly made-up doe eyes drop to my outfit. 'Um . . . is that what you're wearing? Because you know this is Vegas, right?'

I look down at my crew-neck Rask summer dress and gold wedges. Since I didn't pack anything other than work and travel clothes, it's the best I've been able to manage (along with cool tone make-up and a braided bun), although it's actually perfect since I don't want to be noticeable tonight. I want to blend in with the crowd. It's my only hope of dodging Leif.

'I know.' I feign a look of regret. 'I packed in a hurry.'

'Don't worry. I brought a back-up.' She rifles in her suitcase. 'We're about the same size. Here, try this.'

'Oh, I don't know.' My eyes widen as they take in the one-shouldered, dark purple bodycon dress she's holding out to me. It's gorgeous, but . . . *definitely* noticeable. 'I don't want to stretch it.'

'You won't, and this colour will look great on you.'

I'm too tired to think of any more excuses so I change quickly and then head downstairs with her into a ginormous, crowded ballroom. Merchandising have gone all out here too. The walls are streaming with Rask banners and the waiters are all dressed in racing overalls. Suddenly I feel grateful to Emika for not taking no for an answer. There are so many glamorous outfits that I would have been more noticeable in my plain one.

'You know, if someone had told me in May that we'd be hosting a party like this by October, I would never have believed them.' Emika swipes a pair of champagne flutes off a tray. 'We've come so far this season! If we keep it up, we could be real contenders for the podium next year.'

'I hope so,' I murmur, though I'm distracted, looking for Leif. There's no sign of him yet, but he must be here.

'Hey, ladies . . .' Yuto appears through the crowd, stopping briefly to give us a twirl in his burgundy suit. 'What do you think? Pretty hot, right?'

'Scorching.' I give him a thumbs-up, then drink half the contents of my champagne flute in one go. It's probably not a good idea on top of nerves and an empty stomach, but I feel like I need it.

'So, Vienna wants us to mingle and tell everyone how excited we are about Quinn,' Yuto says. 'And if we stop smiling for even a second, we're all fired.'

'Got it. Hey, have you met Quinn yet?' Emika asks. 'She was in a meeting with her race engineer when I went to find her earlier.'

'Yeah, she's over there talking to one of our IT sponsors.' Yuto points to the opposite side of the room. 'Come on, I'll introduce you.'

'Great. You coming?' Emika looks back over her shoulder at me.

'Not right now.' I wave them away. 'You go. I'll mingle.'

I drink some more champagne and try to pull myself together. I can see some representatives from another of our sponsors, a financial services company, a few feet away. I should probably go and reintroduce myself. Plus, there's a scattering of journalists I want to thank for supporting us when the Philip Sawyer article came out. I just need to get my professional face on and –

'Ava?'

I jolt and turn around slowly, my skin prickling at the sound of Leif's voice. He's standing an arm's length away, dressed in a classic black tuxedo and looking so handsome, I'm pretty sure my heart actually stops.

'Leif . . .' I swallow. 'Hi.'

'Hi.' He holds on to my gaze, his own guarded.

I say the first thing that comes into my mind. 'I've missed you.'

I know that I'm being a hypocrite, that I'm the one who's been avoiding him, but I still mean it. Looking at Leif now, I realize just how unhappy I've been for the past two months. Part of me wants to throw my arms around him, only we're surrounded by hundreds of people, and even if we weren't, I can't. We need to talk first.

'Have you?' He sounds suspicious. Hurt.

I give a jerky nod. 'I'm sorry I've been –'

'Busy.' His voice hardens.

'Yes. It's complicated, but it's not –'

'*Don't.*' His eyes flash. 'Don't say "It's not you, it's me".'

'I wasn't going to,' I lie. 'I was going to say that it's not what you think.'

'Then tell me what it is.' He closes the distance between us, his gaze laser-focused. 'Ava, I've been going out of my mind. What happened? Why did you stop answering my calls?'

I throw a quick look around. The tension between us is obvious and people – worse, *journalists* – are beginning to notice. 'Leif, I can't talk about it here,' I say quietly. 'Not now. We're making a scene.'

'Then let's go to my room.'

'We *can't*.' Despite everything, a shiver of excitement snakes its way down my spine. The thought of being alone with him is so tempting, but if we end up in bed together, things will be even more confusing. 'You need to be here, representing the team, especially now Corey's out of action. We'll talk after the race.'

'Ava!' I hear Emika's voice. 'Look who I found.'

I take a step away from Leif. She's walking towards us, arm in arm with a petite, dark-haired woman in an elegant, floor-length black dress.

'Hi.' The woman holds out a hand with a smile. 'I'm Quinn.'

'Good to meet you.' I shake her hand and try to smile back, but my facial muscles are stiff and I feel like every part of my body is straining towards Leif. He's standing right beside me, so close I can feel his body heat on my bare shoulder.

'You're friends with Maisie and Gio, right?' Quinn has a soft Scottish accent. 'I'm so grateful to them both. I had some problems when I first joined Fraser, but they've been so wonderful and supportive.'

'They're a great couple.' I manage to smile properly this time. She sounds genuine, like she'd be horrified if she knew she'd caused any angst for them. 'And the whole team at Rask is ready to support you too.'

'They already are. I was pretty intimidated coming here, but everyone's been so nice. I'm feeling a lot better now.'

'I'll drink to that.' Emika lifts her champagne flute. 'Does that mean you're ready to score us some points this weekend?'

Quinn laughs. 'Fingers crossed.'

I turn my head towards Leif, but he's staring at the floor, frowning, not joining in with the conversation. He's behaving just as he did on the evening we first met in Monaco, only this time I'm the one at fault. Because I've done this to him. And I'm still doing it. And it's not just about us any more. What I'm doing is affecting the whole team.

'Leif. Quinn.' Vienna appears suddenly, accompanied by a tall, silver-haired man. 'Have you met Helmut Moran? He owns our favourite frozen yogurt company.'

I take the opportunity to break away. I'll probably get in trouble for it later, but I can't stay here, networking and pretending that everything's all right. I'll have to tell Vienna I got sick, after all.

I practically sprint for the exit. This is going to be a long few days.

With a 3.8-mile street track, Las Vegas is one of the longest and most exciting races in the F1 calendar, with drivers hitting speeds of up to 217 mph.

@ MotorsportEchoNews, 18 October

TWENTY-SIX

I UNDERESTIMATED. THIS HASN'T been a long few days, it's been a soul-sucking eternity.

At this point I'm ready to join Vienna in tracking Corey down and breaking his other leg. Thanks to him, I've spent the past seventy-two hours doing damage limitation over reports of a smashed-up hospital room. I know he must be feeling pretty devastated right now and I feel bad for him, but his behaviour still reflects on the team and we're busy enough fielding questions about Quinn. Most journalists are asking the same thing, about why she was chosen to stand in, as opposed to any other available driver. Nobody actually says it out loud, but the words '*female* driver' are implied. It's like nobody can believe she's here on the basis of talent alone.

On top of that, there's been practice and qualifying. Fortunately, I've been so busy in the Media Centre I haven't had to venture anywhere near the garage. I've caught brief glimpses of Leif from a distance, but so far I've managed to successfully avoid him. The fact that he hasn't sought me out either makes me wonder if he's avoiding me now too, but I've no headspace left to ponder the implications.

At least it's finally Saturday, which means the media's attention is shifting away from the personalities and politics to the actual race. The usual suspects (Marr, Gio and Shimizu) occupy the top three spots, while Leif is in P10, his worst qualifying position in eight races, and Quinn is P17, not bad for a debut, but not exactly great for the team.

Ten minutes before the race, I head into the communications office at the back of the Rask motorhome to find Robbo, one of the technicians, glaring at a TV screen.

'Hey. Are you all right?' I follow his gaze. The picture changes as I look, but for a split second I thought I caught a glimpse of Leif.

'Mmm?' Robbo gives a start, like he didn't notice me come in. 'Yeah, sorry. I was just thinking about something I heard.'

'Anything juicy?'

'More disappointing.'

'Oh, really?' I wait for him to say more, but he's busy glaring at the screen again. 'So are we all good to go?'

'Pretty much. Both cars are in grid position.'

'Great.' I curl up on the sofa in the corner. 'Would it be rude to nap?'

'I won't tell anyone.'

'Thanks.' I rest my head on a cushion. I've never slept through a race before, and I really don't want to miss this one, but I'm so exhausted I can't resist. After four days of incessant activity and continued emotional turmoil, I can barely keep my eyes open, let alone think straight. I'll watch the replay later. Right now, I need to recharge my batteries a little.

It's the last thing I think before I drift off, though it feels like only seconds later that a hand shakes me awake again.

'Huh?' I lift my head groggily. 'What is it?'

'Ava, wake up! You need to see this.' Emika's tone is serious. 'There's been an accident.'

'What?' I break into a cold sweat as I see a group of people gathered around the TV screen. They're all standing very still and a few have their hands pressed to their mouths. 'Who?'

'It's more like who isn't involved. Twelve cars just went out.'

'Leif?' I get up and stagger forward, my pulse thumping so hard I feel dizzy.

'No.' Yuto puts a hand out to steady me. 'Neither he nor Quinn were involved.'

I feel a rush of relief, immediately followed by guilt. There are twenty other drivers to think about. 'Is anyone seriously hurt?'

'We don't think so. The race has been red-flagged and the medics are out there, but it looks like everyone's OK. It's a total mess, though.'

I drag in a breath as my eyes focus on the screen. Yuto's right: the track is in total chaos. There are bits of carbon fibre and rubber everywhere.

'What happened?'

'It was one of the Gold Darts,' Emika answers. 'Both the Fraser and Quezada cars had just pitted so the field was crowded. Erikkson went too tight into the bend and connected with Marr and Shimizu. Then Gio and Zaragoza went into them. It was like a whole chain reaction. Most of the front-runners are out.'

'Is Gio OK?' Fear grips me again.

'Yes. He's standing over there with Marr, look.'

I heave a sigh of relief, not just for Gio but for Maisie

watching back home. She must be a nervous wreck right now. I'd call her, except she's probably waiting for a call from Gio himself.

'Wait!' A new thought hits me. 'If twelve cars are out, that means –'

'There are only ten left.' Emika's eyes connect with mine. 'So everyone who finishes the race will be in the points.'

'Which means another double points finish for us.' Yuto looks around the room. 'We're allowed to feel good about that, right? I mean, since it looks like nobody's injured?'

I don't answer because the accident is being replayed in slow motion on the screen. The thought that Leif was only a couple of seconds behind makes me feel sick. I have a powerful urge to run to the garage to make sure he's all right, but he'll be waiting with his car for the restart. Short of elbowing his mechanics out of the way and smothering his helmet in kisses, there's no way for me to reach him.

At this point, he probably wouldn't want me to anyway.

'What lap was it?' I ask, pushing that last thought from my mind.

'Thirty-nine,' Emika says. 'So there'll only be eleven left if they can clear the track in time.' We all turn to look at the clock. If a race has no stoppage time, the limit is two hours. With stoppages, that extends to four. Right now, we're only ninety minutes in.

'So we're looking at a likely restart. What positions are Leif and Quinn in now?'

'Leif's second and Quinn's seventh.'

'Leif is second?' I need a moment to process. If he stays there, he'll be on the podium again for the first time since Australia.

'We could get a win if he overtakes Cooper.' Yuto sounds like he's trying to restrain his excitement.

'It's possible.' I feel a surge of adrenaline because it really is. Leif is one of the best drivers on the grid, in one of the best cars now too. If he's in the right frame of mind, he could win the whole GP . . .

If . . .

But I daren't think about that, because I have a horrible feeling I might have messed up his chances already.

'I CAN'T WATCH.' EMIKA buries her face in her hands. 'Tell me when it's over.'

'One more lap.' Yuto clutches my arm. 'This is so exciting!'

'I know!' I clutch him back. After half an hour of clearing up the track, the race restarted with the drivers in the same positions they were in before the accident. Some commentators were expecting a procession, with none of the drivers prepared to take risks for fear of losing guaranteed points, but it's been the complete opposite. With all the cars on new tyres, the last ten laps have been some of the most exciting in the whole year, more like a sprint race than a Grand Prix.

Cooper is still in the lead, but Leif is relentless. I want him to overtake, but I also don't want him to do anything reckless. If he were to miss out on a podium at this point, it would be gutting for everyone. Meanwhile, Quinn has overtaken three cars already, putting her in fourth place, and the way she's driving, a podium finish isn't out of the question for her either.

There are two corners left. Leif comes up behind Cooper, turns on the inside and then . . .

'He's done it!' I spring into the air with Yuto as the whole motorhome seems to shake with the volume of cheers. 'He's overtaken Cooper!'

'Leif?' Emika peers out from between her fingers.

'Yes!'

'No way!' She wraps her arms around us so that we're all jumping up and down together when he passes the chequered flag, closely followed by Cooper and then . . .

'Quinn!' Emika's screech is so loud it's amazing the screen doesn't shatter.

'First and third!' Yuto throws his head back and gives a loud whoop.

I want to stay.

The thought pops into my head with such clarity that I know it's the truth. I want to stay with Rask, with this team, these people, this family. My life isn't going to fall apart if I revise my plan. It's got me this far, but now all it's doing is holding me back, trapping me in a past I've finally outgrown because I'm not the person I was when I first set my mind on Quezada. I'm happier and stronger, someone who ought to be free to change her mind if she wants to. And I won't be doing it for a man, but for me, because Rask is where I can have a career and friendship and fun, as well as love too.

My eyes well with tears as I watch Leif pull into parc fermé. Everything is so clear now. I feel like a burden has been lifted from my shoulders and I can finally stand tall, look up and see the world properly again. I'm in love with him. I refused to let myself acknowledge it before, but I am. So now it's time to set my old plan aside and make a new one. One where I stay with Rask and Leif, and we get a ton more podiums and become the best damn team in Formula 1. Together.

'Go!' I push Yuto and Emika towards the door because if I keep hugging them any longer I'm going to erupt into sobs. 'Go and congratulate them. I need to post about this, but I'll celebrate with you later. Just remember to send me some shots from the podium!'

I sit down the moment they're gone, wiping my hands across my cheeks as Leif gets out of his car, hugs Quinn and then flings himself against the barrier and into the arms of his mechanics. I wonder if he's looking for me among them. I wish I could go out there and join in, but I can't, not yet. I know I have a lot of explaining to do and I don't want an audience.

Soon, I tell myself. I'll wait until the cameras have gone and then I'll go and explain – and hopefully fix – everything.

AN HOUR LATER, I stretch my back, slip my laptop into my bag and throw one last look around the office to make sure nobody's left anything. It's incredible how fast motorhomes are packed up after a race, ready for shipping on to the next Grand Prix. If I don't hurry, they'll be taking the walls down around me.

'I think that's everything,' I say, checking my phone one last time. Race reports are sent, press releases are written, social media is all up to date – for half an hour or so anyway – and I've spoken with Charlotte, updating her on all the drama. I've also got about a hundred messages from Vienna, Yuto and Emika telling me to come and join the celebrations in the garage and I've finally responded to say I'm on my way.

'I guess.' Robbo heaves himself out of his chair. Weirdly, despite our P1 and P3 result, his expression is as brooding now as it was before the race.

'Come on.' I smile encouragingly. 'There has to be some champagne left.'

'You go.' He slings a bag over his shoulder and heads for the door. 'I'm going to bed.'

'Are you kidding?' I blink at him. 'This was a great day for us. Rask's very first win!'

'I know.' He stops in the doorway. 'I just wish it was the other way round, you know. Quinn instead of Leif in first place.'

'That's a bit harsh.' I frown. 'I mean, obviously it's great to finally have a female driver, but –'

'It's not that.' He interrupts me. 'I'm pissed off that in a week's time nobody's going to be talking about us winning a race any more. It's all going to be about Leif going to Fraser. We'll be old news.'

'What?' I feel like he just threw a bucket of icy water into my face. 'Who says that Leif is going to Fraser?'

'Apparently he had dinner with Giovanni Bauer and Mark Haddon last night.'

I stiffen because that does seem a little odd. Why would Leif be dining with the Fraser team principal instead of Bastian the night before a Grand Prix? There has to be a reason. If Leif wasn't prepared to move to Quezada, then why would he go to Fraser instead? Especially after he gave Bastian his word.

'I'm sure there's an explanation,' I say. 'Leif is totally committed to Rask.'

'Then why hasn't he signed the contract yet?' Robbo sounds like he's enjoying his own conspiracy theory. 'It's October. This should have been dealt with months ago. Why are things still up in the air?'

'Because his agent is probably stalling, trying to get more money,' I say, remembering what Leif told me. Although it's certainly unusual to leave things this late in the season...

'*Or* he wants us to *think* his agent is stalling and he's just been waiting for Fraser to make a decision about Hayden Quaid.'

I feel a prickle of discomfort. 'Have they?'

'Yep. They're not renewing his contract. It's going to be announced on Monday.'

'Shit.' I sit down again. 'Are you certain?'

'A friend who works in their engineering department told me. It's a shame. He seems like a nice guy.' Robbo shrugs. 'The whole thing leaves a bad taste in the mouth, you know. People were finally starting to take us seriously again and now Corey's broken his leg and our best driver is leaving. So I'm not in the mood for celebrating.'

'But none of this is confirmed...'

'It will be. Trust me. By the end of next week, we'll be looking for another driver. And hey, I'm not blaming Leif. Fraser are a great team. It just sucks for us.'

'Right.' I stare down at the floor, my shoulders slumping like a new weight has settled across them. It seems too ironic to be true, that I find out Leif is leaving Rask at the same time I decide to stay.

'Sorry.' Robbo's expression turns contrite. 'I didn't mean to bring you down. And maybe things will work out, you know. If Corey's back next year, he and Quinn might make a good pairing.'

'Uh-huh...' I'm barely registering his words now. 'Maybe.'

'Anyway, I'm heading back to the hotel. The airport bus isn't until 6 a.m. so we can still get a few hours' sleep.'

'Yeah . . . See you.'

I sit completely still for a few seconds, waiting until his footsteps have receded before reaching for my phone. There's only one person I can trust right now to tell me the truth.

'Congratulations!' Maisie answers on the second ring. 'Wait – why are you calling me and not celebrating?'

'First, because I need to make sure you're OK after what happened to Gio in the crash. Second, because I have a question and I need you to be completely honest with me.'

'That's so sweet of you.' I can hear the smile in her voice. 'I was a bit shaken at first, but he called me and we're both fine. And I promise to be honest.'

'Thank you.' I take a deep breath. 'Is Leif going to Fraser?'

There's a long, telling moment of silence.

'Maisie?' My limbs feel heavy all of a sudden. 'Are you still there?'

'I'm here.'

'Is it true?'

'Honestly . . . I'm not sure. All I know is that Hayden Quaid's contract isn't being renewed and Gio's been pushing for Leif. They've had a few meetings.'

'When?'

'Over the last month. Gio said he and Leif had a long talk about it in Austin.'

'That was two weeks ago! Why didn't you tell me?'

'I couldn't! It was all confidential. Plus, I figured it was up to Leif to tell you himself.'

'He told me he was staying at Rask,' I say bitterly.

She pauses. 'Well, look, as far as I know, nothing's definite yet. Maybe he really is staying.'

'Is it true he had dinner with Gio and Mark Haddon last night?'

'Ava...'

'Did he?'

She sighs. 'I think so, yes.'

'Right.' I swallow heavily, feeling numb all over. 'I have to go.'

'Are you OK?'

'I will be. I just need to get out of here.'

'Text me. As soon as you get home. I'll come round with anything you need. Ice cream, chicken-noodle soup, gin, whatever. I'll bring it.'

'Thanks.' I end the call, grab my bag and hurry out of the motorhome into the night air. I can't believe it. Leif said he was staying at Rask. He was so definite. How could he have changed his mind and not told me?

Because you haven't been answering his calls, my brain taunts me. *Or his messages... Maybe you're the reason he's leaving.*

'Ava?' A man's voice makes me jump.

'Yes?' I whip my head round and gasp. I hadn't even noticed I was passing the Quezada motorhome, but there's a man sitting outside. 'Jasper!' I drag my scattered thoughts back together. 'I mean, Mr Ramirez. How nice to see you.'

'Jasper is fine. And it's good to see you too. Congratulations on today.'

'Thanks. I'm so sorry about what happened to your cars.'

'Me too, but that's the way it goes sometimes.' He smiles. 'You must be on your way to celebrate, so I won't hold you up. I just wanted to tell you to keep an eye on your inbox.'

'My inbox?'

'For your contract. You already aced the interview, remember?'

'Oh ... that's ... I mean ...' I stutter incoherently because I can't deal with this right now. My mind is too full of Leif and Rask. 'Sorry, I'm just so tired. It's been a rough week.'

'I get it. The situation with Corey. Poor guy.' Jasper shakes his head. 'If you see him, give him my best, and I'll see you soon, OK?'

'Yes. Great.' I nod emphatically. 'Thank you.'

My phone buzzes again as I walk away. It's another message from Emika telling me to hurry up, but I definitely can't celebrate now. If I see Leif, I won't be able to stop myself from confronting him and I don't want to spoil the party for everyone else.

Instead I text to say I'm too tired, then turn my phone off and head back to the hotel. The paddock is still bustling with people, but I keep my head down, weaving my way determinedly through the crowd. Now the first shock has passed, I'm left with anger. I thought Leif was devoted to us – to Rask, I mean. After everything he's said about Bastian giving him a chance in Formula 1, about loyalty and family, how can he just walk away? Maybe my behaviour hasn't been the best either, but I thought he was the kind of guy who could be trusted.

Now, it turns out I didn't know him at all.

With a podium finish for both their drivers, Bastian Aalto and the whole Rask team have silenced their critics – and Philip Sawyer – once and for all. They must be on top of the world!

@ MotorsportEchoNews, 19 October

TWENTY-SEVEN

I HONESTLY INTENDED TO pack. Only when I passed through the casino on the way back to my hotel room I decided that losing some money at blackjack was a much better idea, after which I felt compelled to continue my streak of poor life choices by raiding the mini bar and brooding.

So now it's 5.30 a.m. and I finally *am* packing, stuffing my belongings into my bag with no regard for my usual system. I'm not even folding. Me, Ava Yearwood, *not* folding! If Dan could see me now, he'd call a doctor.

'There you are!' Emika bursts into the room. 'I can't believe the airport bus gets here in thirty minutes. You missed such a great party! I haven't slept all night!' She swaps her Rask T-shirt for a clean one and then starts flinging clothes into her suitcase, running back and forth between the wardrobe and the bathroom. 'How are you feeling? You must have been really exhausted yesterday.'

'Something like that.' I sit down on the edge of the bed. 'I had a private party. Very exclusive. Just me and the mini bar.' I hiccup. 'Don't worry, I'll pay.'

'Wow.' She stops to look at me, her fingers making a circular motion in the air. 'It seems like we ought to talk about this – whatever *this* is – but there's no time right now.'

'Don't worry about it. I'll meet you down in the lobby.'

'Are you sure?' She gives me a suspicious look.

'Yes! I haven't drunk that much, honestly.' I hold a hand up. 'Look, five fingers!'

'*OK.*' She picks up her suitcase and heads for the door. 'Don't make me come back up here!'

'I won't,' I promise as I lie back on the bed and close my eyes. She's right – I should get my shit together and go down to the lobby with everyone else, but this is so much more comfortable.

I twist my head sideways at the sound of a knock. I'd prefer to ignore it, but since it's probably Emika again, back to collect the oversized denim jacket she's left hanging on the chair, I get up and drag my feet to the door. I'm already there by the time it occurs to me she could have just used her key card.

Cautiously, I place my eye to the peep-hole and then wrench the door open.

'You!' I glare at Leif.

'Yes, me.' He doesn't wait for an invite, pushing his way into the room and slamming the door behind him. 'Ava, where the hell have you been all night? I've been up here at least half a dozen times, looking for you.'

'Not that it's any of your business . . .' I thrust my chin into the air, vaguely remembering some knocking. 'But I've had things to do.'

'Oh, really?' His jaw clenches. 'You know, I get that you don't care about *me* any more, but I thought you'd at least come and celebrate with the team. It's our first win.'

'*Our* first win?' I repeat scornfully. '*Our?*'

'Yes! Bastian booked out a whole restaurant. Everyone was there.'

'Not everyone.' I waggle a finger in front of his face. 'Robbo went to bed.'

'Robbo?' He looks confused. 'From tech?'

'Yes! He didn't want to celebrate with you either.' I push my face up to his. 'Do you want to know why?'

'Why?'

'Because he *knows*.'

'Knows what?' Leif sounds exasperated now. 'Ava, you're making no sense.'

'That you're going to Fraser!' I practically shout at him.

He sways away from me and goes very still. 'Where did you hear that?'

'It doesn't matter. The point is, after everything you've said to me about loyalty, you're leaving Rask! And I refuse to celebrate a win when you're about to abandon us.' I toss my head. 'Or are you going to deny that you had dinner with Gio and Mark Haddon the other night?'

'No.' His expression doesn't alter.

'Or that they offered you a job?'

'No.'

'So it's all decided?' His calm demeanour is maddening. 'I can't believe you're so . . . so –' I wave my hands in the air – 'disloyal!'

'Disloyal?' He gives a short laugh. 'Are you really going to lecture me about loyalty?'

I stiffen as a tendril of worry penetrates my mildly intoxicated brain. 'What's that supposed to mean?'

'Just that maybe you ought to try looking in the mirror.'

'I don't know what you're talking about.'

'No? Be honest, Ava. What are you really upset about: the idea that I might be leaving Rask, or that it's Fraser we're talking about and not Quezada?'

My chest contracts so violently I have to take a deep breath in order to speak again. 'How do you know about Quezada?'

'Formula 1 is a small world. I recently found myself in a bar with Jasper Ramirez. Apparently you're going to be a great addition to his team.'

'When . . .?' I clear my throat, feeling extremely sober all of a sudden. 'How long have you known?'

'Since Mexico.'

I stare at him in dismay. '*Before* Austin?'

His gaze flickers. 'What does Austin have to do with it?'

'That's when Gio asked you to join Fraser! Is that why you're doing this? Because you're mad at me?'

'Ava, I'm not leaving Rask.'

'But you had dinner . . .'

'With Gio and Mark? Yes, I did. Bastian and Quinn were both there too. It was a pleasant evening. If you hadn't been ignoring me, you could have joined us.'

'But Gio . . . and Maisie . . . She said he's been trying to persuade you.'

'He has, and I've been saying no. I'm going to keep on saying no. Because I gave Bastian my word and that means something to me.' He folds his arms over his chest. 'You know that, Ava. I told you about Britta.'

'Oh.' I sink back down on to the bed. My voice is so quiet it's barely above a whisper. I can't believe I got this so wrong. 'I'm sorry.'

'Yeah, well, I guess neither of us know each other as well as we thought.'

I flinch at the bitter tone of his voice. 'The thing is –' I make an attempt to explain '– the whole Quezada situation predates Rask. I had an interview in January and Jasper Ramirez told me to come back in December.'

'And you didn't tell me this *because*?'

'Because it wasn't a certainty. For all I knew, it was just another interview. He didn't offer me a job until the football match. And by then I thought you were going to Quezada too. People were talking like it was a done deal. So I thought I would tell you when you told me.' I press my hands to the sides of my head. 'It all seemed so perfect, because I thought if we were both going to Spain then I wouldn't have to . . .'

He lifts an eyebrow when I stop. 'You wouldn't have to what?'

I wince because I get the feeling that backtracking now isn't an option. 'Choose.'

'Choose?' His brow creases and then clears abruptly. 'So that's what you've been doing all this time?' He backs away from me. 'You know, I thought I'd scared you away when I suggested we tell people about us. I thought I'd asked for too much, but it was what I said about staying at Rask, wasn't it? You couldn't choose between me and a job with Quezada?'

'It's not *only* a job!' I surge back to my feet. 'Quezada are important to me. I've wanted to work for them since I was fifteen. I've been working towards it ever since. I had a plan! I thought you could fit into it, but –'

'But then I decided to stay at Rask and mess everything up?' He laughs, though there's no humour in it.

I hang my head. 'I needed time to think, that's all. I just didn't see how we could stay together, working for competing teams.'

'Then I guess that's the difference between us. Because I didn't need time. I knew how I felt about you. I thought we had something special.' He starts pacing up and down. 'You know, when we first started seeing each other, I *was* thinking about signing for another team. Nathan kept on at me about it. But I would have talked to you, asked how you felt, worked out a way for us to stay together before I made a commitment to any team but Rask, whether it was confidential or not.' He pushes his hands through his hair. 'If you'd just told me about Quezada, told me it was your dream job, I would have seriously considered going there. Even after I gave Bastian my word, I would have done that for you. But you shut me out.'

'You're right. I should have told you everything before.' I wrap my arms around my waist. I've never heard him say so much at once and every word is making my stomach churn with guilt. He obviously thinks I've already signed a contract with Quezada, and I need to tell him I haven't, but there's so much to explain. 'I was confused. I needed to get things clear in my own head first. And I was going to talk to you about it as soon as we got home – I promise.'

'So after two months of ignoring me, you finally decided *you* want to talk?' He stops pacing to look hard at me. 'Just answer one question. Why did you really want to keep our relationship a secret, Ava? Was it truly because you didn't want anyone to treat you differently? Or was it because you didn't want Quezada to find out about us?'

'It was both,' I admit. 'I thought it would . . . complicate things.'

He flinches like I've just struck him. 'You know, when you grow up in care you get used to not belonging, to not feeling wanted, to relying on yourself and nobody else. At Rask, I thought I'd found a place I could finally belong, with somebody I belonged with, somebody I could open up to. I never expected her to treat me like some dirty little secret.'

'No!' My heart squeezes. 'Leif, it wasn't like that.'

'How do you think it's been for me these past months, trying to concentrate on driving while you ignore my calls? Do you have any idea how many times I've almost got on a plane because I've been so *desperate* to talk to you, but knowing if I do you'll only make up some excuse not to see me? And then, just when I think I can't feel any worse, I have to hear from Jasper that you're taking a job with him?'

'I'm sorry. I didn't think.' I swallow the lump in my throat. 'But I'm not taking –'

He interrupts me. 'You know, for a communications officer, you're pretty fucking terrible at communicating. I don't even know what I mean to you. All I know is that if you can shut me out of your life like this, then it can't be very much.'

'Leif, wait.' I put a hand on his arm as he strides past me towards the door. 'I didn't want to shut you out, but I told you at the start. I'm not good at relationships. I find it hard to trust.'

'Why? Have I *ever* given you a reason not to trust me?'

'No.'

'Then what else are you not telling me?' His jaw flexes as I recoil from him. 'I can't do this, Ava. I hope you're happy in

Spain. Nobody at Rask knows about us and they won't hear about it from me. You can leave with a glowing reference. I'm sure you'll be running Quezada in no time.'

'Leif . . .' I can feel panic growing inside me. I can't believe I've messed this up so badly. I took him for granted, expecting him to still be around when I made my decision. Maybe if I tell him the reason I find it so hard to trust I can still fix this . . . Only I can't. I don't talk about it. I did once, but I don't have the words any more. 'I'm sorry. I know I've been completely insensitive, but I never meant to hurt you.'

'Maybe not, but you still did.' He lifts a hand towards my face, gently brushing a tear away from the curve of my cheek with his thumb. 'Besides, what is it they say? That relationships are a two-way street? If you can keep something like this from me, how am I supposed to ever trust you again?'

'Hey, did I leave my jacket in here?' Emika barrels into the room suddenly, her cheeks flushed like she's just run all the way along the corridor.

I jolt away from Leif, but it's too late. Her shocked expression tells me she's already seen us.

'Here.' I pass her the jacket.

'Um . . . Thanks.' She reaches a hand out slowly, her gaze flicking from me to Leif and then back again. 'I was just . . . because the bus is coming soon.' She retreats to the door. 'So I'll see you in the lobby?'

I open my mouth to say yes, but she's already gone.

'I guess I should go after her.' I turn back to Leif.

'I guess so.' His face is a mask.

'Can we talk some more when we get home?'

He stares at me for a long moment before twisting away. 'What else is there to say, Ava?'

Then he's gone too, and I realize I never even told him my decision. That in the end I chose to stay at Rask with him, after all. And now it's too late.

After Rask scored forty points this weekend, the big question in the paddock is whether there's still time this season for the underdogs to take third place in the Constructors' Championship. With over a hundred million dollars at stake, the pressure is greater than ever ...

@ MotorsportEchoNews, 20 October

TWENTY-EIGHT

'HOME SWEET HOME.' YUTO throws his arms up to stretch as we climb out of the minivan that's brought us back to Rask HQ. A ten-hour flight, combined with an eight-hour time difference, means we took off from Las Vegas at 9 a.m. on Sunday morning and landed back in the UK around 3 a.m. on Monday. Thanks to Customs and the drive, it's now almost 6 a.m.

'You know this is only the place we work, right?' Emika jumps out beside him.

'Yes, but we spend so much time here, I've almost forgotten what my actual home looks like.' He yawns widely. 'At least we get today as holiday. Maybe everyone will start acting normally again tomorrow.' He looks accusingly between us.

'We're being normal,' I answer defensively.

'*Please.*' He snorts. 'You two have been acting weird the whole way home. Whatever's going on, deal with it.'

'We're just tired,' Emika protests.

'If you say so.' He waves to the second minivan that's pulled up beside us and then heads off across the car park. 'See you.'

'Yeah, so ... Bye.' Emika hurries after him, like she doesn't want to be left alone with me.

I watch her go and then head towards my own car. We've both been pretending nothing happened ever since I caught up with her in the hotel lobby in Las Vegas. In some ways it's a relief because I have no excuse for my behaviour, and explanations will only make me look bad, but I also hate this new atmosphere of tension between us. It's bad enough knowing Leif thinks I betrayed him. I don't want to see the same expression on her face too.

'Hey, Ava!' Kayleigh, one of the marketing assistants, calls after me. 'Vienna wants a word.'

'Now?' I stop by my car.

'She says it's important.'

My heart sinks as I look across the parking lot to where Vienna is marching into the building, a phone pressed to her ear.

'Did she say why?' My throat feels very dry suddenly.

'No, just that it won't take long. Why, what have you been up to?' Kayleigh starts to smile, then does a double-take when she sees my expression. 'Whoa, what *have* you been up to?'

'Nothing.' I shake my head quickly. 'Enjoy the rest of the day.'

'You too.'

I follow Vienna into the building, my footsteps heavy. I guess Emika must have told her what she saw at some point on the journey home. Maybe she emailed her from the airport lounge, where we were sitting in opposite chairs, avoiding each other's eyes. It seems out of character for Emika, but I can't exactly blame her. She probably thinks Vienna has a right to know. Which she does. I should have told HR about my relationship with Leif a long time ago. Now I'm probably about to be told how disappointed everyone is in me, not that it matters any more. There's no way I can stay at Rask now. My only hope is that I'll be allowed to resign rather than be fired.

'Hi.' I catch up with Vienna just as she reaches her office. 'You wanted to see me?'

'Sit down.' She waves me in, throwing her coat off at the same time. 'I'm sure you're keen to get home so I'll make this quick. You can probably guess why I want to talk to you.'

'Yes.' I perch on the edge of a chair. I've already decided I won't object or try to defend myself when she shouts at me. It's only fair. Honestly, if she wants to throw the employee handbook at me, I'll sit here and take it.

'Because I've been hearing a lot of things about you.'

'A lot?' I give a startled jolt. Do *other* people know?

'And everyone says the same thing. You're a huge asset to this team, Ava, and we'd be fools to let you go.' Vienna spreads her hands wide. 'So your trial period is officially over. I'd like to offer you a permanent contract.'

'You want me . . . to stay?' I feel completely disorientated, like I've just blinked and found myself in a different room.

'Fuck, yes. You work harder than anyone else, you're a team player and you have great ideas. Don't tell the others, but you're one of the best employees I've ever had.' She leans forward over her desk. 'Remember when I hired you, how I said we needed to turn this team around? Well, full disclosure, I didn't think it could be done. I had no idea if any of us would have jobs by the end of the year. Yet, somehow, we've done it. Philip Sawyer's done his worst and we're still here. And we just won a fucking GP! Who knows what we can achieve next year? So I want the best possible team around me, and that includes you.'

'Wow.' I splay a hand across my chest. I'm so touched by her words I can feel a lump in my throat. 'That's . . . I don't know what to say.'

'Say you'll sign and stay,' Vienna answers emphatically. 'Say you'll accept a raise and a better job title. Senior communications manager – how's that? I'll even throw in a designated parking spot.'

'That would be . . .' My voice trails away. *Amazing*, I was going to say, because it *would* have been amazing. If I could rewind time to immediately after the Las Vegas GP when I knew how much I wanted to stay at Rask, it would have been perfect. Then I could have run to the podium and told Leif how sorry I was for the way I'd treated him and pre-empted our whole argument. But I can't, and now I feel flattered and heartbroken at the same time.

'I can't.' I dip my chin. 'Vienna, I'm sorry. I really appreciate the offer, but . . . I just can't.'

Her face falls before she rallies again. 'Well, there's no need to rush. Take a couple of weeks to decide. After that I'll need to start advertising for your replacement, but until then . . .' She winks at me. 'Pick an office. Any office you want. Except this one.'

I get up and walk to reception in a daze. I was so sure that I was about to be sacked. Instead I've been offered a better job, with more money and responsibility than anything Quezada will probably offer me. But it's too late for me to accept because I've already ruined everything with Leif and there's no way we can keep working together now. Even if we keep things professional, the thought of being around him is too painful. I've become expert at burying my feelings over the years, but I know I won't be able to repress that. I've no choice but to move on.

I step outside and let Rask's front door slam shut behind me.

'WAIT, DON'T TELL ME!' Dan opens his front door wearing a navy fleece dressing-gown and holding a bowl of cereal. 'Alice? Annie? I know I recognize you from somewhere . . .'

'Haha.' I shuffle my feet. 'I'm sorry I haven't visited in a while.'

'And you thought 7 a.m. on a Monday morning was the best time to fix that?' He chuckles. 'It's OK. You've been busy.'

'I still should have come after Hailey . . . you know.'

'Flew off to Australia and forgot about me?'

'Right.' I give him a sympathetic look. 'So I know it's early, but –'

'Actually, you're in luck. I'm working from home today.' He steps aside. 'Come on in.'

'Thanks. How are you doing?'

'Better than I was. Congratulations on Las Vegas, by the way.'

'Did you watch?'

'No, but I saw some clips online.' He leads me through to his kitchen. 'So when did you get back?'

'About an hour ago.' I look around quizzically. 'Have you decorated?'

'Yes. I've wanted to do it for ages, but Hailey and I could never agree on a colour scheme. Now I only have myself to please, so . . .' He shrugs. 'Silver linings, I guess.'

'It's very blue.'

'I like blue.' He puts his cereal down and reaches for the kettle. 'Tea?'

'Please.' I hop on to a stool. 'Have you heard from her?'

'No, but according to Instagram she loves Melbourne.' He makes a face. 'I've decided to restrict her posts for a while.'

'That's probably a good idea.'

'Yep. So . . .' He gives me a narrow look as he braces his hands on the counter between us. 'What's the matter?'

I try not to flinch. 'What do you mean?'

'Because you look like crap, no offence, and you clearly haven't been home yet.'

I glare at him. I admit the combination of stress, a prolonged hangover and jet lag means I'm not looking my best, but I don't think I look so bad in my travel outfit of baggy jeans and a grey Henley. 'Your house is on my way home, so I thought I'd pop in, that's all. And can't I look like crap and still want to visit you?'

'Nice try, but I know you. Something's wrong.'

'OK, fine.' I fling my arms out. 'Leif and I broke up.'

'Shit. Sorry.' His brow furrows. 'What happened?'

'I messed up. I couldn't make up my mind between staying at Rask with him or taking a job with Quezada in Spain, so I kind of . . . ignored him for two months.' I wince at how awful it sounds. 'Then he found out the reason.' I give a brittle-sounding laugh. 'And the ironic thing is that I'd just decided to stay with him at Rask.'

'Really?' Dan draws his head back. 'What about your plan?'

'I changed it.'

'Ava, that's brilliant!' He breaks into a wide smile. 'You have no idea how much I hated the plan.'

'Excuse me?' I'm offended. 'It was a great plan! It helped me get back on my feet.'

'I know.' He raises a hand. 'Hey, I'm not saying it wasn't effective. I mean, you've gone from A to B to C, doing everything perfectly for the past few years. And maybe it was what you needed at first. It just got a little bit predictable.'

'Are you calling me boring?'

'Not you *personally*. Only your approach to life. You know, it's possible to be *too* in control.'

'Well, all I know is that I would have been a lot happier if I'd stuck to being boring and predictable. If I'd kept to the plan, I wouldn't be looking like crap! Thanks for that, by the way.'

'Yeah . . . sorry.' He scratches his neck. 'So what are you going to do?'

'What do you think?' I drape myself across the counter, resting my cheek on the cold marble surface. 'There's nothing I *can* do except go back to the plan you hate so much. I can't stay at Rask with Leif now. He broke up with me because I shut him out and he says he can't trust me any more.'

'He said what?' Dan's expression turns furious. 'The insensitive asshole! After what you went through, how can he expect –'

'He doesn't know,' I interrupt. 'I never told him what happened.'

There's a heavy pause. 'Why not?'

'Because I don't talk about it any more.'

'It kind of sounds like you need to. I know it won't be easy, but if you want to mend things with Leif, you need to explain why Quezada means so much to you.'

'I can't.'

'Look, Ava . . .' He rests his arms across the counter beside mine. 'You don't want to end up with regrets. If there had been any chance I could have saved my relationship with Hailey through a *conversation*, even one that was painful –' he gives me a meaningful look – 'I would have taken it in a second.'

'What if it's too late?' I lift my head tentatively off the counter. 'What if I tell him and he still doesn't want me?'

'It's a risk.' He nods. 'But you're tough. You've picked yourself up before – you can do it again. Even a broken heart heals eventually. Just look at me.' His lips curve ruefully.

'You know, you're pretty wise for a big brother.' I smile back. 'I promise I didn't just come here to cry on your shoulder. I really did want to see how you were.'

'I know. And you can stay as long as you want. If you need company or you don't want to go home yet, it's fine.'

'Thank you.' I sniff. 'Do you really think that telling Leif the truth might make a difference?'

'It's worth a try. I mean, if you won't do it for yourself, do it for me. It might be cool to have a Formula 1 driver as a brother-in-law.'

'You don't even watch F1.'

'I'll start.' He puts a hand on my arm and squeezes. 'Now, let me make that tea.'

I'm incredibly grateful for the offer, but I've decided to stay with Rask

Ava Yearwood to Jasper Ramirez, 21 October

TWENTY-NINE

BECAUSE MY BODY CLOCK is a mess, I wake up at 5 a.m. on Tuesday morning in Dan's spare bedroom feeling like I've just had a triple shot of espresso. On the plus side, a day of sleep, followed by an evening of pizza and video games with my big brother, followed by yet more sleep, seems to have brought clarity, because suddenly I know what I have to do.

I drive home, get showered and changed, and then drive to Quezada HQ. The journey takes a little over an hour, but I have just enough time to get there and back before work and this is something I should do in person. Unfortunately, it turns out I can't even enter the driveway without an appointment, so instead I stop my car by the side of the road, where a low hedge allows me a view of the building in the distance.

Even from a mile away it's impressive: bright and gleaming like a beacon in the early morning light. Gazing at it reminds me of being fifteen, watching as Salvador Torres took the win for Quezada in Melbourne. That was the first time I'd taken an interest in anything for months and I remember how it felt so clearly, like a faint tendril of sunlight was peeking through the grey clouds fogging my brain. Quezada got me through the worst time of my life. It gave me focus, something to aim for, a reason to get up off the sofa and go back to school. I'll always be grateful for that, but it's also served its purpose. Because now I know with every fibre of my being that if I leave Rask I'll regret it. Whether Leif forgives me or not, no matter how painful it is to be close to him, I want to stay.

I reach for my phone, write a short email to Jasper, take a long breath and then hit send. Quezada will always have a special place in my heart. It's just not where I want to be right now. Maybe some day, but not yet.

THE FRONT DOOR OF Rask is locked and the reception looks empty, which is weird because I'm half an hour late, thanks to traffic, so I have to use my security pass to enter through one of the side doors. I'm still buzzing with energy and purpose, and my pulse is racing. Now I know what I've got to say to Leif, I want to find him as quickly as possible.

But all the corridors are deserted. Ditto the factory. Ditto every single room I walk past. I'm beginning to think I've missed a memo telling everyone to take the day off when I hear the sound of shuffling feet and loud murmurs coming from the canteen.

'What's going on?' I ask the first person I meet.

'It's Leif.' The man – Matt? Martin? Mike? from IT – tips his head towards me. 'He's called a meeting and this is the only place big enough to fit all of us.'

I start tapping my foot at hearing Leif's name. I was half afraid he might not come in today, but if he's called a meeting he must be here. Matt/Martin/Mike is right, though, it seems like every single Rask employee is crammed into this one room. 'Did he say what it's about?'

'The contract rumours probably.' He makes a scornful sound. 'I heard that Fraser have offered him five million.'

'I heard it was six,' the woman next to him chimes in.

'*Six* million?' I gasp. Loyalty or not, how could anyone turn down that kind of money?

My companion looks like he's about to say something else when a hush falls over the room and I turn to see Leif climb up on to one of the counters. My heart somersaults at the sight of him, though for a man who won a GP two days ago he looks pretty terrible. There are dark smudges around his eyes and he clearly hasn't shaved, but his jaw is set with determination.

'Thank you for coming.' He clears his throat. 'I'm sorry to interrupt your work, but I wanted to address the rumours about me moving to Fraser. I'm told there's been a lot of speculation, so I wanted you all to be the first to know that I've just signed a two-year contract with Rask. I'm proud of what we've achieved so far this year and I want to take us even further. I think we can be the best team in F1. So I'm not going anywhere. I'm staying here with you, my Rask family.'

There's a huge cheer, a spontaneous outburst from every corner of the room that gets even louder as he reaches a hand down and pulls Bastian on to the counter beside him.

'I also thank you for coming.' Our team principal looks embarrassed to be the centre of attention. 'And I have another piece of news. I spoke to Mark Haddon yesterday evening and I'm delighted to announce that Quinn Sommers will be staying with us for the remainder of the season.'

There's another even louder cheer. I'm starting to think that Leif should have called this meeting outside because we're in danger of bringing the roof down. As bad as everyone feels for Corey, having a permanent female driver is a big – *really big* – deal.

'So let's keep fighting!' Bastian concludes, a mischievous smile spreading across his face. 'I know we can win again and we're sure as hell going to try. Now get back to work, all of you!'

I don't join in with the laughter. Instead, the moment he and Leif jump down off the counter I fight my way forward, pushing my elbows out and wriggling through the throng of people. Everyone is happy and smiling, but I'm full of butterflies. This is the moment. It's now or never.

'Leif!' I burst through the crowd in front of him, panting with the exertion.

'Ava?' His eyes widen at the sight of me.

'I'm staying too,' I blurt out.

'What?'

'I've turned down Quezada's offer. Not just because of you,' I add hastily, as his brow tightens. 'I want what you said as well, to stay and build a winning team. And if you say our relationship is over, then I'll understand and we'll keep things totally professional, but I'm really hoping you'll give me a chance to explain before you decide.'

'Relationship?' Vienna appears at Leif's shoulder, accompanied by Bastian.

'Yes. I'm sorry.' I lift my chin. 'Leif and I have been seeing each other for a while and I convinced him not to tell anyone. It's totally my fault, and if you need to discipline me I'll understand, but if you could give me a second chance too, that would be great. I'd really love to stay, if you still want me?'

'Well . . .' For once, Vienna is slow to respond. '*I* still want you, but I get the feeling it's not up to me.' She quirks an eyebrow at Leif.

He gives me a long look before breaking eye contact. 'This isn't the place to discuss it.'

'You're right. We need to talk in private.' I gesture towards a storeroom. 'Will you let me explain?'

'Fine.' He walks ahead of me, folding his arms over his chest once we're inside. 'Go on.'

I wring my hands together. Now that I'm here, the words seem to be stuck in my throat again, but this time I know I need to get them out. I have to tell him everything. Dan's right – it's the only way.

'Ava?' Leif frowns at my hesitation.

'Yes. I just need to . . .' I take a deep breath, blow the air out slowly and start talking. 'There's something I should have told you before, the reason I find it hard to trust people.'

'OK?' His brows unclench a little.

'When I was fifteen, I went on a night out with my friend and her boyfriend and a friend of his, a boy I really liked. It was early summer, so we met up in the park with some other people, some I knew and some I didn't, but it was fun. We were just hanging out and drinking. I didn't even have much. It was all so chilled that I thought I didn't need to be careful, but after a while I started to feel . . . confused. I tried to get up, but I was so dizzy and my vision was all blurry. Eventually I blacked out. Luckily my friend called Dan and he came and took me home. They both assumed I'd just had too much to drink, but when I woke up the next morning I was still a mess. Completely disorientated, like I'd been hit in the head.'

'You were drugged?' Leif's jaw is rigid. 'Was it the guy you were with?'

'I still don't know for sure. But he was the one handing out the drinks,' I admit.

'What about the police? Did they do anything?'

'No. Maybe if I'd gone to the hospital straight away and got proof they could have investigated, but I left it too late. And when I couldn't even tell them the names of everyone I was with, they acted like it was my fault for drinking underage in the first place, like I should have been grateful that nothing worse happened. But I still felt violated. Just the idea that somebody could have done that to me deliberately, and for what purpose . . .' I shiver at the memory. 'The doctors said I had a kind of breakdown. I felt so hopeless and depressed and paranoid, like there was a shadow on my soul. I didn't go out for a long time, and when I did it was never at night. I felt like there was something evil out there, waiting to get me.'

'Ava . . .' Leif takes a step towards me, but I hold my hands up because I need to finish.

'I started watching F1 while I was stuck at home. It was the season when Quezada were winning everything and –' I lift my shoulders – 'I guess I got kind of obsessed. But it made me feel better. All the adrenaline and excitement and glamour took me out of myself. And then I thought, why can't I be a part of that world? So I came up with a plan, a way to work for Quezada some day. And I started to feel like myself again. I worked hard because I knew what I wanted, but I never told anyone what had happened to me and I hardly ever dated because the thought of being vulnerable like that again was too frightening. I just threw myself into work.' I pause for breath. 'Then I met you and we had this connection. And I thought I could go to Quezada and be with you too, but then you said you were staying here and I didn't know what to do. I was afraid that if I gave up on my plan I'd fall apart all over again. So that's why I didn't answer your calls. I was so stuck in my own head. And by the time I realized how much I wanted to stay here at Rask, with you, it was too late.'

'I'm sorry.' Leif's voice has a catch in it. 'Ava, I had no idea.'

'I know. And I'm not telling you so you can feel sorry for me. I don't want pity. I just want you to understand why I found it so hard to choose. But I've put that behind me now. And if you'll give me another chance, I want our relationship to be out in the open. We can tell everyone. I'll shout it from the rooftops, if you want. In fact . . .' I run out of the storeroom impulsively.

'Where are you going?' Leif follows after me.

'To make an announcement of my own!' I kick off my heels and climb up on to the same counter he did a few minutes ago. It's not easy in a skirt, but I'm determined. 'Could I have everyone's attention, please?' I call out over the canteen. 'There's something I need to tell you.'

'Ava, you don't need to . . .' Leif reaches for my hand.

'Yes, I do. If you could all look this way for a moment?'

'Hey, everyone!' Emika bellows from the back of the room. 'Ava has something to say!'

'Thank you.' I throw her a smile. 'The thing is . . .' I begin, and then stop abruptly, as it occurs to me that I haven't given Leif an opportunity to say anything back. I've told him my truth, but he hasn't agreed to give our relationship another try.

Oh crap. I twist my face towards the nearest exit as my palms start to sweat and my cheeks turn an even brighter shade than my hair. Maybe I shouldn't have climbed up here. Maybe I shouldn't have sent that email to Jasper either. Maybe I do still need Quezada? Because if this grand romantic gesture goes wrong, I really will have to leave. I'll never be able to live down the embarrassment.

And now everybody's staring at me, because I literally just asked them to, waiting for my big announcement. It's so quiet you could hear a pin drop. But I'm here now and there's still one more thing I need to tell Leif.

If I'm going to make a fool of myself, I might as well do it properly.

'The thing is . . .' I repeat. 'Leif and I have been seeing each other for a few months and I asked him to keep it a secret, but I don't want to do that any longer because I'm in love with him.' I close my eyes for a moment and then look back down at Leif. 'I love you.'

There's a stunned silence, before he climbs up on to the counter beside me.

'You do?' His voice is gravelly.

'Yes.' I throw a nervous look at the crowd and lower my voice. 'You don't have to say it back, but if you could pretend to say something, that would be really great.'

'Are you kidding?' He cups my face in his hands. 'Ava, I've been in love with you for months.'

'Really?' A combination of relief and joy and desire bursts to life inside me. 'Does that mean you want me to stay?'

'Only if it's what you really want.' His expression turns serious again. 'If Quezada means so much to you, then I don't want you to give it up. We can find a way to make this work, even if it means being at different teams, in different countries.'

'Quezada does mean a lot to me,' I admit. 'But you and Rask mean more.'

'Then I guess we're both staying.' He lowers his mouth to mine and our captive audience goes wild.

This must be what winning a world championship feels like.

It's the final race in the season, and with Giovanni Bauer already a double world champion, all that's left to decide is the Constructors' championship. With Quezada currently in first place and Fraser in second, the big question is whether Rask Racing can take third place from Gold Dart. There's only six points in it, and given the performance of their two drivers, Leif Olsen and Quinn Sommers, over the past four races, most pundits are backing Rask. It's hard to remember the last time a team turned their fortunes around so spectacularly within a season. Let's see if they can get their fairy-tale ending today.

@ MotorsportEchoNews, 7 December

THIRTY

'WISH ME LUCK.' LEIF slides an arm around my waist and pulls me against him, kissing me goodbye at the entrance to the garage.

'Good luck,' I murmur, pushing my hands through his hair and lacing them behind his head. It's the last race of the year and I'm here in Suzuka as a spectator for once, as 'Leif Olsen's official, absolutely-not-secret girlfriend', as Emika, Yuto and Charlotte now insist on calling me. The day after my big announcement in the canteen, I arrived at work to find the words engraved on a plaque on my desk. I have a feeling it's going to be a long time before I live that speech down.

'You know, this time in a week, we'll be on a beach.' Leif smiles against my lips. 'I can't wait.'

'Mmm.' I respond by rubbing my nose against his. 'Usually when people say that, they're talking about somewhere warm, not the side of a fjord. How many layers do I need to pack again?'

'Lots. Think thermals and wool. You'll need them for watching the Northern Lights.'

'And husky sledding?'

'And staying in an ice hotel.'

'It sounds amazing.' I sigh blissfully. 'I can't wait to meet your foster family too. I just hope they like me as much as my parents love you.'

'It'll be tough. I mean, I'm pretty *adorable*.' He rubs a hand over his chin and I regret, yet again, sharing Charlotte's description of him.

'Hey, cut it out, you two!' Yuto's voice interrupts us. 'I thought I spoke to you about all the PDAs yesterday.'

'You did.' I step back and attempt to look shame-faced. 'I'm sorry.'

'I'm not.' Leif pulls me back again.

'Just get us more points than Gold Dart and I'll let you kiss as much as you want.' Yuto grins. 'Get on the podium again and I'll carry her up to you.'

'Ahem, what about me?' Quinn appears from the other direction, accompanied by Emika. 'What will I get in exchange for a podium?'

'Will undying respect and gratitude be enough?' Yuto lifts an eyebrow.

'It's a start.'

'Good luck today,' I say to Quinn. 'And congratulations again on the contract for next year.'

'Thanks.' Her smile is strained. 'I only wish the circumstances were different. I can't help feeling like I've profited from Corey's misfortune. It must have been terrible, being told his career is over because of nerve damage. He must be devastated.'

I exchange a quick glance with Leif. According to him, devastated isn't the half of it, but there's no need to tell Quinn that.

'If anyone can bounce back, it's Corey.' I try to sound reassuring. 'I honestly wouldn't be surprised if he's back next year as a pundit.'

'I hope so.' She tips her head towards the garage. 'Now I'd better get in there. Are you going to stay here and watch?'

'No, I'm meeting Maisie in the Media Centre. Neutral territory.'

'Maisie doesn't need your support. Her boyfriend's already a world champion,' Emika objects. 'We're the ones going for third place in the Constructors' Championship.'

'You don't have to remind me.' I place a hand over my stomach. 'I'm nervous enough.'

'It would be pretty amazing, wouldn't it?' Yuto sounds hopeful. 'No pressure on you two, obviously.'

'We can handle pressure.' Leif fist-bumps Quinn.

'Hell, yes.' She squares her shoulders. 'Let's do this.'

'Three minutes.' Yuto waves a finger between me and Leif as he follows Quinn and Emika into the garage. 'Or I'll be back to drag you two apart.'

'You know, you and Quinn make a pretty good team,' I say, looping my arms back around Leif's neck.

'Yeah.' He rests his hands on my hips. 'But I'm worried about Corey too. He was always the positive one, but now . . . Hopefully, we'll see him at Charlotte's wedding, but I doubt it.'

'He needs time to process. If he doesn't come to the wedding, then maybe we could go and visit him?' I suggest, leaning in to give him one last lingering kiss. 'I know it's hard, but just concentrate on racing today.'

I start to move away, but he slips his fingers through mine, circling his thumb around my palm. 'Hey . . . tell me who your favourite driver is again?'

'Isn't it obvious?' I laugh, then throw a kiss over my shoulder as I head off through the paddock. 'You are!'

I'm still smiling to myself when I pass the giant yellow Quezada motorhome, just as the door opens and a group of men emerge, Jasper Ramirez among them. As I watch, he glances in my direction, does a swift double-take, and then raises a hand in greeting. I wait for the pang in my chest, but it never comes, so I smile and wave back, and then carry on walking to meet Maisie.

Life goes on; plans change. Whatever happens in the race today, I know I'll be back at Rask next year with Leif, working to build the best, strongest F1 team we possibly can. I'm excited about what the future might hold. But after today, and for the next few weeks, I'm going to enjoy being on holiday with the man I love.

And absolutely no plan at all.

ACKNOWLEDGEMENTS

Writing this book was a bigger challenge than writing *Lights Out* because it meant going behind the scenes of a sport I'm used to only watching from the outside. So, a huge thank you to all the F1 bloggers, podcasters and fans for providing so much content for research (especially those lovely people who supported my first book!). I couldn't have written this without your help.

Thanks as always to the wonderful and incredibly patient team at Penguin Books: Katie Sinfield, Awo Ibrahim and Jess Mackay, as well as Bex Glendining for the beautiful artwork.

The biggest collective hug to my family. Watching F1 is one of my favourite things to do together, even when we don't agree. A special thank you to Andy for answering all of my technical questions, even when I'm asking for the 100th time.

As in the first book, I've made some changes to the world of F1, especially with the calendar and number of teams, but any mistakes are completely my own.

Finally, a shout-out to three of my favourite, now former, F1 drivers: Kevin Magnussen, Valtteri Bottas and Daniel Ricciardo, this sport won't be the same without you!